Review by Henry Cairney* of "The Mysterious Robbie Gordon" by author Barry Bernhardt.

An intriguing fictional story linking two individuals with the same poems 200 years apart. Similarities in Robert Burns and Robbie Gordon's health and general life linked to farming families, lifestyle and tragedies. Both died relatively young.

Robert Burns was an extremely astute observer of life around and a special relationship relating to everyone and everything and had a history of depression. Robbie Gordon portrays the same attributes with an uncanny ability to recite and produce poetry and song he clearly had no exposure to.

Both had special relationships with the two John Murdoch's in their particular time zones, and the ancestral connection in the story links perfectly with both individuals.

The legal battle for the discovered letter and poem to John Murdoch, captures an intriguing and highly possible scenario, had the documents existed. This ties to the factual discovery in 2008 of fragments of Robert Burns poems which were discovered around his 250 anniversary. The story has been penned after competent research.

All in all, a nice storyline and well written by the author, thoroughly enjoyable.

Henry Cairney*

Henry Cairney was born and grew up in Irvine, Ayrshire, Scotland, the same county that Robert Burns was born and also lived for most of his life. He attended School at Irvine Royal Academy where his English teacher was Willam McIllvanney, a famous Scottish novelist and poet, who always taught Robert Burns in his class.

Henry has attended and spoke at many Burns Suppers and events in both the United Kingdom and North America. He is the Past President of the Robert Burns World Federation, the Robert Burns Association of North America and Calgary Burns Club where he is a Life Member. He is also a member of Greenock Burns Club and a Life Member of Irvine Burns Club and a fervent Burnsian and his works.*

The Mysterious Robbie Gordon

Also by Barry A. Bernhardt

Novel

Galerie Hoffman

Poetry

As If You Were Here

Hands

I Care

I Have No Armour

I Need a Cab

I Should Have Said Something

If I Don't

Looking At Me

The Little Flying Things

To John Murdoch

The Mysterious Robbie Gordon

Copyright © 2019 by Barry A. Bernhardt

All rights reserved

Scholar's Mate Canada

Second Edition
No part of this book may be used or reproduced in any manner whatsoever without the prior written permission of the publisher, except in the case of brief quotations embodied in reviews.

Scholar's Mate Canada
Calgary, Alberta, Canada

www.scholarsmate.ca

ISBN 9781695163058

To Ben

The Mysterious Robbie Gordon

A Novel

by

Barry A. Bernhardt

Scholar's Mate Canada

Acknowledgments

I want to thank Monique Gareau for her inspiration and encouragement in writing this story. I also want to acknowledge the valuable comments and insights of my beta readers, Benjamin Bernhardt, Calen Bernhardt, Monique Gareau and Vince Cryne.

I want to thank Christopher L. Griffin, Visiting Professor and Research Scholar at the James E. Rogers College of Law, University of Arizona for his helpful guidance relating to the law of equity.

I also want to thank Ruth Blake, of Scholar's Mate Canada, for her immense contribution in editing this Second Edition of my manuscript.

Contents

Prologue 3
PART I 4
    Chapter 1 4
    Chapter 2 5
    Chapter 3 9
    Chapter 4 11
    Chapter 5 13
    Chapter 6 15
    Chapter 7 18
    Chapter 8 21
    Chapter 9 28
    Chapter 10 31
    Chapter 11 34
    Chapter 12 36
    Chapter 13 39
    Chapter 14 42
    Chapter 15 44
    Chapter 16 46
    Chapter 17 55
    Chapter 18 58
    Chapter 19 65
    Chapter 20 68
PART II 71
    Chapter 21 71
    Chapter 22 75
    Chapter 23 80
    Chapter 24 84
    Chapter 25 86
    Chapter 26 95
    Chapter 27 98
    Chapter 28 101
    Chapter 29 105

PART III 107
Chapter 30 107
Chapter 31 109
Chapter 32 111
Chapter 33 115
PART IV 118
Chapter 34 118
Chapter 35 124
Chapter 36 126
Chapter 37 132
Chapter 38 136
Chapter 39 141
Chapter 40 145
Chapter 41 150
Chapter 42 153
Chapter 43 156
Chapter 44 160
Chapter 45 164
Chapter 46 166
Chapter 47 168
Epilogue 172

PROLOGUE

At approximately 2:45 in the afternoon of September 30, 2010, the fragile piece of paper trembled in his hand. He became ashenfaced, his body weakened, and he slumped in his chair. She spilled her tea.

PART I

Chapter 1

Sonya had no pain, didn't scream, didn't cry.

He didn't scream or cry either. He slipped into the world with no fanfare. He arrived on January 25, 1951, in the 32nd week of Sonya's term. He was 4 lbs, 5 oz.

His left leg was about one inch shorter than his right and his left foot was pronated slightly inward. The doctors advised Derek and Sonya that he had a moderate respiratory condition. They were told not to worry. At least there was no brain damage. They were relieved.

For the first four weeks of his life, he remained in hospital and was treated with small amounts of oxygen and intravenous fluids.

The nurse had cleaned the baby, wrapped him up and laid him in Sonya's arms immediately after he was born. She nursed him for only a few minutes, then he unlatched, turned his head, opened his eyes and looked at her. They were the darkest blue eyes Sonya had ever seen. They seemed transparent and Sonya had the strange sensation that she could see inside of him. Sonya felt something she could not understand or explain. It was like the baby arrived with his own and another presence. She held him close, kissed his forehead and touched his tender cheek with the back of her fingers. He continued to look at her.

Derek didn't want to hold the baby. He said," I'll hold him when he gets a bit stronger…maybe when he comes home from the hospital."

Sonya didn't understand this.

They named him Robert Allan Gordon. They called him Robbie.

Chapter 2

When Willie was born, Derek and Sonya had already been farming for three years. Their farm was about six miles from Maxville in eastern Ontario. Now they had two little boys and were going to start their sixth year.

Sonya had met Derek Gordon at a dance. She was 16 and he was 18.

When Sonya first spotted him, he looked out of place. Derek had only been to two other dances in his life.

At some point, early in Derek's childhood, a travelling Swedish evangelist had come to Maxville and had conducted a series of five evening rallies at a small tent set up for his sermons. Not many people attended but for some reason, Derek's mom had. Margaret Gordon was frightened and deeply moved by the evangelist's sermons. At the end of the fire and brimstone sermon on the third night, she had raised her hand at the evangelist's invitation, went forward and was 'saved'. She came home that night and announced that she had 'found Jesus and let him come into her heart' and had become a 'born again Christian'.

Derek's father, Dale Gordon, didn't even know what that meant but she prevailed upon him to attend the last two meetings, which he reluctantly did. With equal reluctance, and after some poking and prodding from his wife, he raised his hand and went forward on the fifth night. He then, half-heartedly, 'found Jesus and let him into his heart' too.

Following their conversions, Dale and Margaret Gordon still attended St. Andrew's Presbyterian Church in Maxville. But in less than a year, Margaret decided that the theology at St. Andrew's was too liberal, so she and a few other recent converts left St. Andrew's to found the Maxville Community Church, two blocks away. Derek and his father were dragged along.

During the remainder of his childhood, Derek was forced to attend multiple church services each week, plus Sunday School.

The theology of their new church had dancing and drinking lumped together in the same sin bin as smoking cigarettes and pre-marital sex.

So, the night Derek met Sonya, it was the third time in his life that he had snuck out of their farmhouse to go to a dance. And he had never drank liquor.

This dance was much livelier than the previous two that he had attended. This one had better music and a very pretty girl on stage playing the piano. He wanted to meet her.

Sonya's father, Adam Fergus, also was a farmer. However, he was better known in the community as a fiddle player. And, he called a lively square dance. Adam was in great demand to perform at dances in every town, village and rural community hall from Kingston to Quebec. His farm took second place to fiddling and dancing. And drinking. For Adam, music and drinking came first, farming came second. Whatever income he received playing at dances, was at least halved by whisky.

Adam was very popular and had lots of friends. Not only because he was a well-known fiddler, but also because of his laugh. It was almost as famous as his fiddling.

He had one of the heartiest laughs anyone had ever heard. When he laughed, he would throw his head back, his right leg would pump up and down, he'd slap the table in front of him and tears would run down his cheeks.

When Adam laughed, people around him didn't even have to know what he was laughing at. They would laugh along with him, just because his laugh was so completely contagious. When a group of people are laughing and they don't even know what they're laughing at, it starts to be funny in itself, which brings on even more laughter. It's quite something to see and experience.

When Adam drank, he laughed even louder and longer than when he was sober so, naturally, people liked to be around him when he drank and laughed.

Adam was multi talented, musically. Of course, he was a master Scottish fiddler. He could hack bow, snap bow and pluck the strings of his fiddle, to the delight of his audiences. He could also play the piano, at least chord along to a piece of music at a very rapid pace, and he had pretty good skills on the accordion.

Sonya was Adam and Lilian's eldest of eight children. She, her oldest two brothers and sister were already playing various instruments.

Sonya played the piano. Adam wanted someone in his family to learn to play the piano well, so he had insisted that at an early age, Sonya get lessons from the best piano teacher in the Maxville area. Her teacher was classically trained, so Sonya got a heavy dose of music theory and was exposed to many of the great classic composers. Adam's interest, of course, was not in classical music. He wanted her to play the piano so that she could learn the traditional Scottish folk and dance music that he was known for and accompany him on the piano at his popular dances.

After Sonya, Adam's next two boys were also recruited to accompany him at his dances. Adam had taught the oldest to play the fiddle and the second boy had learned to play the accordion.

Sonya's younger sisters and brothers were likely going to be musical too. All of Adam's children plunked away on their old piano as soon as they were old enough to be able to climb up onto the piano bench. Music was a staple in Adam's house.

Most of the time, Sonya enjoyed playing at her father's dances, but the truth was that she was more or less forced into it, whether she liked it or not. As she got older, there were some aspects about it that she definitely did not like. She was a very pretty girl, the men liked her and Adam knew it. Often, Sonya was disgusted at their behavior.

Sonya had a slim build and was a bit taller than most girls her age. She had perfect posture and with her long, graceful neck, she looked regal when she stood. She had a very fair complexion and wavy light-brown hair that fell to the small of her back. Her eyebrows and eye lashes were slightly darker brown than her hair. She had a straight, slender nose and full pink lips. Sonya's smile revealed a slightly crooked set of perfectly white teeth. She had never worn make up and didn't need to.

But Sonya's attractiveness really was in her eyes. Her eyelids were slightly hooded, and her eye formation was almond shaped. Her irises were a grey-blue colour which glistened like pearls when she looked at you. But for those who could see it, her eyes also had a rare maturity and wisdom in them.

The night she met Derek, she and her two brothers were on stage, accompanying Adam at a dance at the community hall in Maxville. Adam and her oldest brother each played the fiddle, Sonya played the piano and her second brother played the accordion. It was a hot evening in the summer of 1942.

That night she wore a yellow flowered print dress, fitted tightly around her slim body, flaring out at her hips and going down to just above her knees. Her arms and legs were bare, she wore short white socks and white penny loafer flats. She had long slender fingers which glided and bounced over the keys of the old upright piano that had been a fixture in the Maxville Community Hall for 20 years now. It was ever so slightly out of tune, but Adam and Sonya were likely the only ones who noticed or cared.

Every man in the dancehall noticed her. As the evening wore on, many of the alcohol fueled men stared at her and lusted.

Derek wasn't in school any longer. His father had pulled him out two years earlier to help on the farm. His father was basically a grain farmer, but he also maintained a few dairy cows, so there were always plenty of chores to do. Derek was an only child and therefor the only free help that his father had available.

Derek remembered seeing Sonya when he was still in school, but then she was just a cute little kid, two grades behind him. All he knew was that she came from a big musical family.

But that cute little kid had bloomed into a beautiful young woman and now Derek wanted to meet her. Badly.

At the first break, Sonya left the stage and walked quickly out into the crowd, head down, to find her mom. She knew she was being watched by all the men. She was glad that they raised the lighting in the hall during the breaks because if they were still low, she would have had a rougher time escaping wandering hands as she walked.

She was intercepted by Derek.

"Hi," was all he could manage. She lifted her head and looked at him. Her eyes met his. He saw the pearls. His heart beat faster.

"Hello," she responded.

He struggled for a moment, not knowing how to follow up. Finally, he stammered, "I'm... ah, I'm, Derek. I really like your piano playing."

As much as Sonya was pretty, Derek was handsome. He was at least six inches taller than Sonya. As was popular at the time, his blonde hair was cut short in a crew cut and contrasted sharply against his suntanned face. His darker brown eyebrows and eyelashes and his dark brown eyes also stood out to his blonde hair. He was a broad-shouldered muscular fellow.

"Thank you, I'm Sonya," she replied. To Derek, her voice sounded like she was playing another musical instrument, maybe a flute or a harp.

"I remember you from school. Will you be playing all night?" Derek asked.

"I remember you too," she said. "I'm finished playing for the night. Now just my brothers play with Dad," she added.

"Do you dance?" he asked, and immediately felt stupid for asking.

"Of course, I dance," she said.

"Would you dance with me?" he asked.

"If you ask me to, I will," she answered coyly and smiled at him. Derek felt stupid again, but he knew he had made progress. He made a quick glance around, hoping other men might notice his obvious progress with the prettiest girl in the room.

"Ok then, will you dance with me when they start playing again?" he asked.

"Yes, I will, but I'm here with my mom and younger sisters and brothers, so we will be going home soon," she answered then turned away and left to continue the search for her mom. He watched her walk away and she knew he was watching.

She found Lilian sitting at a table near the back of the hall with four other women. A swarm of young children were running, laughing and playing under foot and table. Some of them were her own brothers and sisters.

Lilian was holding the baby who was fussing and crying, while the second youngest toddler sat on the floor, tugging at her leg. When Sonya approached, Lilian was visibly relieved.

"Thank God you're here," Lilian sighed. She handed the baby to Sonya. He immediately stopped crying.

Chapter 3

Lilian had just turned 15 years old when she met Adam. He was playing at a dance in nearby Alexandria. She was absolutely charmed by him. His laugh got her.

Adam introduced her to alcohol that first night. Initially, she had one beer and then he convinced her to try whisky. She had two shots of that and felt quite tipsy.

Adam was the drinker, the joker, the life of the party and the star of every dance he played at. Lilian loved his charm, his popularity and, of course, she especially loved his laugh. Plus, he was the best fiddle player in the country. She attended every dance he played at and spent private time with him after the dances.

Adam and Lilian were married within three months of their first meeting.

One of Adam's drinking buddies liked to say, what he thought was a very clever and funny line, 'It takes nine months to make a baby, except for the first one'. Well, that's exactly what happened with Adam and Lilian.

Sonya was born six months after they were married. Lilian was still 15 years old.

After Sonya was born, Lilian became more of the tolerant wife who stood behind her man, smiled and occasionally rolled her eyes at some of his shenanigans.

More babies came to Adam and Lilian arriving in rapid succession. Lilian's life became increasingly one of devotion to her children and tending to the many household and farm chores that Adam began to neglect. Adam's life didn't change much after the babies came.

As time went on Adam's consumption of whisky increased and Lilian developed a resentment towards him. She was bearing a heavy load while Adam fiddled and drank and laughed.

Somewhere along the line, Lilian had stopped drinking the little bit that she did. It didn't hold the appeal to her that it used to. In fact, it started to represent hardship for her.

Even at the beginning of their marriage, Adam's farm was not a huge success, but it did provide the necessities for Adam and Lilian. Unfortunately, as their family grew, Adam's dedication to farming diminished and his commitment to partying and playing dances, grew. Lilian tried her best to take up the slack.

Adam would often come home drunk late at night after playing at a dance. No amount of laughing made Lilian feel good about his arrival.

Often when Adam got home in his inebriated state, he wanted to have sex with Lilian. She didn't enjoy sex under these circumstances but would reluctantly comply. After all, she thought, she was his wife and it was her duty.

Occasionally, Lilian would resist his advances. He would get angry and demand that she have sex with him then force himself on her. Rape of a wife by a husband was not even a concept in those days.

Gradually, Lilian's resentment of Adam grew to the point where she started to emotionally and physically withdraw from him.

Not unexpectedly, matters deteriorated. Nevertheless, Lilian was shocked the first time he struck her across her face.

Lilian didn't tell a single soul. This was her husband. This was Adam Fergus. He was one of the best known and most popular persons in their part of the country. Who could she tell?

Adam was always repentant the next morning and, for the sake of, now, eight children, Lilian stayed with him. But she felt trapped.

The drunken rages, shouting, forcing and striking continued.

Sonya knew what was happening and had seen enough of the drink to form her own opinions about it. She hated when her father would return home late after a dance, drunk, shouting and, sometimes, hitting her mom.

She vowed never to get entangled in a marriage like that.

Chapter 4

When Adam and Sonya's two brothers started their trek back to the stage, Derek quickly made his way over to the table where Lilian and Sonya were seated. Sonya got up, whispered something in her mother's ear and handed the baby back to her.

Derek reached for her hand and nervously led her to the dance floor. She felt the callouses in his big strong hands.

From the stage, Adam announced that they would start the set with a square dance. There were two minutes of excited pandemonium as many people rushed to the dance floor to get in on the action. It was crowded and chaotic, but multiple squares were eventually formed.

Adam and the oldest brother started wailing loudly on their fiddles while the other brother pumped madly on his accordion and music filled the room. Adam then started calling out the steps and movements and the dance floor became a storm of motion.

Sonya twirled and swirled with ease. Her feet slid and tapped at all the right times. The skirt of her dress flew up to her mid-thigh when she spun.

Derek was completely lost. At first, he just tried to keep moving where, he hoped would be an appropriate place in and out of the lines and square formations. He awkwardly jigged his body in time to the music. If a lady aimed for him with an arm outstretched, he knew enough to link his into hers. He soon realized that *he* didn't need to try to find an appropriate place to locate himself in and out of the lines and squares because he was getting tossed from place to place involuntarily. Sonya had her eye on him the whole time and when they'd meet in the formations, she would laugh in his ear as she spun him around and flung him to his next destination. Derek was horrified and thought this might well be the end, both of his dancing career and his relationship with this pretty girl.

Derek hoped that he might be given a second chance and that, at least, the next dance would be a one-on-one dance. Thankfully, it was.

"It's called a traditional two-step," she said when the second tune started. "Take a step forward with your right foot, like this," as she took a step back with her left foot, "then, even up with your left, then take another step forward with your right foot and then swing your left foot to the side, like this." Sonya was patient with him and taught him as they held onto each other with a respectable amount of space between them.

This dance was less hectic than the square dance and at least he could hold on to Sonya this time. Sonya didn't press him into trying any spins, so they just concentrated on the steps.

With confidence building, Derek now hoped that the next dance would be a slow one. It was.

Now, all Derek really had to do was hold Sonya close and sway back and forth.

He was in heaven. He placed his big hands carefully, one on her upper back and the other on her waist. He cheated just a bit and stretched his left arm as far around her as he could and pulled her close to him. She didn't resist. It didn't last too long though because under Lilian's watchful and protective eye, it was her motherly opinion that they were dancing too close. She purposefully approached the couple and told Sonya that they needed to get on home. They quickly untangled themselves from each other.

"Well, goodnight then," Derek said dejectedly. "I really enjoyed dancing with you."

"Good night, Derek," Sonya said, turned and left him standing, watching her walk away. She knew that he was.

Chapter 5

As the oldest of eight children, one of Sonya's many jobs was to care for her younger siblings. By the time the two youngest boys came along, she was practically like a second mother to them.

In addition to attending to their basic needs, she often sang to them, played piano for them, read to them, told them stories and tucked them into bed at night, with motherly hugs and kisses. She had a special love for those boys, and they loved her back. She had a gift.

Lilian relied on Sonya for much needed help. She had enough to do in raising her large family. She was creative in making ends meet, given their poor conditions, but needed help.

Lilian also had to bear the increasingly heavy burden of coping with Adam's drinking and violence. She became weary and aged prematurely.

In Sonya's teen years, she became more like a friend to Lilian than a daughter. They were only 15 years apart in age. They often talked and laughed together, late into the evening when the other children had gone to sleep.

The night Sonya met Derek, Lilian, Sonya and the five youngest children drove home, all piled up in one of their old farm pick-up trucks. Lilian and Sonya knew that Adam would stay much longer at the dance and have several drinks with his friends before coming home.

Lilian dreaded his arrival. Sonya did too, but Lilian didn't know that because they had never talked together about it. Until that night.

Their farmhouse was a simple two storey frame building with three small bedrooms upstairs and two on the ground level. Sonya shared her bedroom upstairs with her next oldest sister, her two oldest brothers shared one of the other bedrooms upstairs and the last one was shared by Sonya's two youngest sisters. Adam and Lilian slept in the larger of the two bedrooms downstairs and the two baby boys were in the tiny bedroom adjacent to theirs.

After they got all the children tucked into bed, Lilian and Sonya sat down on their thread bare, faded green couch in the living room to relax and visit for a bit before going to bed themselves.

"So, who's the young man?" Lilian asked.

"Oh, him…he's a farm kid from somewhere around here. His name is Derek Gordon," Sonya said, trying to sound disinterested.

"You seemed to be dancing pretty close," Lilian said.

"Not really," Sonya said defensively, "I was just trying to teach him how to dance."

"Uh, huh," mumbled Lilian with a small smile on her face. She reached out and touched Sonya's arm affectionately.

They had intended to visit for only a short time and then go to bed but they ended up brewing some tea and talking and laughing together for a couple more hours.

Suddenly, they heard Adam's truck screeching into the yard. It was 1:00 am. Once the engine noise died, they could hear Adam shouting at his two sons.

"Mom, will you be ok?" whispered Sonya.

"Of course, dear, why do you ask?" Lilian asked, fearing the answer.

"Mom, I don't like it when dad comes home drunk and I don't like his shouting at you," Sonya ventured.

"You hear that?" Lilian asked with a slight tremble in her voice.

"Yes, and sometimes, I hear more than shouting. I hate that, mom," Sonya said more boldly.

Lilian dropped her head and remained silent for a while. When she looked up, her eyes were filled with tears. She quickly tried to wipe them away with the back of her hand, looked at Sonya and said, "Don't worry about it sweetheart, I'll be fine. It's just who he is."

Sonya didn't know what she hated more: how her father treated her mom or that her mom accepted it.

Lilian and Sonya could hear their footsteps getting closer to the porch door. They both stood up and anxiously waited.

"Quickly now, go up to bed dear," Lilian said giving Sonya a quick hug then a push in the direction of the stairs.

Sonya quickly undressed and climbed into her bed. She could hear her father shouting downstairs as her brothers quietly came up to their bedroom.

She pulled the covers over her head, closed her eyes tight and covered her ears with her hands.

Chapter 6

When Sonya's oldest sister was able to start caring for the younger children, Sonya took a part-time job at Drader's General Store in Maxville. Her small salary contributed to their meagre family income.

After their first meeting at the dance, Derek would go into the store, pretending that he needed to buy something, but it was really to see Sonya. Often, she was busy with other customers, so he would stand near the back of the store in the housewares section and look at her. He hoped that she wouldn't see him, but she knew he was back there watching her.

One time, Derek had lost sight of her for a moment and was surprised when she tapped him on the back of his shoulder and said, "Hi there, can I help you find something?"

He had been caught off guard and was a bit embarrassed. He spotted a pink wool blanket on the shelf in front of him and quickly pointed to it. "I was looking to buy this blanket," he said and awkwardly pulling it off the shelf and handing it to her.

"A pink wool blanket, eh? That's a lovely color for a boy," she said mockingly. "That should keep you warm this winter."

He knew that she was aware that the pink wool blanket was a cover-up, but now he had to buy the thing and figure out what to do with it when he got home.

Sonya was still in school and Derek was pretty much full time helping his father on the farm. Apart from their meetings at Drader's, the only time they saw each other was at dances, which Derek started to attend more frequently. He did an extra-ordinary amount of shopping at Drader's.

The situation at Sonya's home was worsening. Adam went into alcohol fueled fits of rage more often. His violence had now expanded beyond Lilian to include his two older sons. He never touched Sonya or any of her sisters, but she started to hate him.

Derek didn't drink and she was very happy about that.

Sonya and Derek continued to see each other. They didn't consider themselves a couple, but they both knew that they were on to something.

In the autumn of 1942, some of Derek's friends were enlisting in the army. Only a few months after meeting Sonya, Derek decided to join his friends and sign up. Many Canadian farm boys saw it as an opportunity to see the world and have an adventure. They didn't think of it as going to war, nor did Derek.

Derek went to the recruiting station in Kingston. The officer behind the desk asked, "What's your birthdate son?"

Derek answered truthfully, "March 23, 1924."

The officer wrote down, March 23, 1921 and winked at Derek. He then handed him a piece of paper and said, "Welcome to the Canadian army young man."

Derek saw Sonya the day before he left for basic training. "I want to see the world. If I just stay home and farm that will never happen. I'll miss you but I'll come back with great stories of my travels," he said.

Sonya was disappointed but understood. "I'll miss you too, so hurry home," she said bravely. They were standing on the sidewalk on Main Street just in front of Drader's, so their hug was necessarily short for appearances sake.

During the three years Derek was away, they did correspond, but it was a slow and unpredictable way for Sonya to learn what his status was. Sonya got more information from the radio and newspaper reports than she did from Derek's letters. She learned that his unit had been called up to serve in the joint Allied Italian campaign. She studied maps of Italy at school while trying to imagine where he might be and what adventures he might be experiencing.

But, she also worried.

During Derek's absence, Sonya kept herself busy. She continued to help out at home, obtained her high school diploma, then took two six-week summer courses to obtain a temporary teaching certificate. Sonya started teaching Grade 2 at the Glengarry Public School 30 minutes from Maxville.

She continued to play piano on weekends at her father's dances. She always had many a man's eyes on her during these dances, which became ogling eyes and roaming hands as the evenings wore on.

She also had many potential suitors during this period, but always kept her distance, hoping that Derek would come back safe and sound. He did, more or less.

Derek was one of the lucky ones returning to Maxville in the early autumn of 1945. He had sprained his ankle at a scrub baseball game during his extended training in England and experienced a bout of yellow jaundice in North Africa. His only serious injury was during the Battle of Ortona, Italy during the Christmas of 1943 where he had taken some shrapnel in his left forearm and elbow. It left a nasty scar from his wrist to just above his elbow. He could still flex his elbow but did experience pain. After the injury occurred, the field medics had given him morphine, but they told him that he'd probably have some amount of pain for the rest of his life.

Upon arriving back in Canada, he immediately returned to the farm. Of course, his parents were thrilled to see him and thankful for his safe return. But really, the first person he wanted to see was Sonya. He made inquiries and learned that he could find her at the Glengarry Public School.

Derek hopped in his father's pick-up truck, broke all the rules of the road and made the half hour drive in 19 minutes. He roared dangerously into the school's dirt parking lot, dust billowing as he braked hard to stop.

It was 11:15 am and Sonya was still in class. Derek had to wait until noon to see her.

When the bell rang for the noon hour break, Derek rushed into the school, weaving through a gaggle of elementary school kids in the halls, and quickly found her classroom. He saw her and stopped in the doorway. For a moment he just stood there looking at her. She was seated at her desk, head down, looking at some papers with very large-printed letters and numbers scrawled on them. She held a red marking pencil in her hand. Sensing that she was being watched she lifted her head and her eyes met his. He saw the pearls again. He walked slowly toward her. She rose from her chair and took one step toward him. Derek reached both arms out to her. She did the same until their hands touched. They stayed that way for just a moment and then they embraced with disregard for the amount of time it lasted or for who might be watching. They kissed for the first time.

Four months later, Derek and Sonya were married by Reverend Fraser at St. Andrew's Church in Maxville. Lilian had made most of the arrangements and it was a wonderful wedding. Sonya's oldest sister served as her bridesmaid and one of Derek's army buddies was his best man. Sonya was happy.

The reception was at the Maxville Community Hall. After dinner, speeches and toasts, the music and dancing began. Sonya's father and her brothers provided the music while the liquor flowed. Of course, Derek's mom and dad didn't drink or dance. In fact, Margaret Gordon had found an unsuspecting couple, cornered them at the back of the hall and was closing in on a conversion.

Sonya had never seen Derek drink before, but that night was special, and he did.

Derek and Sonya moved into the small bunk house on Derek's father farm. Neither of them minded the modest and minimal living conditions. They were content.

Suddenly Derek was a farmer again and Sonya was a farmer's wife, who also happened to teach elementary school. Life was good.

They talked about starting a family.

Chapter 7

The farm had very humble beginnings. Derek's great grandfather had been a crofter in Scottish Highlands. His family had been forcefully evicted from their croft during the Highland Clearances, where wealthy landowners forced them off the land to make way for large scale sheep pasturing. So, along with thousands of other Scots, many forcefully and others voluntarily, before and after him, he had emigrated. Canada was his destination where he spent a few years in Halifax, working on the docks. The Legislative Assembly of Ontario passed *The Free Grants and Homestead Act* in 1868. The following year he found his way to a Scottish settlement in Eastern Ontario where he applied for and was granted a 160 acre parcel of farmland near Maxville. It was a beautiful piece of land with rich soil. A tiny creek ran through the property which emptied into and formed a small lake making it ideal if he wanted to raise sheep or cattle.

The farm had been passed down through three generations to Dale Gordon and now it was Derek's turn to farm.

Derek was a hard-working man and a good and careful farmer. He was industrious, aggressive and eager to expand the farm. He bought more land with the financial assistance of the Government of Canada's *Veterans' Land Act*. The local Bank of Montreal was quite happy to lend him even more money to buy the latest and best farm equipment.

He grew wheat and barley on a rotating basis. His father had already abandoned their small dairy operation and focused only on cereal grains.

For almost two years after Derek had taken over the reigns of the farm from his father, he and Sonya remained living in the small bunk house. But, when Sonya announced her pregnancy with Willie, Dale and Margaret Gordon decided to fully retire, buy a house in Maxville and yield the main farm house to Derek and Sonya.

Plus, Derek's mom wanted to be closer to and devote more time to the ministry of the Maxville Community Church that she had helped found some years earlier. From their new retirement house in town, she could walk to the church.

The devout congregation had grown to the point where the members felt that they could afford a full-time pastor. They had recruited a young fundamentalist fellow from Toronto to lead the ministry. He was fresh out of seminary and this was his first job. In less than a year, it became clear that he didn't fit into the community and that he really didn't even like being in 'remote Maxville'. One Saturday night, he packed up his few belongings and unceremoniously left town. The next morning, the congregation was shocked to find out that he was gone and that there was no one to preach the sermon. Margaret Gordon was the only one to volunteer to preach. The offer, coming from a woman, even though that woman was the devout Mrs. Gordon, was not well received by the three male deacons.

After the scandal of their pastor ditching the congregation, membership dropped off some. But now, with more time available to her in these retirement years, Margaret Gordon was determined to do her part to grow the congregation, bigger than it ever been before. If it hadn't been against the church's theology and the position of the deacons, she would have gladly taken over the role of pastor!

Sonya and Derek moved from the bunk house into the main farmhouse. Initially they had only the bare necessities for furniture, but the one thing that Sonya insisted they purchase for their new larger house, was a piano. She hadn't had one now for a few years and longed to return to playing. Derek ordered a brand-new upright piano for her through the new Sears desk at Drader's General Store.

Sonya loved the farm and the surrounding scenery. The only thing she didn't like was that the farm yard was too close to the small lake that was on the property. She had always had a fear of water and now that she was pregnant with their first child, the prospect of raising a family so near water frightened her even more.

About this time, a group of local businessmen met to discuss ways to preserve and promote their Scottish heritage and traditions. In 1948, they formed the Glengarry Highland Games.

The Games were a natural and welcome fit for Sonya and Derek.

Sonya was asked to head up some of the musical events and she began to contact various pipe bands, Highland Dance groups and fiddlers, from near and far, to participate and compete in the games. She even recruited a well-known piper in Glengarry County to teach some of the local men and boys to play the bagpipes and, for those who already had some skills, to help improve them. The response was overwhelming, and his efforts eventually led to the formation of an award-winning pipe band.

Of course, the natural adjunct to a good Scottish pipe band is dancing. Sonya organized a Scottish Country Dance group from the men, women, boys and girls in the community, who had some background in the steps. Sonya had only ever danced to the traditional and country music that her father had played at his dances, but after watching the Highland dancers do their beautiful and intricate steps, she was determined to learn them herself after her baby was born.

Derek was known in the community to be a strong young man so he was asked to help organize some of the traditional heavy events for the Highland Games. It didn't take him long to develop a list of events. He contacted groups from various communities in Eastern Canada and even in New York state, inviting them to participate in such competitions as hurling cabers, throwing iron hammers, warring at rope tugs, and other manly games.

The inaugural Glengarry Highland Games were a huge success and shockingly, some 10,000 participants and spectators descended on the small village of Maxville.

Sonya had even arranged for her father's band to play at the wind-up dance on the Saturday night of those first games. Adam's fame had continued to grow, and he now called his band, 'Adam Fergus Fiddle & Dance Band'. The band had been expanded to five members, Adam and two new fellows on the fiddles, Sonya's oldest brother on the piano and her next brother on the accordion. The dance was also a great success and with the largest audience he had ever had, Adam's fame and popularity grew even more.

Derek and Sonya were busy with their careers and had little time for a social life. But occasionally, they would meet up with some of their friends at one of Adam's dances.

Derek began drinking more often, but never in excess and only just before he went to bed. He said it helped relieve the pain in his arm and helped him get to sleep.

Sometimes Derek would wake up in a sweat in the middle of the night, shouting. One time she thought she could hear him sobbing quietly.

Sonya wondered if Derek's drinking was linked somehow to his war-time memories. She had heard the expression "shell shocked" but until now she hadn't thought about it in connection with Derek.

One morning after he'd had one of his nightmares, she asked him if he was having bad dreams about experiences he'd had during the war. He quickly denied it and said that he didn't want to talk about it.

He didn't have to admit to it, though, for her to wonder.

In fact, other than almost side comments now and then, Derek never talked about anything related to his actual war-time experiences. She learned sometime later, that this was not uncommon for veterans who had experienced trauma at war.

Another thing that struck Sonya as a bit odd was that, as manly a man as Derek was, and living on a farm, he refused to allow guns in the house. Almost every farm had one or more long guns: shotguns, .22s and even big game rifles. But there weren't any of these in Derek's house.

Chapter 8

William Dale Gordon was born in 1948. He was a big healthy baby and grew quickly. Derek had bonded with him right away.

Robbie came three years later, and Sonya bonded with him right away.

Willie drew heavily from his father's gene pool, while Robbie looked more like his mom.

The boys appearance and mannerisms were so different that no observer would peg them as being brothers.

Willie had blond hair with brown eyes and an olive complexion. As time passed, he grew to be a strong, handsome boy.

Robbie had dark blue eyes and straight medium-brown hair, which contrasted to his very fair complexion. He was a beautiful boy, almost feminine in his facial features.

Robbie's personality and characteristics began to show from a very young age. He was quiet, sensitive and almost never cried.

Over the years he grew but remained slight, frail and pale. He didn't start to walk until almost two years old. But by this time he was already talking and had an impressive vocabulary, quite beyond his age. When he did finally start to walk, he did so with a slight tilt and his left foot remained pronated inward. The local doctor had ordered special shoes for Robbie from a firm in Toronto that made various prosthetics. There had been no prior fitting or sizing of the shoes. They had simply been fashioned by the Toronto firm, based on photos of Robbie's foot that the local doctor had mailed to them. They were designed to provide an additional bit of height for his shorter left leg, as well has redirect his left foot back to a normal, non-pronated position. The shoes were ugly and very stiff. They caused Robbie so much pain that Sonya couldn't bear to see him wear them. So, she abandoned them and let him go back to his normal soft shoes at cooler times and barefoot in summer.

Sonya's motherly instincts were well honed from her teen years. As she had done with her baby brothers, Sonya talked, sang and read to her sons.

As an avid reader, she had plenty of books of her own that she had collected through the years. Some were novels and books of poetry that she read for her own enjoyment. Many were children's books that she had collected and read to her younger siblings when they were growing up.

Another common activity for the boys and their mom was time at the piano. She would seat Willie close by her on the piano bench and put Robbie on her lap. They both made their contributions to her playing by plunking their little fingers on the keys. The boys loved those times with their mom and Sonya cherished those memories.

Sonya was a strong believer in talking to her boys, right from birth on. When she talked to them, she did not use baby-talk. She used adult words and full sentences. Both boys learned to talk earlier than most, particularly Robbie who, one could say, was positively precocious.

Bedtime was always special. Sonya would gather the boys together for whatever was on the agenda for that night.

She showed them picture books, read stories from children's books and if she had the energy, she would make up stories from her own imagination.

As the boys got older, she read increasingly advanced stories and the occasional poem. Willie wasn't much for the poems, but Robbie would often ask for them and seemed to prefer them to the stories.

When Willie started Grade 1, he decided he was too grown up to share Sonya with Robbie for bedtime events. So, she started splitting her bed time sessions, one with each boy.

It wasn't really until she started spending one-on-one time with Robbie at bedtime that she started to notice some of his 'out-of-the-ordinary' behaviours.

One night when Robbie was three years old, she read to him,

From a Railway Carriage by Robert Louis Stevenson:

Faster than fairies, faster than witches,
Bridges and houses, hedges and ditches;
And charging along like troops in a battle,
All through the meadows the horses and cattle:
All of the sights of the hill and the plain
Fly as thick as driving rain;
And ever again, in the wink of an eye,
Painted stations whistle by.
Here is a child who clambers and scrambles,
All by himself and gathering brambles;
Here is a tramp who stands and gazes;
And there is the green for stringing the daisies!.
Here is a cart run away in the road
Lumping along with man and load;
And here is a mill and there is a river;
Each a glimpse and gone for ever!

When Sonya was finished reading, she looked down at Robbie laying in his bed. His eyes were closed, and he was whispering, "Tick-tick…Tick-tick…Tick-tick" over-and-over again while waving his slender hand quickly back and forth over his face. Sonya silently watched him do this for at least a full minute.

Finally, she whispered, "Robbie, what are you doing?"

"I'm on the train. It's going very fast."

"You have a great imagination Robbie…good for you."

"No, I'm on the train."

A bit confused, Sonya said, "You're in your bed love." Then she caught herself and said, "Yes, honey, you are on the train."

After another minute or so watching him continue down the track, she said, "Ok, sweetheart, it's time to go to sleep. Sweet dreams."

He didn't respond so she leaned over him, tucked his little hands under the covers and pulled them up to his chin. She kissed him on the forehead, walked to the door, turned out the light and looked back at him just before leaving his room. She could still hear a soft, "Tick-tick.... Tick-tick...Tick-tick...." She could just make out his hand moving quickly under the covers.

These types of occurrences were not uncommon or infrequent.

One night, in particular, stuck in Sonya's memory. She had read to Robbie,

A Red, Red Rose by **Robert Burns:**

O my Luve's like a red, red rose,
That's newly sprung in June:
O my Luve's like the melodie,
That's sweetly play'd in tune.

As fair art thou, my bonie lass,
So deep in luve am I;
And I will luve thee still, my dear,
Till a' the seas gang dry.

Till a' the seas gang dry, my dear,
And the rocks melt wi' the sun;
And I will luve thee still, my dear,
While the sands o' life shall run.

And fare-thee-weel, my only Luve!
And fare-thee-weel, a while!
An I will come again, my Luve,
Tho' 'twere ten thousand mile!

Robbie sat up in bed as she read it. When she finished, he asked her to read it again. She did. He closed his eyes and tipped his head back ever so slightly while he listened.

She never read that poem again to Robbie. He had memorized it from her two readings of it. From that night on, Robbie could often be heard reciting it around the house, in the yard, in bed. Wherever he went, that poem went with him. Somehow, that Robert Burns poem had struck a chord with him.

Following story time or whatever else Sonya did for the boys at bedtime, she often sang the Brahms Lullaby before tucking them in for the night. Only, the Brahms Lullaby. One night, she had sung the lullaby to him and given him his good night hug and kiss. He had closed his eyes and she thought he was asleep. But as she was leaving his room, she heard him softly humming Schumann's Traumerei. She was shocked. She recognized the beautiful piece from her days of piano lessons, but the last time she could remember playing it, was well before Robbie was even born. She was also certain that she had never even hummed the tune to him at bed time, or any other time, for that matter.

She turned back and asked, "Robbie, what are you humming?"

"I don't know the name of it, but I love it," he said softly and kept humming the tune.

Sonya was speechless and couldn't decide what to do or how to respond to this, so she just turned his light out and left his room. Robbie was still humming.

Another time, Sonya overheard Robbie talking to Willie, "Mom showed me a book of famous paintings."

Willie, then 7 years old and going through his 'I'm a big boy and you're not' phase, answered, "Yea, so what about it?"

Robbie continued, "One of the paintings was of a ship in a storm on the sea by a painter called Rembent."

"You can't even say it right, it's '*Rembant*,'" Willie said with a sense of superiority, but also saying it wrong.

"Last night I had a dream and I was painting that same storm," Robbie said.

"You're weird," Willie concluded.

Robbie smiled and limped away.

Robbie had a lot of dreams like that.

Then there were times when Robbie seemed to know about things that were about to happen. Often, when Sonya told one of her made up stories, Robbie would interrupt her and tell her the end of her story, exactly how she had intended it to go. Sometimes, Sonya would dismiss it as intuition, maybe something he could have figured out from the context of the story. But other times when it happened, she decided that it was just plain premonition. There was little chance of any normal person, let alone a child determining the outcome.

Sonya wondered how in the world he knew how she was planning to end that story. Did he have some secret source of knowledge? When she asked him and he would shrug his thin little shoulders and say, "I just knew."

That kind of thing also happened frequently.

Robbie didn't play with toys like other boys did. In fact, he did very little that boys his age would normally do. He mostly talked to himself and told himself stories.

Sometimes he talked to plants and animals.

One summer day, from her kitchen window, Sonya was watching Robbie sitting on the prickly pine needles next to the trunk of a large spruce tree in their yard. He reached out toward the tree, opened his hand and placed his palm against the trunk. He remained in that position for as long as Sonya watched him. She could see his lips moving and his head nodding and shaking. It looked to Sonya as if he was engaged in an intense conversation. She watched this for several minutes and then decided to go out and talk with him. She approached him quietly. His eyes were closed, and he didn't see or hear her coming. He was talking.

"Why?" he asked. "I didn't know," he added, "How long?"

Sonya watched and listened for a minute or two and then came up to him and tapped him on the shoulder. He opened his eyes and looked at her, and she said, "Robbie, dear, who are you talking to?".

"To one of my friends," he answered.

"Oh, what friend is that?" she asked.

"To this friend," he said, and he removed his palm from the tree's trunk and pointed his little finger to the tree until he touched it again.

"What were you talking about?" she asked.

"He told me that he is sad because many of *his* friends are being killed in the forests," he said.

Sonya wasn't sure how to respond to that, so didn't.

On other occasions, she would observe Robbie talking with ants, spiders, caterpillars, butterflies and other creatures in the yard or in the house.

One time he said to Sonya, "Mom, did you know that caterpillars turn into butterflies?"

"Yes, I did, honey. It's a beautiful thing, isn't it?" she said.

"What do we turn into?" Robbie asked.

'Yikes', she thought, 'How do I answer that?' Sonya decided that she'd stick with the butterfly theme and said, "Well, I don't know, sweetheart, but maybe we turn into something beautiful just like the caterpillars do."

Robbie seemed to like that answer and smiled at her and began to hop around in small circles, tilting slightly to one side, and bobbing back and forth. He stretched his arms out, started flapping them up and down shouted, "See mom, I'm a butterfly."

Sometimes, he would pretend he was a character from a story or poem that Sonya had read to him. Often, he would stay in character for the whole day. To Sonya, what seemed especially strange about that was that Robbie seemed to believe he really was that character…it seemed like he was more than pretending.

One day, when Robbie was four or five, he was alone in his bedroom and she could overhear him talking. She had heard that often enough, but this time was different. She heard two distinct voices, one low pitched and the other higher:

"Why is a raven like a writing-desk? Have you guessed the riddle yet?" the lower voice asked.

"No, I give it up, what's the answer?" the higher voice answered.

"I haven't the slightest idea," answered the lower voice.

It was almost as if Robbie was channeling these voices.

Then she heard Robbie giggle in the higher voice.

Sonya recognized that this dialogue was from *Alice in Wonderland*. The characters were the Mad Hatter and Alice. Again, she knew that she had never read anything from that book to Robbie. She also knew that Derek would never have read it, or anything else for that matter, to him.

She knocked quietly on his door. There was no response. She put her ear to the door and knocked again. Still no response, so she slowly opened it. Robbie was lying on the floor, again with his eyes closed. He appeared to be in a trance. She softly said, "Robbie." There was no response. She approached him and knelt down beside him. He was silent and motionless. She touched him on the shoulder. He slowly opened his big dark blue eyes and looked at her and smiled. His eyes seemed transparent. As she had from Robbie's birth, Sonya again had the sensation that she could see right through his eyes into his mind, but she couldn't understand what she saw.

"Robbie, sweetheart, were you pretending?" she asked.

"No."

"What were you doing?"

"We were talking. It was funny!", and he giggled, this time in his normal voice.

"Who was talking?"

"We were."

"Do you know who they were?"

"Yes."

"Who were they?"

"They were my friends."

Robbie closed his eyes again and Sonya remained by his side and looked down on him for a bit longer.

She couldn't explain what was happening, but a strange sense of understanding came over her. Her understanding took the form of acceptance. She reached down and touched Robbie on the cheek, leaned toward him and kissed his forehead.

She didn't know what else to say and left Robbie's room. She could hear him continuing in conversation with different voices and giggling from time to time.

Sometimes Robbie would almost completely withdraw from everyone and everything around him. He seemed to be very sad. He would become silent, had no appetite and had trouble sleeping. On those nights, Sonya would hold him and try to rock him to sleep.

Sonya thought that, even though he was just a boy, it appeared as if he was depressed.

Sonya felt that even though many of Robbie's behaviours were very different from those of most children, at least he seemed happy some of the time. For that, she was at peace. While she couldn't explain it, Sonya was increasingly experiencing a sense of understanding and acceptance of his behaviours, so she was less troubled. She accepted the fact that Robbie was mysterious and different.

What she was not at peace about was Robbie's periods of withdrawal and his apparent depressed states. These worried her.

She would periodically try to discuss Robbie's behaviour with Derek, but he was always dismissive. He'd say, "Ach, he's just a kid with a big imagination and he's lonely. He'll snap out of it once he goes to school and starts playing with other kids."

Sonya knew in her heart that this wasn't likely to be true but held her tongue, partly because she didn't have any better solution to offer.

Sonya was reluctant to use, or even think, the word, but she knew Robbie was 'abnormal'. Somehow special and gifted, but abnormal.

During one of Lilian's visits with Sonya, she had suggested that Sonya consider taking Robbie to some kind of medical professional to be assessed and maybe given some kind of treatment. Lilian didn't really know what type of professional or treatment that would be. Sonya knew that this would be a psychologist or psychiatrist but didn't want to use these words in front of her mom. In 1955, there weren't any of these types in the Maxville area anyway. She'd have to go into Kingston, or even Toronto.

But Sonya was reluctant to think further along these lines. She intuitively felt that one of the reasons she was on this planet was to protect Robbie. She feared what could happen to him if a professional subjected him to some kind of treatment that was in vogue in those circles at the time.

Secretly though, Sonya wondered and worried.

Chapter 9

Sonya's teaching career had been interrupted with the birth of her boys, but she hoped and planned to return to it someday in the future.

Willie started Grade 1 at Glengarry Public School where Sonya had taught. He had been anxious to start school, he fit in quickly and did very well.

When Willie started school, Sonya knew all of the teachers from her recent teaching days. She got along fine with all of them...well, all of them except one. Sonya couldn't put her finger on it, but she disliked Miss Greta Schnurenberger, a Grade 3 teacher.

With Willie now in school, Robbie didn't even have Willie to keep him company at home, not that they were close anyway. Willie had seldom played with Robbie. When they did, it was short lived. Throughout their childhood, Sonya would often manufacture circumstances to encourage the boys to play together, but the togetherness usually lasted only a few minutes. Willie would leave Robbie and go off playing on his own, sometimes cowboys and Indians, shooting, yelping and riding his pretend horse. Robbie would sit on the floor with his eyes closed, talking to himself.

Robbie didn't have any other friends either, not human friends anyway. Living on the farm he, of course, had his tree and creature friends. But the only other interaction Robbie had with children his own age was the occasional time that Derek and Sonya brought the boys to Sunday School at St. Andrew's in Maxville.

Derek was not much for attending church. He had quit shortly after he turned 18. He had rebelled against all things relating to church after his mother had 'found Jesus'. He thought that the litany of dos and don'ts was excessive and foolish.

Attending church had never played much of a role in Sonya's life. Dances were what her family attended, not church. So, Derek and Sonya seldom went, but when they did, they went to St. Andrew's.

After the service on one of the Sundays that they did attend, Reverend Campbell approached Derek and Sonya and greeted them. Reverend Campbell was a somewhat portly fellow, with a full head of white hair and was nearing the end of his ministerial career. He was experienced in dealing with sensitive matters and would normally have been quite comfortable with what he was about to do, but now seemed nervous.

He asked, ever so carefully, "Would it be possible for you to meet with me privately at the church one-day next week? I'd like to speak with you about Robbie.

Derek responded with some agitation and, Sonya thought, unnecessary brusqueness, "What do you want to talk about?"

"I'd rather we talked in private, if that would work for you folks," Reverend Campbell said.

Sonya said, "Yes, that would be fine with us."

Sonya and Reverend Campbell set a time for the three of them to meet the following Tuesday.

Derek was not happy and mumbled curse words under his breath on the drive back to the farm. Sonya had only heard him curse a few times before and knew that he was quite perturbed. Sonya remained silent and stoically stared out the window as they drove.

At the appointed time, Derek, Sonya and Robbie arrived at St. Andrews Church. Reverend Campbell greeted them and asked if it would be ok if Robbie played with some toys in the church nursery while they spoke.

Sonya knew that Robbie wouldn't play with any of the toys, but she also knew that he was perfectly capable of occupying himself for any amount of time that he was in the nursery. She told Reverend Campbell that would be fine, so he led Sonya and Robbie to the nursery.

Once Derek and Sonya were seated in the Reverend's small office, he started, "As you probably know, Mrs. Anderson is Robbie's Sunday School teacher. She came to me a few weeks ago, somewhat troubled by Robbie's behaviour in her class."

"Oh, what happened?" Sonya asked, already anticipating what was coming.

Reverend Campbell said, "Of course Robbie is not in Sunday School very often but, apparently, he still seems to know more about the Bible stories than Mrs. Anderson does."

The Reverend seemed uncomfortable, but carried on, "He often corrects her 'errors' in class and sometimes tells more of the story than she even knows. She finds that to be disruptive and embarrassing. On the one hand, she is pleased that he knows so much about these Bible stories. On the other hand, she is puzzled, as am I, as to how it is that he knows so much. She asked me to speak to you about it."

"What?" Derek barked, visibly irritated to even be there let alone hear this complaint, which didn't make any sense to him, on a number of levels.

"Well," Reverend Campbell continued, "I'm happy that Robbie knows these wonderful stories from God's Holy Word. I commend you for teaching them to him?"

"We don't!" Derek said curtly.

"You don't?" Reverend Campbell said with some surprise, "How then, does he know so much about them?" He then turned and looked at Sonya, suggesting that it was her turn to shed some light on the situation.

Sonya knew she should say something but didn't know what, so she just sat still waiting for the next exchange.

After a few uncomfortable moments of silence, Reverend Campbell said, "Well, I think it's wonderful that Robbie is learning these stories. All I can ask you to do is encourage him not to disrupt Mrs. Anderson. She's getting up there in age and has less patience with these young ones than she used to have."

"Yes, we'll do that Reverend," Sonya finally spoke.

All three of them rose. Derek headed for the door. Sonya held back for just a moment and shook Reverend Campbell's hand and said good-bye.

She quickly went back to the nursery, collected Robbie and went to join Derek, who was already in the car, again mumbling curse words under his breath.

Sonya had hoped that things would be different when Robbie went to school. But they weren't.

Chapter 10

Robbie, as Willie had done three years earlier, started Grade 1 at Glengarry Public School.

Unlike Willie, Robbie didn't seem to care if he went to school or not. He was indifferent about it.

A typical after school conversation between Sonya and Robbie would run something like this: "How was your day today sweetheart?"

"Ok."

She pressed, "What did you learn today?"

He would shrug and say, "Nothing new," and disappear to his bedroom.

Sonya was non-plussed.

Robbie's performance in school was always acceptable, in fact it was above average, but not because he tried, but because he just seemed to absorb what came his way in some kind of mysteriously, passive way.

Robbie had no friends at school either. He was a loner, both by his own choice and the choice of other kids who generally found him to be odd and didn't befriend him. This troubled Sonya.

During Robbie's time in public school, the meeting with Reverend Campbell was played out many times with every teacher that Robbie had. Only the issues and concerns varied. Derek never attended the meetings. He had said that the meeting with Reverend Campbell had cured him for life and he never wanted to endure another foolish session like that.

Sonya somehow managed to get through the meetings without making an attempt to explain what she understood and accepted about Robbie. She felt that his behaviour was a private matter between Robbie and whoever or whatever energy surrounded him. Sometimes she thought she could actually sense that energy herself. Whatever it was, she accepted it but wasn't about to try to explain it to anyone.

In these meetings, Robbie's teachers were polite and broached each meeting with sensitivity. There was, however, one teacher who did not, Miss Schnurenberger. She was Robbie's Grade 3 teacher.

She was a bit of an outsider to Glengarry County. No one seemed to know much about her or where she was originally from.

Miss Schnurenberger had the most training of any teacher at Glengarry Public School. She not only had the requisite teachers' certificate, but she also had a bachelor's degree in Education from the University of Ottawa.

Miss Schnurenberger was a sturdy, stout and stern 36-year old spinster. She was clearly going to be a career school teacher. She spoke with a heavy German accent and was known to be a severe disciplinarian. Her students feared her. Most parents feared her. The other teachers avoided her.

The day Miss Schnurenberger called for a meeting with Derek and Sonya, Sonya was already bracing herself for some discomfort and possible confrontation.

Of course, Derek refused to attend.

When Sonya met with Miss Schnurenberger, the latter started right in with what was on her mind. She said, "I'm sure dat you are vell avare dat Robbie iss a problem in de school."

"No, I'm not aware of that, at all," Sonya replied, her body stiffening, readying herself in defence.

"Vell he iss. He tinks dat he knows everytink dat I'm going to teach unt he's disruptive unt frankly I'm not prepare to tolerate it," she continued.

Sonya already knew this wasn't going to end well but kept her composure. She calmly said, "What do you suggest we do, Greta?"

In a parent-teacher meeting of this nature, Miss Schnurenberger didn't like being called by her first name and scowled. She continued, "Look, Mrs. Gorton, sometink has to change unt I'm recommendink to de principal dat Robbie be seen by a psychiatrist unt get some kint of treatment or medication. You know dat dey haf lithium now for people like young Robbie, right?"

Sonya bristled and decided right there and then to cut this meeting short. She said, "Robbie does *not* need to see a psychiatrist! Now I'm going down to see Principal Brown and request that Robbie be transferred out of your class into Miss Robertson's Grade 3 class. I'm sure you'll be happy with that."

"Vy, yes I vill," Miss Schnurenberger snorted.

Sonya rose up from her chair without saying another word. As she left, she heard Miss Schnurenberger mumble, "Dickköpfig!" Sonya didn't know what it meant, but was pretty sure that it was not, "Have a nice day!"

Before that day was over, Robbie had been transferred to Miss Robertson's Grade 3 class.

When she returned home, Derek had already been drinking. She related the account of her meeting with Greta Schnurenberger and Derek's response was, "Sure, take him to a shrink. It might do him some good."

Sonya choked and couldn't speak. She clenched her fists and walked away.

There were occasions when school kids made fun of Robbie, sometimes to his face, most times behind his back. It never seemed to bother Robbie though.

But there was no bullying. Word had spread throughout the school that Willie was Robbie's older brother. Willie already had a reputation for being the unofficial enforcer on the playground. Kids, teachers and parents all knew that it would not be a good idea if someone messed with Robbie. Even mild teasing was a significant risk for the perpetrator.

Chapter 11

Derek was a good father to Willie. He had a very close relationship with the boy and spent a lot of time with him. They played cops and robbers, cowboys and Indians and cars and trucks. They wrestled together and in the dog days of summer they'd swim together in the little lake on their farm then play catch afterwards. As Willie got older, Derek would get him to help with chores on the farm and in organizing events for the Glengarry Highland Games. Willie loved spending time with his dad and Derek with his son.

It pleased Sonya to see Derek and Willie spend time together. One thing did, however, make her nervous and that was the times they spent down at their little lake, swimming. When Willie was younger, she had insisted that he get swimming lessons at the public pool in Glengarry, so at least he knew how to swim. And, of course, Derek was always with him when they went down to the lake. But, with Robbie's respiratory problems, he wasn't permitted to take swimming lessons. So, whenever Robbie was outdoors, Sonya warned him not to get anywhere near the lake and she kept a watchful, nervous eye on him to make sure he didn't.

Instead of swimming lessons, Sonya gave Robbie piano lessons. She was his teacher and he was her exceptional student. He learned everything she taught him without much repetition. It was uncanny how quickly he absorbed the music.

It was quite evident that if one of the Gordon boys was going to take over the farm, it wasn't going to be Robbie, it would be Willie.

Derek spent very little time with Robbie. In fact, it was quite clear that Derek avoided him. That did not please Sonya.

One late summer evening, Derek and Sonya decided to attend a dance at the Maxville Community Hall, sort of a pre-harvest kick-off. Adam Fergus Fiddle & Dance Band was playing. They hadn't attended one of his dances for several months. Sonya had tried to avoid them because the few times that they did go, Derek would drink and that made Sonya uncomfortable.

At one of the breaks, Derek was talking with a group of his farmer friends. As usual, they were talking about farming. On this occasion, they talked about whether they would have enough help and equipment to get the harvest in that year before the snow fell. As Sonya had feared, Derek had been drinking. She overheard him say, too loudly, she thought, "Yeh, I've got one good little helper, but that other kid of mine will never be good for anything, I'll tell you that much!"

Sonya was hurt, for herself and for Robbie.

It probably wasn't the best choice for timing, but later that same night, when they had returned home from the dance, Sonya confronted Derek, "Why did you say what you said about Robbie to your friends tonight? I was hurt and embarrassed. Plus, it was disrespectful to Robbie!"

Derek struggled to get himself out of the chair he had fallen into. He staggered towards her with a grin on his face, reached out for Sonya, wrapped his big arms around her and pulled her roughly into his body. He said, again too loudly, "Don't worry about it. Let's go to bed." He bent forward and kissed her sloppily on her mouth. Sonya's body stiffened and she attempted to resist.

Suddenly Sonya felt nauseous. She had a flash-back to her father.

Chapter 12

It was literally the day after Sonya's meeting with Greta Schnurenberger that she decided she did not want her boys continuing on in the Ontario public school system. She wanted something different for them.

She would do some research. After all, she was a teacher and she should be able to find a good quality private school. The farm was quite successful, so they had the money for the expense of tuition and room and board at a private school.

Sonya's research eventually led her to a boarding school of some reputation situated on Lake Ontario in the City of Kingston. The school was called Banffshire Academy for Boys and offered "...*seven Levels of advanced education for gifted and talented boys aged 6 to 18.*" What were called "Grades" in the public-school system in Ontario, were called "Levels" at Banffshire. Sonya learned that a boy could advance from level to level based on their individual progress, not on the school's calendar year. A starting student at Banffshire, was in Level One, not Grade Seven, as they would have been in the public system.

Banffshire was founded in 1848 and had roots from a predecessor school in the whisky town of Keith, Scotland. It had a reputation of providing a rigorous and thorough educational program with not a small dose of Scottish discipline to boot. Most of the professional staff at the school were of Scottish heritage and everyone of them had master's or Ph.D. degree.

If the boys could get accepted into Banffshire, Willie could start that fall. Robbie would have to wait three more years. Sonya could live with that as long as Miss Greta Schnurenberger was not in the picture.

In the early summer, after Willie had finished Grade 6, Derek, Sonya and Willie visited the school in person. They met the Headmaster, Dr. Fraser, who gave them an overview of the educational program. He provided a summary of each year's compulsory courses and all the electives. The school did not have a semester system, every course was a full year course. Sonya asked all the questions and was quite satisfied with Dr. Fraser's responses.

A young staff person was commissioned to guide the three of them around the campus and provide a tour of the buildings.

The campus of the Banffshire Academy for Boys was a 30-acre trapezoid shaped parcel located on the shores of Lake Ontario, just before it started to funnel into the St. Lawrence River.

The one and only entrance was off Front Road at the north end of the property, the smaller part of the trapezoid. The curvy southern shore line was the broader part. There was a paved parking lot to the east side of the building cluster.

The campus had five Gothic Revival limestone buildings, crafted by Scottish stone-masons at various times during the history of the school.

The first building on the campus was nothing more than a one-storey ten-room building with eight classrooms and two offices in which the original teachers had small desks. The building was constructed from local limestone in 1865 and had a modest sign above the double front door which simply said, 'Banffshire School For Boys'.

The building faced north and had been modified and added onto through the years. The original building was altered to become a three-storey structure with a spire rising to just over 40 feet. It was given the somewhat ostentatious name of 'Banff Hall' and the name of the school was amended to 'Banffshire Academy For Boys'.

Later, two large wings were added to Banff Hall, one on each side of the centre building. The wings housed classrooms and teachers' offices. The centre portion was modified to become a large meeting area called the 'Great Assembly Hall'.

Later still, four additional buildings were built around Banff Hall, two dormitories at the south end, near the lake and an administration building and a library at the north end. The five building complex formed a large rectangular shape with well-manicured lawns, shrubs, trees and cobblestone paths in the courtyard mall throughout the inside of the rectangle.

The campus had a rather grand appearance as one entered the property.

The library was, by far, the most beautiful of all of the buildings on the campus. It was named the 'Inverness Library'. It was an octagonal shaped building with a high dome shaped roof. There was a small rectangular vestibule at the front of the octagon with an exterior set of double brass doors and an interior set of solid oak doors.

The interior of the Inverness Library was completely encircled with book shelves, with the exception of the vestibule side. None of the shelves were adjustable but they were built at varying heights to accommodate smaller or larger books, as required. There were between 12 and 16 tiers of honey-oak colored shelves, depending on the height of each shelf. They started a foot above floor level and went up about 15 feet.

Around the perimeter of seven sides of the octagon were rails upon which long dark oak colored ladders slid to access the dusty books on the upper shelves.

Above the bookshelves, on each of the seven sides of the octagon, were two stained-glass windows which had been made by skilled French window makers in Montreal. Each of the fourteen windows was about three feet in height and featured a well-known 16th, 17th or 18th Century intellectual or academic formed into the stained glass: Galileo Galilei, René Déscartes, Nicolaus Copernicus, Thomas Hobbes, William Shakespeare, Francis Bacon, John Locke, Voltaire, Immanuel Kant, Walter Scott, Adam Smith, Jules-Jacques Rousseau, Robert Burns and Jeremy Bentham. One larger stained glass window occupied the space on the side of the octagon above the vestibule. The upper two thirds portrayed The Holy Trinity and the bottom third depicted the saltire.

The maple parquet floor of the main library was split at various points. The floor was worn and faded to a greyish color in the high traffic entrance area and under and around the tables. Only a few places remained where one could see the original dark stain of the maple.

Located about six feet from the inside perimeter of the octagon were seven large, rectangle mahogany tables arranged equidistant from each other. Each table had two green banker's lamps, one at each end. The middle portion of the surface of the tables had originally been inlaid with burgundy colored leather, but they had suffered wear and tear over the years by students and had now been replaced with flush walnut inserts. Each table had eight heavy oak captains' chairs, four on each side. They originally had a medium brown stain, but they too, especially the arms, had faded through the years to, now, a light oak color. In between each table was a globe mounted on a heavy wrought iron tripod. The maps of many of the countries on the globes were now outdated but the globes were beautiful, and the school's trustees and administrators had decided to keep them. The students could consult up-to-date atlases if they really wanted to know what was where and what it was called.

The inside of the dome consisted of intricate marquetry comprised of various colored stains of inlaid mahogany, oak, walnut, rosewood and elm wood. The exterior cap of the Inverness Library was copper and had matured into a bluish-green color.

Throughout the campus were mature maple, oak and tamarack trees thoughtfully placed and planted through the years by skilled groundskeepers. The only indigenous trees on the property were those near the water. There were dense stands of deciduous and coniferous forests a few feet off the rocky shoreline of Lake Ontario: ash, maple, oak, hickory, hemlock, balsam fir, spruce and cedar.

There were pine flower boxes under the massive ground floor windows at the front of Banff Hall and below the smaller windows of the two wings running out from the centre block. From late spring to early fall, they were filled with colorful geraniums, peonies, petunias and occasionally tulips.

Derek, Sonya, Willie and their tour guide walked through the beautiful campus and its buildings. Sonya was enthralled by the physical beauty of the place. Of particular interest to Willie was the dorm where he and the other junior boys would live. Of the two dormitory buildings, the senior boys' dormitory was the closest to the lake. The junior boys' dormitory was set back a bit from the water.

Willie met a few foreign students in the dorm who were still there for the summer. He liked the boys and what he saw of the dorm.

Kingston was two hours away from the farm and, although it was painful for both Derek and Sonya, they saw Banffshire Academy as an investment in Willie's future. They made the decision to make an application for Willie.

He was accepted, so in September they drove him to Kingston and bid him farewell, Sonya with tears, hugs and kisses, Derek with a manly handshake. They watched him disappear into the junior boys' dormitory that he had visited two months earlier.

Chapter 13

Willie thrived at Banffshire Academy as he had done at Glengarry Public School. He was popular with the teachers and the other boys. They looked up to him as a kind of leader. He was developing his father's powerful physique and was strong as an ox. No one messed with Willie.

One teacher, an English teacher, by the name of Dr. John Murdoch, had made a particular impression on Willie. Willie talked about him several times during the Christmas break of his first year at Banffshire.

Sonya looked forward to meeting him one day.

She did. Sonya met John Murdoch when she and Derek picked Willie up on the last day of that school year. In fact, it was Willie that engineered the meeting. He told Dr. Murdoch that he would like him to meet his parents when they picked him up. He had responded by saying that he would be happy to meet them.

When they met, Derek pumped John Murdoch's hand in the manly, farmer way that he did with every other man. Dr. Murdoch's wire-rimmed glasses slid a bit down his nose during the vigorous ordeal. Sonya thought that he looked like he was trying to protect his arm from injury and withdrew it as quickly as he could.

When Sonya shook his hand, she felt an immediate warmth, not only from his hand, but also from his smile and his eyes. When their eyes met, John Murdoch was struck by Sonya's eyes. They were like pearls.

Unlike Derek's rough calloused hands, John Murdoch's hand was warm and soft. He was about the same age as Derek but couldn't have looked more different.

John Murdoch looked every part the professor. That day, he wore a light brown herring bone wool sport coat with dark brown patches at the elbows. He was of average height with a slight build. He had the requisite professor's beard, neatly trimmed and fine, thin eyebrows. He had a high forehead and light brown hair that matched his eyes of the same colour. He wore a pair of wire rimmed-glasses. He had let his hair grow a bit over his ears, as was the fashion for many young men after the Beatles hit the world's stage. In fact, he looked a little like a shorter John Lennon with a beard. He even had the same long thin nose. He already had a slight bit of grey at his temples, but it was mostly hidden by his longer hair. The color of his beard matched his hair, but also had specks of grey throughout.

Sonya was curious about this man that had impressed Willie, so she studied him a bit longer than she would normally have done. She instantly liked him and intuitively felt that this was a man she could admire and trust.

In Willie's second year at Banffshire, he increasingly found himself in a position of leadership with the other Level two boys. Some of them looked up to him, some of them feared him. Willie's classmates elected him as the Level two representative to the school's student council.

At the end of Willie's second year, Derek was unable to make the trip to pick him up. Sonya made the trip by herself in their new salmon colored Pontiac sedan. As she drove, she wondered if she'd see John Murdoch again. She hoped so.

When she pulled the car into the school's parking lot, chaos reigned. Boys were running helter-skelter in and out of buildings and all over the campus, trying to find their friends and teachers to say their good-byes. Slowly, the confusion morphed into another melee of boys trying to gather up their belongings and to find their parents and parents to find their boys.

During all of this, Sonya kept one eye out for Willie and the other for John Murdoch. She eventually spotted Willie and he ran to her and gave her a short hug and tugged her towards his dorm room to gather up his things.

She still couldn't spot John Murdoch.

Finally, she had Willie and his possessions stowed here and there in the new car. Sonya felt disappointed that she had missed John Murdoch. With a twinge of guilt, she asked Willie, "Did you say good-bye to Dr. Murdoch?"

"Yeh, and he asked if you were coming to pick me up," Willie said.

A lump formed in Sonya's throat and her heart began to beat faster. She said, "It's too bad that I've missed him. I looked for him but couldn't see him."

"I think he went back to his office," Willie said.

Sonya wanted to immediately go to the Administration building and find him. She was confused as to why she wanted to see him. She rationalized that he was Willie's teacher who had been an important influence on him and that she should seek him out and thank him. Another part of Sonya knew, however, that that was not why she wanted to see John Murdoch. Sonya was confused and feeling increasingly lonely and detached from Derek. He was drinking more, and they were growing apart emotionally and physically.

Sonya hoped that if she saw John Murdoch again, she would feel the warmth of his hand and his presence that she had felt when they first met. She didn't want to admit it to herself, but she longed for that warmth. She hadn't felt that from Derek for quite some time now.

Sonya sat in the car thinking these thoughts and suddenly came out of her melancholy reverie and shook her head. She realized that it would look odd to Willie, and any other person who saw her, if she were to dash into the Administration building just to find John Murdoch. So, she resigned herself to the fact that she had missed this opportunity to see him again, started the engine and began driving out of the parking lot.

They were almost off the school's property when she spotted someone in her rear-view mirror standing in the parking lot waving their hand. Sonya had no idea who it was or who he was waving at. She told Willie what she saw, and he turned to look. "That's Dr. Murdoch!" he exclaimed.

Sonya hit the brakes much too hard, the car's tires squealed, and boxes, bags and Willie lurched forward as the car came to an abrupt stop.

Sonya didn't even pull over…she just opened the door, got out and walked towards John Murdoch who was walking toward her.

"I'm so glad to have caught you before you left," he said as he extended his hand to her.

Sonya reached out her hand and accepted his. They didn't shake hands, they simply stood there for a moment their hands clasped together. She felt the same warmth from his hand that she had when they first met. He reached out with his other hand and placed it over both their hands. He looked again into her eyes. Those pearls!

Sonya finally found her voice. "I looked but couldn't find you. I had hoped to see you again" was all she could manage.

Willie had also got out of the car and watched his mom and Dr. Murdoch standing there holding hands. He had a slightly puzzled look on his face.

When Sonya became aware of Willie observing them, she quickly withdrew her hand from his, stepped back two steps, waved awkwardly at him and said, "Ahh…well, I just wanted to thank you." She didn't quite know how to follow up on the thank you. What came next was what she really wanted to say, "I'll be back this fall and I hope to see you again then, Dr. Murdoch."

"Yes, well, Willie is a very well-liked student here at Banffshire and, indeed, I do hope to see you again this fall," he said, and he awkwardly returned her wave.

Now Sonya was completely flustered and managed to say, "You can, ahh, please call me Sonya."

She turned and walked back to the car. He watched her walk away. She knew that he was watching.

Several times during that summer Willie recounted things he had learned at school that year. Sometimes it related to English literature, other times it would just be useful bits and pieces of information, most of which Willie credited to Dr. Murdoch. This gave Sonya a sense of satisfaction and made her happy. But more than that sense of satisfaction, was her desire to see John Murdoch again.

That autumn, Derek and Sonya drove back to Banffshire to return Willie for his third year. Sonya was disappointed that Derek had decided to take the day off from readying for harvest. She had hoped to make the trip alone with Willie. She didn't make any attempt to see John Murdoch and didn't.

Sonya did, however, find reasons to return to the Banffshire two or three times during the school year, including the Christmas break. She made the trips alone and they were made ostensibly to see Willie for special school functions, or whatever other excuse she could muster. Of course, she did see Willie, but she also made no effort to conceal her attempts to find John Murdoch. Each time, she did, and their meetings became a bit longer each time. They enjoyed each other's company and their hand-holding handshakes evolved into short embraces when they greeted and again when they parted.

Chapter 14

For Sonya, there really was no decision about Robbie also attending Banffshire. Derek didn't care one way or another.

Sonya completed the application form and Robbie was accepted into Banffshire Academy for Boys.

Early in the summer preceding Robbie's first year, Sonya made arrangements to take him to the school for a meeting with Headmaster Dr. Fraser and tour of the campus, as they had done with Willie three years earlier. The morning of their planned trip to Kingston, Derek announced that he was too busy to go. Sonya was a little disappointed, a little not. But she was not surprised.

Of course, Sonya also hoped to see John Murdoch again.

As had happened three years earlier, a junior staff person toured Sonya and Robbie around the campus.

Robbie seemed to especially admire the trees, particularly, the indigenous trees near the lake. Sonya thought to herself, 'I'm guessing that Robbie will be having a few conversations with those trees while he's here.'

When they approached the dormitories, Sonya was having a discussion with their tour guide about the proximity of the junior boys' dorm being so close to the lake. Sonya's fear of water welled up again and she told the guide that for some reason she was uneasy with the dorm being so close to the lake. She hadn't been uneasy when Willie lived there but she was now. Robbie would be living there in September.

As they were talking, Robbie had wondered off. When they realized that he wasn't with them, Sonya called out is name. There was no response. Sonya and the guide started walking together in search of him. Still they did not find him or hear anything. The very unease she had been describing to the guide was now a distinct fear. They decided to split up and continue their search. Sonya began to panic a bit and hastened the pace of her walking and searching.

Then she saw him. He was lying on his right side on the rocky shore his back towards the campus, facing the lake. He was inches away from the water. She cried out, "Robbie! Robbie! What are you doing? You're too close to the water? Are you ok?" He didn't respond.

Sonya ran to him, knelt down beside him and leaned over to look at his face. His eyes were closed, and his lips were moving.

He still didn't respond. He remained laying there with his eyes closed. A wave lapped up to him, splashing water on his right side and his face.

"Robbie!", Sonya was almost screaming.

Slowly he opened his eyes and said, "I was just talking with my friend."

At that point, Sonya didn't have the patience or will to inquire as to who that particular friend was or what they were talking about. All she wanted to do was get him away from the water.

Of course, Sonya had seen this kind of behaviour from Robbie many times before. But this time, she was alarmed, both out of a sense of fear for Robbie's well being so far away from her watchful eye and care, but out of a sense of worry about how Robbie would fit in at Banffshire if other boys observed something like this.

She had hoped that Robbie would make some friends at Banffshire. He never had at Glengarry, but she hoped he would here. But if the kids saw him do this kind of thing or hear him talk like that, he might not only not make friends, he might also be in for a rough ride.

The junior staff person had caught up with Robbie and Sonya and he looked at the strange scene, a bit baffled. "What is he doing? Is he ok?" he asked.

"Yes, he's fine," Sonya answered, then turned back to Robbie.

"Please get up, Robbie. It's time for us to return home," she said.

Robbie slowly stirred and got up. His entire right side was wet from the wave. Sonya thanked the young guide and quickly led Robbie to the car.

Sonya was flustered and just wanted to get home. She reluctantly abandoned her hope to see John Murdoch on that trip and drove home. He probably wasn't even at the school for the summer, she thought.

In September, Robbie was off to Banffshire Academy for Boys with Willie.

Chapter 15

John Murdoch had been told by his father that he'd come from a long line of English school teachers.

What 'long line' really meant was that his father had birth records from St Mary's Cathedral in Kingston, Ontario for John, for himself and for his father. All three had been born and raised Catholic in Kingston.

His father claimed that John's great grandfather was born in Keith, Scotland but he had no records. John was born in 1926, and he knew the birthdates of his two Canadian Murdoch ancestors, so he estimated that his great grandfather would have been born in the 1850s in Scotland. Someday, he would check into it.

After John's father passed away, he had no more oral stories or traditions to provide any further information on his Murdoch ancestry.

John's mother's name was Alice Brennen. Her ancestry, apparently, was from the Newcastle area in England but she never seemed to be interested in talking about it beyond the account of her own mother. Both Alice and her mother had been born in Canada and neither of them seemed to have any further interest in England or things English. They had both become thoroughly Canadian. His mother passed away seven years after his father had.

He always planned to investigate his Scottish ancestry further after he retired, but never did. He also planned to go to Scotland after he retired, but he never did that either.

John, like his father and grandfather before him, had graduated from Queen's University and taught English literature at Banffshire Academy for Boys.

John's father claimed that when John's great grandfather had arrived in Canada from Scotland, he had taught French as well as English. However, in eastern Ontario, there were many native French speakers who were more competent teachers of the French language than a Scot fresh off the boat. So that particular skill had disappeared from the Murdoch resume.

John Murdoch had gone further in his education than any of his forefathers. He earned a Ph.D. at Queen's in English Literature. His thesis on 18th century Scottish poetry, with a focus on Robert Burns, had been published as the feature article in the Winter, 1951 issue of the prestigious London based Journal of English Literature.

After graduating, John was immediately hired as an Assistant Professor at Banffshire Academy teaching English literature.

When John Murdoch began teaching at the school in 1951, the student population at Banffshire was approximately 300 and the academic staff numbered about 25, 21 men and 4 women. By the time he retired in 1991, both the student and staff populations had quadrupled. The ratio of men to women in the ranks of the professional teaching staff remained about the same.

Barry A. Bernhardt

Boys came to Banffshire from all parts of Canada. There were some boys from the United States and a few from the United Kingdom, often sons of families who had some connection or other to Canada or Scotland. Most of the boys came from families with at least some amount of Scottish ancestry. About 65% of the surnames of the students were Scottish.

Most boys also came from well to do families. Banffshire Academy was a private school with no public funding source. In its early days, it had had some financial support from the Presbyterian Church of Canada but that had long since been discontinued. Thus, the tuition and residency fees were high. That also explained why the student attrition rate was low…parents 'committed' their boys to the school, whether they liked it or not.

During his 40-year career at Banffshire Academy, John Murdoch had seen every conceivable type of student. He estimated that he had taught English Literature to some 3,000 boys. John Murdoch had taught all types: diligent students, lazy ones, naturally talented boys and ones who survived the rigorous school program only due to much hard work.

Of course, there were some boys who stood out in John Murdoch's memory for one reason or another. For example, Patrick McKenzie had committed suicide, Morley Anderson, a so-so student, had gone on to be the Minister of Finance in the Government of Canada. Lawrence Mallory had become a Justice of the Supreme Court of Canada and James Fillmore had been convicted of three counts of 1st degree murder.

John Murdoch's favourite memories, of course, were of students that had had shone or at least had taken an interest in his English classes. He took a special interest in those students who had followed up with careers in some related field. Arnold Cryne had gone on to be a successful journalist with the Globe and Mail, Vince McKillop had become a New York Times bestselling novelist and Peter Faraday had gotten a Ph.D. in English Literature from the University of Toronto and was now Professor Emeritus (Victorian Novels) at Harvard University.

Then there was Robbie Gordon.

Chapter 16

Robbie Gordon arrived at Banffshire Academy in September 1963. The trees on the campus were in the early stages of putting on their spectacular annual autumn exhibition. The maple leaves were still a mix of green, orange and red.

Dr. John Murdoch had already been teaching at Banffshire for 12 years.

On his first day, Robbie was fitted with his school uniform. He was given the smallest size available. The uniform consisted of dark blue trousers and a matching vest. The color matched Robbie's dark blue eyes. The vest had brass buttons down the front. Each brass button featured the Banffshire logo in low relief. The shirt was collared and white, mated with a dark blue necktie, which also contained the school's logo. The logo was a stylized red lion on a saltire, below which were the Latin words "*Educatio – Provectus*": Advanced Education. Black shoes and black socks were compulsory. Navy blue winter coats were issued to each student and completed the ensemble of school issued garb.

During the long cold winter months in Kingston, Ontario, the only thing that distinguished one Banffshire student from another was the color of their toques and gloves. For some reason, the school had never standardized these items, so to provide some individuality, each boy took great pride in collecting the loudest and strangest of these items that he could find.

Robbie had learned of this wonderful opportunity from Willie. Willie had gone for three years with a crimson red color. Robbie had chosen a purple and yellow toque with matching purple woolen gloves. He was looking forward to the winter days when he could wear them.

Later that same first day of school, Robbie was approached by three new Level 1 boys. They seemed to all know each other and looked like a sort of club. One of them shouted out to Robbie, "Hey kid, you look pretty enough to be a girl. You know this is a boys' school." Robbie just walked away.

About a week later, Willie, who was now in Level four at Banffshire, heard about this incident, not from Robbie, but from some bystanders who had witnessed the event. Willie purposefully found the three boys and asked them to follow him. Willie said, "Hey guys, there's something I want to show you."

The boys hadn't yet heard about Willie Gordon, so they didn't fear him. They also didn't know that Willie was Robbie Gordon's brother. They obediently followed Willie, nervously snickering amongst themselves and speculating as to what this big Level four student was going to show them. Willie guided them to a secluded, heavily treed spot on the south-west corner of the campus, near the lake. Once assembled and without saying anything to them, Willie, in rapid succession, punched each of them once in the nose. They all immediately began to cry. They weren't sure whether to run away and risk being chased, and suffer further pain, or to stay and hope that this ordeal was over. Willie then calmly gave them three suggestions: first, that they never talk to Robbie Gordon again, the way they had; second, that they tell all their friends the same thing; and third, that they tell anyone who asked, that it was Willie Gordon that punched them in the nose. They were now all snivelling and wiping blood and snot from their noses while nodding vigorously in agreement with each of Willie's suggestions.

Robbie never had any similar problems for the rest of his time at Banffshire.

But Robbie never had any mates either. He remained a loner, as he had been his whole life.

On the second day, there was a general assembly in the Great Assembly Hall. Following many introductory comments and announcements, new and returning students were welcomed, and the academic staff was introduced.

That was the day Robbie Gordon first saw Dr. John Murdoch. He had heard about him from Willie and was curious.

At the beginning of his third day, Robbie attended his first class at Banffshire Academy.

"Good morning sir," was the united chorus of the 40 boys in the Level 1 *Introduction to English Literature*" class, in response to Dr. Murdoch's, "Good Morning boys."

This Level 1 English course was one of the compulsory courses for every first-year student and was held in one of the school's three large theatre type classrooms. Dr. Murdoch had been assigned to teach this course and for 6 years now, he had done so.

John Murdoch learned over the years not to expend too much energy in getting to know the names and faces of the boys in this large classroom environment. He saved that energy for the smaller classes of the many English electives that would follow. Notwithstanding that experience, he couldn't help but notice one frail looking lad on the extreme left side of the theatre, near the back. His pale complexion almost shone in comparison to the sea of other ruddier faces.

He had also learned not to make any attempt, at least in the early days, to meet any of the boys after the lectures of these large classes. There would be plenty of opportunities for that during the balance of the school year. But on that particular day, for some reason, he ranged off his normal course.

The pale boy was one of the last to leave the theatre and Dr. Murdoch caught the boy's eye, pointed to him and beckoned him with his index finger to come to the front of the room. The boy slowly made his way towards the front of the theatre. John Murdoch noticed that he tilted a bit to the left and walked with a slight limp.

That morning John Murdoch and Robbie Gordon met.

"Good morning young man. What is your name?" Dr. Murdoch asked.

"My name is Robert Allan Gordon, but my mom calls me Robbie," Robbie answered.

Based on Robbie's appearance, he doubted it but asked anyway, "Are you related to Willie Gordon?"

"Yes sir, he's my brother," Robbie replied.

John Murdoch was taken aback. In their several meetings, Sonya Gordon had never mentioned that she had another son let alone that he'd be attending Banffshire.

"Well, then," he continued, "It's great to have you here at Banffshire"

"I write poetry," Robbie said.

John Murdoch hadn't asked for that bit of information and was immediately interested in following up. "I see. Do you know much about poetry?" he asked.

"Yes sir, I do," Robbie said.

"How do you know about poetry?" Dr. Murdoch asked.

"It's just in my head," Robbie answered.

"In your head?" Dr. Murdoch asked with a puzzled look on his face.

"Yes sir," Robbie said.

John Murdoch didn't know how to respond to that, so he said, "That's wonderful. We have lots of time so let's get to know each other and we'll see how your interests and skills develop."

Robbie said, "Thank you sir," and he left the theatre.

Dr. Murdoch watched him walk away, again with a slight tilt to the left and a limp.

Each first-year student was permitted to choose one elective for a second English Literature course. These courses were limited to 10 students and Robbie chose 18th Century English Language Poets. What Robbie didn't know when he'd made the election was that Dr. Murdoch was the teacher for that course as well.

On Robbie's fourth day he entered the small classroom for the course on 18th Century English Language Poets. There were only 7 boys in the class.

When John Murdoch saw Robbie enter, he smiled and greeted him, approached him and touched his boney shoulder making sure that he made eye contact. He couldn't help noticing Robbie's striking dark blue eyes. He said, "I'm happy to see you in my class. I look forward to helping you explore your interest in poetry."

Robbie, said, "Thank you sir, I'm happy to be here."

In the compulsory "Introduction to English Literature," John Murdoch surveyed all genres of English literature, from works in predecessor linguistic forms to modern English. He started with Widsith, Cædmon's Hymn and Beowulf, then progressed down through the years to include Shakespeare, Milton, Austen, Dickens, Bronte, Wilde, Yeats and Kipling, among many others. The course covered the evolution of the English language itself, the development of different styles of writing, the political and economic context that existed when the works were written, among other topics.

Many students found the course quite boring…Robbie Gordon did not.

One of Dr. Murdoch's philosophies of teaching was to expose his students to as many writers and as many forms of literature as he could. His view was that even if they retained only a small part of what they learned in school, it would enrich their lives forever.

Another philosophy of his was to push the boys to develop their creative writing skills. He felt that if they were not pushed, those skills would lie dormant. And, for some of his best students, he noticed that the more he pushed them, the more curious and talented they became in their writing skills.

One of Dr. Murdoch's exercises in his Introduction to English Literature class was to challenge the students at various points during the year, to take any collection of words from a contemporary text and create a composition using an earlier form of the language. He felt that this exercise would help them develop an appreciation for the historical roots of the English language.

Robbie seemed to have a knack for writing in old English and old Scots. In fact, he was so skilled that Dr. Murdoch wondered if he'd had some experience with the early forms of those dialects before he had arrived at Banffshire.

Another exercise he used in the compulsory introductory English course was to ask the students to write a romantic poem using only words from a modern, non-creative text. He felt that this would give his students an appreciation of how the same words in the English language can be used in flexible and multiple ways and convey very different emotions and messages.

That was one of the early term assignments Dr. Murdoch gave to the students in the year Robbie Gordon was in that class.

The source work that Dr. Murdoch chose for that year's assignment was from a legal document called a "Trust Deed." It ran like this:

> *I, John Doe (the "Trustee"), hereby agree to act as a trustee for you, Lawrence Peabody (the "Beneficiary"). In the exercise of the rights, duties and obligations prescribed or conferred by the terms of this trust, I shall act with honesty and in good faith with a view to your best interests and shall exercise the care, diligence and skill of a reasonably prudent trustee. I shall only be liable for my own wilful acts and defaults. I shall give substantially all of my professional time and attention to my duties as trustee. When performing my duties hereunder, I shall not be liable for any act or default on the part of any agent or co-trustee, or for having permitted any agent or co-trustee to receive and retain any gain or benefit that is attributable to me hereunder, except as aforesaid.*

Using only the words found in this Trust Deed, the students were now to write a romantic, love poem.

He carefully read each of the 40 compositions. Many of the students struggled with the exercise and came up with simplistic three or four-line poems. One example was:

> *I hereby agree*
> *To be your trustee*
> *And only that, I'll be.*

Hardly romantic, John Murdoch thought. He wondered if that student even knew what a trustee was.

Then he came to Robbie Gordon's poem:

I CARE

> *My only obligation is to you.*
> *My honesty is my default.*
> *I care, I care.*
> *My only obligation is to you.*
>
> *My only duty is to you.*
> *My skill is for your benefit.*
> *I care, I care.*
> *My only duty is to you.*
>
> *My best attention is for you.*
> *My diligence is for your gain.*
> *I care, I care.*
> *My best attention is for you.*
>
> *My only interest is to retain you.*
> *I perform to gain your faith.*
> *I care, I care.*
> *My only interest is to retain you.*

He carefully analyzed Robbie's poem. Every single word of the poem came from the Trust Deed.

He saw a maturity to Robbie's poem that no other student matched. The poem made it appear that this boy of 12 years old had actually experienced some type of romantic love. He wondered how that could be.

In the 18th Century English Language Poets class, he had a more focused syllabus. Because it was a course restricted to the genre of poetry He surveyed the likes of Ramsay, Dryden, Blake, Burns, Wordsworth, Scott, Keats, Coleridge, Shelley and Stevenson.

An integral part of this course was to encourage the students to write their own poetry, about any topic that they wished, just to experiment with the art of writing poetry. Robbie loved these exercises.

On one occasion early in the year, John Murdoch reviewed one of Robbie's works and again, was impressed with its maturity. It read:

AS IF YOU WERE HERE

I'm talking to you
as if you were here,
as if you could hear,
as if you were near.
But you're not.

I reach for your face
as if I could touch
again, even once
again, I could touch.
But I can't.

I tug at your heart
as if it could feel,
as if I could will,
will it to heal.
But it won't.

Again, John Murdoch wondered what experience a 12-year-old boy could have had to write such words. Or did it just come from his head, as Robbie had told him it did. It was almost as if Robbie was channeling someone or something external to himself.

During that school year, he became increasingly fascinated by and interested in Robbie. He saw a talent in Robbie that he had never seen in any other student in his years of teaching. He decided to press Robbie, even more than the other students, to see what he might create. Instead of bucking the pressure, Robbie seemed to yearn to learn more and more. His curiosity to learn was insatiable. He soaked in everything that John Murdoch taught him.

Sometimes, however, it seemed to John Murdoch that Robbie was also absorbing knowledge from another mysterious and unknown teacher. He knew more than he was teaching him.

John Murdoch often invited Robbie to stay for a few minutes after class to discuss a bit further what they had been talking about in class. He was pleased with how perceptive and interested Robbie was.

Robbie spent many hours in the Inverness Library. He always sat at the same table, in the same chair. His spot was directly underneath the stained-glass window of Robert Burns, next to one of the old globes at the lamp end of a table. If Dr. Murdoch ever wanted to find him, he knew exactly where to look. He often did just that. Robbie was almost always reading poetry, often the 18 Century poets. That was something very few students would ever voluntarily do. The Inverness Library only had two books of Burns poetry and one or both of them could often be seen lying on the table near where Robbie sat. John Murdoch would often sit down at the table with Robbie. They would quietly talk and read together, sometimes for hours.

Robbie had a particular love for Robert Burns poems and would recite many of them from memory to his teacher. In John Murdoch's lifetime, he had attended several Burns functions in Kingston and even as far away as Toronto and had heard people recite Burns poems from memory, even some of the longer ones such as Tam O'Shanter. That was an amazing accomplishment, but young Robbie Gordon could recite dozens of Burns poems by heart. John Murdoch wondered.

Early in the mornings or late in the evenings, Robbie could often be seen walking slowly around the campus on the cobblestone pathway that ran around the circumference of the property. Sometimes, he would stand on the lake shore, for long periods of time looking out onto the water. He was always alone. He had no friends, so sometimes when John Murdoch spotted Robbie walking, he would join him, and they would walk and talk together.

On one of these occasions, Robbie wanted to go off the path into one of the forested areas of indigenous trees near the lake. John Murdoch walked with him. Robbie walked up to an old maple tree sat down beside it and placed the palm of his hand on the trunk of the tree. The tree was very old, near the end of its life and its branches were mostly bare. Robbie remained silent in that position for several minutes. John Murdoch waited in silence watching him. Tears began to form in Robbie's eyes, and a few fell on the leaves where he sat. Finally, John Murdoch said, "Robbie, what is happening?"

Robbie looked up at him and said, "This tree is angry and sad at how people treat trees and cut down the forests."

He did not know how to respond to this, so simply said, "I see. Yes, that is a tragedy."

They remained at the maple tree for a few more minutes then returned to the cobblestone pathway and walked on further.

During the school year, a relationship developed between Robbie Gordon and John Murdoch. It was more than a teacher-student relationship. It was a friendship. Robbie had never really had a friend before and for the first time in his life he started to reveal himself to another human being, his first real friend. He had not done that before, even to his own mother. He began to expose his inner self to John Murdoch. It was as if Robbie was willing to share his secret things only with someone who knew and understood them or else he would choose to be alone.

During these one-on-one times, at the library or walking, John Murdoch and Robbie would have wide ranging discussions about literature, especially poetry. They would talk for hours, something that John Murdoch had never done with any other student. Gradually, Robbie began to open up to John Murdoch about other topics as well.

Robbie told him about his frequent dreams, when he would do amazing things.

He told him about the times when he 'became' another person.

He told him how he could sense things that hadn't happened yet.

He told him about his friendship with trees and creatures.

John Murdoch would listen and wonder. He had never experienced anything like it. He had never known anyone like Robbie Gordon.

He also began to develop a sense of understanding and acceptance of Robbie's strange and wonderful accounts and behaviours. He couldn't explain it, he just understood that there was something mysterious, magical and special about Robbie Gordon. John Murdoch not only had a sense of understanding and acceptance about these things, he felt that he somehow had a special mission in his life to nurture and encourage this boy.

It was shortly after the session with the old maple tree that Robbie wrote an unsolicited poem and handed it to Dr. Murdoch during one of their walks. It read:

I SHOULD HAVE SAID SOMETHING SOONER

I should have spoke out earlier,
now I'm 300 years old.
What was once full, green and clean
is now bare, brown and dry.
I should have said something before.

Of course, I've sensed things myself
and my friends have told me things.
Years have scarred the tenderness.
The music is now garbled noise.
I should have done something before.

But now I do speak...I speak to my friends
"Be aggressive, if you are able!
You must make bare, brown and dry,
full, green and clean again."
I wish I had spoke out earlier.

I'm near the end now.
Wiser than before, but
I can't see color, and little light.
The variety and array have dwindled.
I should have said something sooner.

What will happen in the next 300 years?
I won't see it. Do I want to?
My roots are tired, and my branches are bare.
Damn, is it too late?
I should have said something sooner!

John Murdoch read the poem and wondered at the maturity of its author. Then another thought struck him. He wondered if the poem was a reflection of what the maple tree had said to Robbie that day he saw him talking with it.

Chapter 17

The night before the 1963 Banffshire Christmas break, Derek came home late and drunk.

They had planned to drive to Kingston early the next morning to pick Willie and Robbie up from school.

Sonya laid awake in bed waiting for him and worrying. As the hours passed, her worry changed to anger. When he finally came home, he noisily undressed and crawled into bed with her. She pretended to be asleep. He stunk. He immediately fell asleep and started snoring loudly. Sonya quietly left the bed and went into Willie's room where she finished out the night with little sleep.

Early the next morning, Sonya got out of Willie's bed and returned to their bedroom to wake Derek up. "Derek, you need to get up. We're supposed to be in Kingston by 10 o'clock," Sonya said and jiggled his exposed bare shoulder.

Derek opened one eye, "You gotta be kidding," he mumbled.

"No, I'm not, now get up," she said.

"Hey, don't get bossy with me woman," he slurred, "Let me be." It had only been three hours earlier that he had come home, and he was clearly still drunk.

"I can't believe you," Sonya said angrily. "You get drunk the night before we're supposed to go pick the boys up. Never mind, I'll drive there by myself."

"You're not takin' my new car. No, yere not!" Derek slurred.

"Don't be ridiculous Derek," she shouted back. "How do you expect me to get there? Do think I'm going to drive that old pick-up truck all the way to Kingston and back. It's filthy dirty and probably won't even make the trip."

"You're not taking the truck either," he continued, with raised voice. Derek then tried to get out of bed and fell down onto the floor. He was naked. He had developed a beer belly, from drinking. He finally found his feet and stood up. Sonya shuddered and turned away.

He started to stagger out of the bedroom towards the kitchen.

"Where are you going?" Sonya shouted as she followed him.

Derek didn't answer. Once he had made it to the kitchen, he reached into the large open bowl on the counter where they kept various keys. He grabbed the car keys and the keys to their old pick-up truck and stumbled back to the bedroom clutching them in his big fist. Sonya followed him, dumbfounded.

"Oh my god," said Sonya, "You are a child. Do you expect me to get a taxi? There are no cabs around here."

"You figure that out," he sneered and then rolled over and immediately fell back asleep, snoring loudly.

Sonya was confused and completely exasperated. For a moment she simply stood there looking at him wondering what had just happened. Derek had been drinking more and more but he had never acted belligerent or unreasonable like this before. Something was clearly bothering him and whatever it was, it was bothering Sonya just as much.

When she regained her composure, she realized that she had to somehow find her way to Kingston. She was embarrassed to call anyone for help. What excuse would she give?

Then she decided that she was going to have to find a cab somewhere in the region. She knew that there weren't any cabs in Maxville. She went back to the kitchen and took out the regional phone book and started looking through the yellow pages. It looked like the closest cab company was in Cornwall, at least 30 minutes away. If she called right away and if they could come, she might still be able to make it to Banffshire by 10 o'clock.

She called and about 40 minutes later a rickety pale green colored cab drove into their farm yard. In faded red letters on each side of the car it said, 'MIK'S Cab Service.' Derek was still sleeping.

Sonya had a sense of deep sadness as she climbed into the cab. Her eyes filled with tears.

She left the farm in a dilapidated taxi-cab that billowed out black smoke when it accelerated.

When she arrived at Banffshire, Sonya was motivated to collect the boys as quickly as possible so as to avoid any questions about her mode of transportation. She was even prepared to forego seeing John Murdoch, although on this day, she yearned to see him more than ever before.

She directed the cab driver to park his unsightly cab near the back of the parking lot. She got out and waited for the boys. When she saw them, she waved vigorously to get their attention. When they saw her, she beckoned them to come quickly to the cab. Willie excitedly ran to the car with a big grin. He had never been in a cab before. "What's this, mom?" he asked.

"Oh, I couldn't get the car today, so I thought we'd have an adventure in a taxicab," she answered.

The driver invited Willie to sit in the front with him. Sonya and Robbie sat in the back. During the trip back to the farm Willie asked a lot of questions of the driver and studied the meter and two-way radio. The driver let him talk to the dispatcher in Cornwall. Willie was thrilled.

Sonya looked over at Robbie. He was typically quiet but looked more somber than usual. Sonya laid her hand on Robbie's arm and asked, "Is everything ok, Robbie?"

"Yes," he said then paused before continuing, "Is everything ok with you mom?"

"Of course, it is dear," she lied.

Robbie looked directly into Sonya's eyes. His eyes filled with tears as he looked.

Sonya suddenly had a terrifying thought. 'Does he know what has happened, just like he knows the endings to my stories before I tell them? Oh, please God, he's too young to be burdened with this.'

Willie kept up his excited jabbering for the entire two-hour ride back to the farm.

Robbie was silent the remainder of the trip.

Chapter 18

After the Christmas break John Murdoch looked forward to continuing his journey with Robbie. He was increasingly drawn to the boy. He was amazed at his nascent abilities as a poet, his sensitivity and his tenderness as a human being.

He was also astonished at some of the strange things that Robbie told him about himself. He was beginning to see Robbie's strange behaviour as a gift. A mysterious gift from some unknown person or energy source.

But he also wondered if Robbie was altogether okay. Whatever was going on in the boy's mind certainly wasn't affecting the boy's performance at school, but John Murdoch became increasingly concerned about his ability to survive in the harsh environment that this world offered.

Shortly after the boys returned from Christmas break, John Murdoch decided to discuss Robbie with his parents. Plus, he wanted to see Sonya Gordon again.

He called the Gordon house one evening and Sonya answered the phone. He knew her voice right away. He thought it sounded like a musical instrument. For a moment, a lump caught in his throat and he couldn't speak.

Finally, he found his voice and said, "Oh, I'm sorry, hello, Mrs. Gordon this is John Murdoch."

"Hello, Dr. Murdoch, its very nice to hear from you," Sonya said.

"Yes, its nice to hear your voice again too, Sonya," he said. He wanted to say more along those lines but decided not to. Instead, he continued, "I don't know if you are aware of this, but I have Robbie in two of my classes. I must say, he is a very special boy."

"I knew he was in your English class, but I didn't know he was in another of your courses. Yes, he is special, isn't he?" she said, "I was wondering how long it would take you to call me." Sonya laughed nervously into the mouthpiece of the telephone and pushed her lips into it.

"I was wondering if you and your husband could meet with me to discuss a few things about Robbie," he said.

"Yes, I would love...I mean, of course, we would be happy to meet with you," she said.

"Could you come up to the school one day this week?" he asked.

They set a meeting date and time.

"I look forward to seeing you again," she said.

"I look forward to seeing you, as well," he replied.

Derek wasn't home when John Murdoch had called. He was in town at the bar. His drinking had continued to escalate, and Sonya had grown increasingly distant from him. She was heart sick at what was happening to Derek. She was very familiar with this behaviour from her years of experience with her father, and she feared the consequences.

Whenever she broached the subject of his drinking with Derek, he would always blame it on the pain in his arm. She believed that. She would often see him wince in pain when he'd lift something heavy or bump his arm.

But she wondered if there were other reasons.

She had discussed war time memories with him before, but he denied that he was troubled by anything like that.

Sonya knew that Derek was unhappy and uncomfortable about Robbie. That thought troubled Sonya. Not infrequently, he would make some snide comment about Robbie to Sonya. Then there were those times he would even say derogatory things to his friends about Robbie. He never spent much time with Robbie and seemed embarrassed to be seen with him in public. Sonya wondered if that contributed to his drinking.

When Derek returned home later that evening, he was more than a bit tipsy. She told him about Dr. Murdoch's call and the scheduled meeting. Derek didn't see the need to attend. More accurately, he didn't want to attend. He said to Sonya, with some amount of slurring, "If the guy wants ta talk about the kid, I a'ready know how weird 'e is, so wha's the use? I'm not goin."

Sonya winced but realized that it would probably be better for her to meet with John Murdoch alone, anyway. In fact, she preferred to see him alone. So, she didn't argue.

Two days later, she drove to Kingston alone in their new light blue Buick. She was looking forward to seeing John Murdoch again.

Before she met him that day, Sonya had the strange feeling that somehow Robbie was going to bind them together forever.

When Sonya arrived, she had expected to have to announce herself at the reception desk of the Administration building and then be escorted to Dr. Murdoch's office. She was surprised to see him waiting outside the doors of the building, ready to greet her.

His hair was shorter than when she had seen him last and he had greyed a bit more around his temples. She thought she could notice more fine lines at the corners of his brown eyes and between his eyebrows. She suddenly became aware that she was studying his face longer than she should have. He was watching her look at him. She averted her eyes downward and now, somewhat more discreetly, she thought, looked over the rest of him. His lean body had filled out a bit. He also looked taller than she remembered.

When she looked up, she realized that he had been studying her as she had been, him. She instinctively brought her hand up to her hair and gently flipped the side of it. She also gave her head a little shake.

One thing about him that hadn't changed was the sense of warmth that she had experienced at their previous meetings.

She extended her hand to him which he gently brushed to the side and he leaned towards her and gave her a very quick embrace and said, "It's very nice to see you again, Sonya."

Sonya's body immediately relaxed into him with a return embrace and said, "I am very happy to see you again, too."

"Please come with me," he said gently taking her arm just above the elbow guiding her into the building to his office. Now fully at ease and with anticipation, Sonya let herself be guided by him. He took her coat, hung it on his mahogany coat tree and closed his office door.

Dr. Murdoch was now a full professor at Banffshire and with that status came a quite comfortable office. In it was a large oak desk with a generously padded buttoned green leather chair behind it. In front of his desk were two maple client chairs. A small, upholstered chaise lounge fit perfectly into an alcove on one of the side walls. The chaise lounge faced a window on the other side wall, which looked out onto several mature trees on the campus.

Without her coat, he was now able to study Sonya more fully.

She was smartly dressed. She wore a white long-sleeved blouse with the top two buttons undone. Around her neck hung a single fine silver chain with a small silver locket hanging down just to the top of the curve of her breasts. She wore a navy-blue skirt with matching pumps. She too had greyed a bit and wore her hair a bit shorter than when he'd first met her. But her beauty was still there. The trials of life, whatever they were, had left her face without a trace.

Then it was his turn to realize that he had been studying her for just a bit too long and averted his eyes.

He asked her to sit down on the chaise lounge, which she did modestly crossing her legs, folding her hands and resting them in her lap.

He rearranged one of his client chairs to face Sonya and sat down in it. For a short moment, their eyes met and held. Again, he admired her pearls.

Finally, he said, "Mrs. Gordon…" Sonya interrupted him. "Please call me Sonya," she said.

He looked pleased, nodded and said, "Very well then, Sonya, I will do that, if you agree to call me John."

"Thank you, I will," she said.

"Before we talk about Robbie, will you forgive me if I say, I'm so happy that you could come and visit me, Sonya," John said. "But of course, I also wanted to talk to you about Robbie," he added.

Sonya smiled and said, "I was waiting for your call. How have you been?" she asked.

"I've been well and very busy. I have a full course load, but I enjoy it very much. How have you been Sonya? I think of you often," he ventured.

"Life is changing for me and….," she said as her voice drifted down to silence. Her head dropped for a moment and she just looked down to the floor.

"Is it something to do with Robbie?" John asked.

"No, it's nothing to do with Robbie. Sometimes I just get a bit down. Please excuse me," she said softly, still looking down.

"I'm sorry for whatever it is, Sonya," John said in a comforting voice. "If you ever need to talk, I will be here for you," he added.

"Thank you so much. I very much appreciate it," she said as she raised her head and again met his eyes with hers.

"Should we talk about Robbie then?" he asked. "As I said to you on the telephone, he's a very special boy," he added.

"I know. Robbie is different, isn't he?" she said.

"Yes, he is different and very special" he replied. "If you don't mind me saying Sonya, I've taken a real interest in Robbie and I believe he to me."

He continued, "I believe that Robbie has a special gift. I'm not sure where it comes from, but he has some kind of secret experience and knowledge that is a mystery to me. I wonder how Robbie knows what he knows. You are his mother so I'm certain that you know what I'm talking about."

"Yes, I do. Robbie has been unusual from birth. His childhood was full of unexplainable behaviours," she said.

Sonya then related in some detail some of Robbie's behaviour over the course of his childhood. John followed up with his own accounts of Robbie while at Banffshire.

"In the short time that he has been here at Banffshire, I have seen many of the same things that you've just described, Sonya," he said, "It's as if he has a secret source of knowledge. I find it absolutely amazing and wonderful."

Sonya said, "I have had people advise me through the years that I should take Robbie to see a professional psychologist or psychiatrist. I have never done that. What do you think?" she asked.

"Hmm," John put his finger on his chin as he thought about that. "I don't think that I would want to see that happen. Robbie is a gifted, fragile human being and I would hate to see someone tinker with his mind and damage his special gifts," he concluded. "Am I correct in saying that you would agree with that and that's why you've never taken him to such people?" John asked.

"That is exactly how I feel, John," she said as she simultaneously realized that this was the first time, she had called him by his first name. It felt comfortable to her. She liked it and immediately wanted to say his name again, over and over.

But she didn't instead asking "Is Robbie ok, here at Banffshire?"

"I do have a concern about how other people regard him and his lack of relationship with the other students. They shy away from Robbie and he seems quite happy to be alone. The staff here at Banffshire is well aware that sometimes some of the kids make fun of him behind his back but no one dares do or say anything to his face for fear of reprisal from his protector…his big brother Willie."

Sonya smiled at that.

John continued, "Of course, I fear that the environment here at Banffshire will be writ large in the harsh world out there when he leaves."

Sonya's head dropped again, and she said quietly, "Yes, I worry about that too. What kind of future will Robbie have? I love that boy more than I love myself." Tears welled up in her eyes and she lifted her head and looked at John. "What can we do to protect him?" she asked.

John was only two feet away from her and he leaned forward and placed his hand on her folded hands resting on her lap. He said, "I care very much for Robbie too. He and I have developed a very close relationship in this short time that we've been together. He tells me things about himself that I'm sure he has never told anyone, other than, perhaps you, Sonya. His mind is full of some kind of energy that you and I can't explain, but from it, he has a gift."

He paused for a moment in deep thought, as if he'd just had a revelation himself. He continued, "Yes, Robbie has a gift and one of the wonderful consequences of his gift is that he is able to produce beautiful and mature poetry. I would not want to do anything to interfere in any way with that gift."

Sonya pulled one of her folded hands from under his and laid it on top of his and said, "John, what should we do?" She pressed down on his hand.

He suddenly became aware of the escalating level of emotion and intimacy between himself and Sonya. He knew that he should be careful not to cross a line, so he gently pulled his hand from between hers, got up and opened the door to his office.

When he returned, he sat in his buttoned leather chair behind his desk and proceeded, "Mrs. Gordon, I think that you and I should just continue to love, nurture and protect Robbie as best we can. Let's see how he's doing by the end of the school year. Of course, we can always meet and talk again, if anything changes. I'd like to do that anyway." Then he added, "Even if nothing changes, I'd like to see you again to talk things over. Would that be alright with you?"

Sonya, too, had become very aware of the raising level of intimacy between them and of John Murdoch's attempt to now get control of it. She wasn't sure that she wanted it to be controlled but knew that it was the right thing to do.

She adjusted herself, wiped her eyes with her now empty hands and replied, "Yes, Dr. Murdoch, I do agree with that." They both realized that they had returned to calling each other 'Mrs. Gordon' and 'Dr. Murdoch' instead of 'Sonya' and 'John'.

When she got up, John helped her put on her coat and then faced her, placed his hands on her shoulders, looked into her eyes and said, "You and I have a bond in Robbie. I like that."

She started to tear up again, turned and left John Murdoch's office. He was watching her walk away and she knew he was.

In one of the exercises near the end of that school year, in his 18th Century English Language Poets class, John Murdoch had asked the students to write an original poem during the 50-minute class period and try to replicate the language and style of one of the poets they were studying.

Robbie's composition was:

TO MISS BURNS

Like to a fading flower in May,
Which Gardner cannot save,
So Beauty must, sometime, decay
And drop into the grave.

Fair Burns, for long the talk and toast
Of many a gaudy Beau,
That Beauty has forever lost
That made each bosom glow.

Think, fellow sisters, on her fate!
Think, think how short her days!
Oh! Think, and, e'er it be too late,
Turn from your evil ways.

Beneath this cold, green sod lies dead
That once bewitching dame
That fired Edina's lustful sons,
And quench'd their glowing flame.

John Murdoch read each of the 7 students' compositions and when he read Robbie's he was puzzled.

He had a faint recollection of seeing this poem before but couldn't quite place it. For two days he was troubled by his memory of the poem. Then it came to him that this may have been a Robert Burns poem that he had once seen during his university days at Queens. He went to the Inverness Library and found the two Robert Burns books of poetry on the table where Robbie always sat. Robbie was not there. John Murdoch reviewed the Table of Contents of both books but could not find a poem entitled 'To Miss Burns.' He looked through the entire list of poems for other titles that could have been the same poem but found nothing close. Now his curiosity was aroused, and he decided to attend the Queen's University Library. In the general collection he found several books relating to Robert Burns and complete works of his poetry. Not a single one contained a poem entitled 'To Miss Burns'. Next he went to the W.D. Jordan Rare Books & Special Collections and there he found a book of Robert Burns poetry published in 1843 which contained a poem entitled '*To the Memory of the Unfortunate Miss Burns.*' It was the same poem that Robbie Gordon had written. Now John Murdoch was shocked.

The next day, John Murdoch asked Robbie to see him after class. John Murdoch handed him the poem and asked him, "Robbie, is this your poem?"

"Yes sir."

"This is your own creation?"

"Yes sir."

"Robbie, I think that you have seen this poem before and that you have memorized it"

"No sir, I've never seen it before, it's my poem."

John Murdoch was perplexed. He doubted very much if Robbie had ever seen the poem before, as it was hard enough for him to find, let alone Robbie, who he was quite certain had never been off the Banffshire campus. But how could Robbie have written an identical poem to a Robert Burns poem written almost 200 years earlier. This was one of the strangest things John Murdoch had ever experienced in his teaching career, or his entire life, for that matter!

"Robbie, this is not your poem. I asked you to replicate the language and style of a poem by one of the poets you were studying, not to simply reproduce an actual poem by that poet"

"No sir, I didn't. This is my poem," Robbie insisted.

John Murdoch became a bit flustered and said, "Robbie, this is not your poem. It is a poem written by Robert Burns. How did you....where did you.... You are a very talented boy, and you're developing into a fine poet, but you are not telling me the truth, and this is not your poem."

Robbie Gordon, looked straight into the eyes of his teacher and friend. Tears welled up and he said, "I'm very sorry sir, but this is my poem."

John Murdoch was uncertain as to what to do. Should he have the boy disciplined in some way? The school had a strict policy against even the slightest hint of plagiarism. This was not a hint, this was a full scaled copying of someone else's work. But how did he do it? Even if he reported this incident to Headmaster Fraser, how would he explain it?

Both John Murdoch and Robbie stayed silent, for several minutes. Suddenly, John Murdoch had a sense of understanding and without planning to do so, stood up and hugged the tearful boy and said, "I know it was your poem, Robbie."

Chapter 19

Robbie Gordon's health deteriorated after the Christmas break that year at Banffshire Academy. He was in and out of hospital in Kingston four times that winter. Sonya came to visit him every day when he was in the hospital. Derek came to visit him once.

Of course, Robbie missed several classes during that period. John Murdoch went to visit him often. He hoped he would see Sonya during his visits, but he always missed her.

The doctors reminded Derek and Sonya that Robbie's lungs had been damaged from birth and advised them that they were weakening as he got older.

When Robbie returned to school in between his hospital stays, John Murdoch spent increasingly more time with him. Their friendship continued to grow.

Robbie's ability to compose beautiful and profoundly mature poetry grew, especially over the last few weeks of the school year.

But in June, with only three weeks of classes left, Robbie's mood suddenly turned dark and he started to sink into, what John Murdoch could only assess as a depression.

In his frequent one-on-one times with him, Robbie became less and less responsive and seemed to withdraw into the lonely boy he had been when he arrived at Banffshire. He even began to withdraw from John Murdoch.

On the second last day of class that school year, John Murdoch had given to the seven boys in his 18th Century English Language Poets class their final assignment. They were to create a poem during the class hour that expressed their own personal feelings and emotions.

Robbie's poem was this:

I NEED A CAB

I need a cab.
I'm on the ledge, I'm in the rain.
I'm on the edge, I'm in some pain.
I need to get out of here.

I need a cab.
My umbrella failed, failed years ago.
My cheeks are wet. The tears, they flow.
How do I get out of here?

I need a cab.
My feet are stuck. I can not move.
I died inside. There's no more love.
Where do I go from here?

The Mysterious Robbie Gordon

I see a cab.
Can I now escape from this?
How do I forget, the things I'll miss,
when I'm gone from here?

I'm in the cab.
I said, "Drive me far away."
He asked what I'll do there. I couldn't say.
As long as I'm away from here.

This poem was so dark. It troubled John Murdoch greatly.

Banffshire Academy had a farewell general assembly on the afternoon of the last day of school. John Murdoch intended to locate Robbie and talk to him about his poem after the general assembly.

John Murdoch looked for Robbie in the noisy, happy confusion following the boys' dismissal. As occurred every year, there was the chaos of students and staff saying their good-byes and students and parents trying to find each other.

He couldn't find Robbie in this rabble.

He did find Sonya though. She had arrived alone to pick the boys up.

Together Sonya and John began to look for Robbie. More boys and their parents were connecting and were leaving the campus for the summer.

Once all of Willie's friends were gone, he joined in the search as well.

John led Sonya to the places where he would often find Robbie when he went looking for him. They went into the Inverness Library to the table where Robbie often sat reading poetry. He wasn't there.

They looked for him on the cobblestone path encircling the campus. They didn't find him.

They quickened their pace and went down to the junior boys' dormitory and entered Robbie's room. He wasn't there either.

Sonya panicked as she had the previous summer. She worried that he may have gone down near the water. She and John rushed down to the lakeside and paced up and down the shore shouting out his name, "Robbie, Robbie." But he wasn't to be found.

After an hour or so, all the kids, moms and dads had left the campus and the staff members had either escaped to their offices or to their favourite pubs in town to celebrate the end of the year.

The campus was eerily silent, but Sonya and John had still not found Robbie. They were now clearly worried.

By late afternoon, John had called the authorities. Sonya was nearly hysterical with panic. She called home to tell Derek, but he didn't pick up. She guessed that he was at the bar.

The authorities formed a search party consisting of members of the Kingston police service and fire department. The search continued into the night. Around midnight, the police added two of their dogs to the search team.

Sonya and John never stopped in their search and continued through the night, tired and stressed.

About 5:00 am, just as light was starting to break on that early summer morning, they heard a shout then several shouts coming from the shore of the lake

John Murdoch never talked to Robbie about his dark, last poem.

Robbie Gordon's body was found in Lake Ontario. He was 13 years old.

Chapter 20

Three days after Robbie's body was discovered, Sonya called John Murdoch.

Sonya sobbed, "John, Robbie never really had any friends, but you were not only a very special teacher to him, but you were also his friend. For that I will be eternally grateful. John, would you consider speaking at Robbie's funeral?"

He could barely choke out a response, "Of course, I will Sonya. I'm so sorry for your loss…for our loss."

The service was held at St. Andrew's Church in Maxville. Reverend Campbell officiated. John Murdoch gave the eulogy.

The Kingston Whig-Standard carried a brief story of Robbie's drowning and made reference to the eulogy being given by Dr. John Murdoch of the Banffshire Academy.

A few days after the funeral, Sonya called John Murdoch and said, "John, thank you so much for the kind words you said about Robbie. Nobody understood him like you did. John, I've just found something in Robbie's things from his dorm room that the school brought to the house yesterday. Could I come to Kingston tomorrow and see you?"

"Of course, I'll be home. I'd love to see you. Would 2 pm work for you?" He gave her his address.

"Yes, I'll see you then," she answered and hung up the phone.

At 2 pm, Friday, July 8, 1964 Sonya was seated in a chair in John Murdoch's living room. John sat across from her on his sofa.

She handed him a sealed envelope. He immediately recognized Robbie's handwriting. It was addressed to 'Dr. John Murdoch'.

He opened the envelope and in it were two items. The first was a piece of paper folded into thirds, the second was another smaller sealed envelope also addressed to 'Dr. John Murdoch'. They were both in Robbie's handwriting. John unfolded the letter and read it silently:

> *June 26, 1964*
>
> *Dear Dr. Murdoch,*
>
> *I wanted to be a poet before I met you, but you taught me about the great poets, how to create, dream and how to write. I think, now, I truly am a poet.*
>
> *I don't know if I'll see you again, so I'm writing this poem to you.*
>
> *Thank you.*
>
> *Your adoring student and loving friend,*
>
> *Robbie Gordon*

John's eyes filled with tears and he tried to wipe them dry so that he could continue on with the second envelope.

He finally composed himself and reached into the first envelope for the second envelope.

He opened the second envelope and in it was another piece of paper folded in thirds as the letter in the first envelope had been. He carefully unfolded it. It was a poem, also in Robbie's hand-writing.

Again, he read it silently:

TO JOHN MURDOCH, MY TEACHER, MY FRIEND

By Robert Gordon

By John Murdoch I am bless'd.
By John Murdoch I was test'd.
He came whereo' I nest'd.
Lookin'. Wha' he found:
thrissles; my mind was mess'd.
He planted i' my ground.

In my ware he gently nurs'd it.
In simmer whipp'd and press'd it,
my mind he would no' rest it.
Wi' Dryden, Ramsay, Pope
he did his best to best it.
He never ga'e up hope.

By John Murdoch I am bless'd.
By John Murdoch I was test'd.
By hairst my mind conquest'd,
wi' his canie words
tha' he taught wi' pest an' zest.
I thank 'im wi' my words.

By John Murdoch I am bless'd.
By John Murdoch I was test'd.
Sae, my teacher lo'ed and trust'd,
I'll be indebt'd.
For wha' i' me he vest'd:
Curiosity whet'd.

The poem touched John Murdoch deeply and he now openly wept.

He handed the letter and poem to Sonya. She read them and also wept.

She rose from her chair and sat beside John. An unusual mix of profound grief and joy settled over them both. They wrapped their arms around each other and sobbed together for several minutes.

John Murdoch and Sonya Gordon never revealed the poem to anyone for the next 47 years.

PART II

Chapter 21

Ann Benoit had graduated from the University of London with a Bachelor of Education degree with honors. She had a major in French and a minor in English Literature.

She was now looking for a job and spotted the following ad in the Evening Standard:

> The highly reputed St. Germain École des Garçons is seeking candidates for a teaching position to commence September 2008 for Years 7 and 8 French language instruction. A high level of spoken and written French is required (preferred native speaker, but not necessary).

As French was her mother tongue, she would be well qualified for the job. Plus, it was close to where she lived in Marylebone.

Ann did some research on St. Germain before applying and learned that the school traced its origins in London back to 1805. The school's website said the school had its beginnings when its founder, Louis Chartier, a bilingual French and English language school teacher in Paris, escaped the post-revolutionary turmoils in France and emigrated to England. He began his London career by simply offering his services as a French language tutor.

When **Louis Chartier** arrived in London, there were other French language schools and tutoring of various sorts and sizes, but they were mostly led and taught by Englishmen, whose skill in French was often minimal.

The school's website went on to describe the years that followed and the growth and success of the school until today, when it was considered to be one of the top private French language schools for boys in London.

Ann applied for the job at St. Germain and her application was successful.

Her principal, Dr. Pierre Gingras, approached her and asked if she would be interested in earning some extra money by working over the summer to cull through the school's 100 plus years of archives, organizing and cataloguing them so that they could be properly managed and preserved for future years. Dr. Gingras told her that another teacher, Jules Marchand had agreed to the task and that if Ann was interested, she and Jules would be working together.

Feeling quite secure in her job at St. Germain, Ann had recently entered into a lease of a small flat on the rather posh Baker Street but could certainly use some extra cash to furnish the place properly. So, she readily accepted the summer job.

Besides, Jules Marchand was not hard to look at. The thought of rummaging through dusty old boxes in narrow aisles in a back room in the school all summer with Jules Marchand, appealed to her.

Unlike many women she loved her appearance and especially her body. She had an olive complexion, green eyes and dark brown hair. Her father's side gifted her with a strong nose. She got her body from her mother. Ann was especially proud of the shape she was in. She biked, worked out and ate well. She was slim and knew that her best feature was her legs. She often wore short skirts or short shorts to provide maximum exposure to those assets. It had served her well during her partying university days, but now she had somewhat, but only somewhat, lost interest in that scene and was looking more for a long-term mate.

Ann not only had the looks but also the attitude. She knew that when she walked into a room, especially a bar, every man stared at her. She had that sassy attitude with men that said, 'Hey, I've got it, I know it and I'll flaunt it'. No man, in Ann's experience, ever complained about that.

The summer job started the first week of July and she and Jules were given some basic instructions and an organizational chart by Dr. Gingras. They were then basically left alone for the rest of the summer.

Jules was also a relatively new teacher at St Germain. He was one of those stereotypical handsome, romantic and well-dressed Frenchmen. He was also some flirtatious.

Ann found it a challenge to resist the temptation to sneak looks at him throughout their summer workdays. So, for the most part, she didn't. What she didn't initially realize was that Jules was doing the same. Once they both realized that they were sneaking lustful looks at each other, the fix was in!

Only one week into the summer, they each seemed to be quite able to find reasons to frequently get close enough to the other that made bumping and touching inevitable. Of course, all this bumping was quite understandable because the job entailed fiddling with the boxes, files and other materials in the very cramped quarters of the archive room.

It was a hot, humid summer and there was little air conditioning in their little archive room. Thankfully, for Jules, Ann wore shorts or short skirts to work most days. She had great legs and they affected his ability to concentrate. Jules not only caught the vibe but actively encouraged it. For his part, there was nothing quite as sexy as a sassy, curvy French woman. Ann more than caught the vibe, she was emanating it from every pore of her body.

In the second week, Jules asked Ann if she'd like to join him for drinks after work. She readily agreed and Jules took her to Lord Byron's. He seemed to know his way around that particular establishment. Ann had never been there before and was amused with its mantra, "...*better beer and whisky for everyone.*"

Ann knew nothing about whisky so ordered a beer. Jules, who declared that he knew quite a bit about whisky ordered a Chivas Regal. He waxed eloquent about the Strathisla Distillery in Keith, Scotland where it was made. She feigned interest in his account but was more interested in his touching of her hand or her arm, which he did frequently during their session together. It wasn't really a date, it was just an after-work drink. Nevertheless, Ann was excited and considered it the starting point. She said to herself, 'He's not only good looking but he's also a touchy-feeling sort of guy. So far, so good!'

By the end of the third week, Jules and Ann had visited Lord Byron's four times and each time lasted longer than the one before and each time there was a bit more flirting and touching.

At the beginning of the fourth week, Jules came upon a box that had documents in it dating back to the 1820s. In one folder in the box was an unopened envelope addressed to:

'John Murdoch, c/o Louis Chartier, 88 Porter Street, London, England'

The envelope had a return address on the back side:

'Gilbert Burns
Bolton, East Lothian, Scotland'

The post mark on the letter was November 21, 1823.

Jules showed it to Ann and together they pondered what to do with it.

Jules said, "I think we need to visit Lord Byron's again and have a drink and decide what to do with this."

Ann happily agreed and hoped for more touching, perhaps crossing into some new territory.

They found a comfortable booth and this time Ann ordered a Scotch to impress Jules. Her hopes of success in that regard quickly vanished after her first sip, because immediately after swallowing a bit of it, she choked and spewed out what was left in her mouth. Jules laughed and encouraged her to keep trying. Hmm.

They talked about everything but the envelope. In fact, they almost forgot what their purpose was for coming there that afternoon.

And yes, there was a fair amount of touching. At one point, mid second drink, Jules left his side of the booth and joined Ann on hers. By the end of the second drink, she was practically sitting on his lap and they had their first, second and third kiss.

Lord Byron's had a fairly sophisticated clientele and Ann and Jules's displays of public affection was amusing and entertaining to some but was becoming a bit much for some of the stuffier senior patrons. Someone near to their booth said, in a very proper English accent, just loud enough for Ann and Jules to hear, "They might well consider taking a room." Even though Ann and Jules both wanted to do just that, neither of them gave a damn and carried right on with their activities.

A server finally came to their booth and asked Jules if he'd like to close the tab. Jules got the message, moved back to his side of the booth and ordered another round.

Finally, Jules said to Ann, "Well, I suppose we should talk about the envelope."

"If we have to," Ann laughed.

So, they reluctantly turned the conversation to the reason that they had come to Lord Byron's that afternoon, namely, the envelope. Jules said, "I think we'll need to open it to see what's inside in order to figure out where it belongs in our organization of things."

Ann still had a clear enough mind to know that this was probably not the right thing to do, at least not then. She responded cautiously, "I think we should discuss this with Dr. Gingras first. I have a good friend who is an archivist at the Avery & Lord firm and if Dr. Gingras agrees, I think it might be wise to contact her and let her have a look." Jules agreed with that.

That was enough conversation about the envelope, and they resumed their previous activities. At least, Jules stayed on his side of the booth.

Chapter 22

Elizabeth Cullen had met Ann at the University of London in a first year introductory Psychology course that they had both enrolled in as part of their respective electives. They sat next to each other on the first day of classes and became instant pals. Up to that day, Elizabeth had only ever been called by her full name, but Ann called her 'Liz' and thereafter, she was known as Liz to Ann.

They spent the next four years studying, partying, laughing and crying together. Of course, Ann was always the ring leader in the partying scene.

Many of their partying escapades started with the girls together and ended up with them separated. Usually Ann ended the night hooking up with some guy or another and Liz going home.

Ann was clearly the looker of the two girls and Liz knew full well that when they partied together, she was the side-kick and Ann was the player. Liz didn't really mind though. She was more the bookish, moderate type. Ann was the wild child. Liz lived vicariously through Ann's recounting of her adventures and frankly, she preferred that role.

Liz was plain, with a fair complexion, a small curvy nose on a face full of freckles, had a head full of orangy-brown hair and was very lean. Liz weighed about 100 lbs soaking wet, on a rainy day in London.

In university, Liz had earned a bachelor's degree with a major in Anthropology and a minor in English Literature, an odd combination but they were the two areas that interested her. She knew full well that there were very few jobs for anthropologists with a bit of knowledge of English literature, but she stuck with it and enjoyed it.

Even before she graduated, she knew she'd have to take some additional training to get into the job market, so she enrolled in a master's degree program called 'Archives and Records Management' at University College London.

Even before graduating from UCL, she had started looking at job postings and spotted one that interested her. The post said:

> *The established firm of Avery & Lord is seeking applications for a junior archivist. Position to start, September 2009. Avery & Lord has a 75-year history of acting as an independent contractor to reputable persons and institutions that require assistance in researching and archiving materials, including arranging, describing and organizing current collections, utilizing current archives best practices as well as in completing loan requests to lend materials to other institutions, and assisting and facilitating donations.*

Liz applied for the job, got it and loved it.

Her very first assignment was to assist The William J. Rose School of Music, in Canterbury, in organizing their 120 years of scores, correspondence, school records, and other materials.

Liz was on that job for almost a whole year. She didn't own a car, so she travelled back and forth from London to Canterbury via train. In the mornings, she'd board the train at St. Pancras International at Euston Road, Kings Cross about 6:30 am and arrive at the Canterbury West Station just before 8 am. In the evenings she would do the same trip in reverse.

The most interesting part of the work, for Liz, was doing research when required to identify the source of some score or other document when the provenance was unknown. She loved the sleuthing aspect of the job and she was good at it.

The Rose School of Music assignment was wrapping up the following July when Ann called.

"Hey Liz, I've missed you. I don't see you at all any more. When was the last time we went out? We'll have to get together again. How are you?" Ann rattled on.

"Hi Ann, good to hear from you. I'm fine, very busy with my job, but loving it. Last Christmas, I think it was," Liz answered.

Ann continued, "I'd love to see you again, and I've got some juicy stuff to tell you about a guy I'm seeing."

'Nothing new about that,' Liz thought.

Ann said, "And, you'll be interested to hear about a summer job that I've taken here at my school. It's right up your alley."

"Really, what are you doing?" Liz asked.

"Well, Jules (I'll tell you all about him when we get together) and I have been asked to do some organizing of all the historical stuff that's accumulated over the years here at St. Germain. We've come across something that I think might be important and I'd like to show it to you," Ann said.

"I'd love to see you again too. Are you free this weekend?" Liz asked.

"I am, but I think I'd better come and see you at your office. I don't want to lose this item or for anything to happen to it, like spilling some beer or whisky on it," Ann laughed. "Would you be available this coming Monday?"

"Ok, I'll be in Canterbury in the morning but returning to London in the afternoon. Could you come at, say, 6 pm?" Liz asked.

Ann said, "Great, I look forward to seeing you again, and, hey, maybe we can go out for a drink after…like old times."

"Sure, I'd like that," Liz said and wondered what kind of trouble this might lead to.

Ann and Jules discussed the find with Dr. Gingras and he agreed with Ann that they should be careful with the envelope and get a professional opinion. He was aware of the firm's excellent reputation and gave Ann permission to take it to her friend at Avery & Lord.

When Ann and Liz met on Monday, they hugged, then gushed, reminisced and gossiped for 45 minutes. Liz heard more than she really wanted to know about Jules Marchand but listened like the good friend that she was.

Finally, Ann produced the envelope.

Liz was immediately intrigued. In the last year she had seen many old documents, but she had never seen an unopened envelope with a post mark of 1823. It was clearly very old. The envelope was brown at the edges and brittle with age. The ink was quite faded, but still legible.

The first thing she did was scold Ann for handling the envelope with her bare fingers. Liz then slipped on a pair of skin-tight surgical type rubber gloves as she had been trained to do when handling important objects, especially paper.

She studied the front and back of the envelope for a few minutes and considered the available information. She had three names, John Murdoch, Louis Chartier and Gilbert Burns. She had two addresses, one in London, the other in Scotland. Then she had the date of November 21, 1823. There was other information, and, with her trained eye, she noted the handwriting, the shape, type and color of the paper of the envelope.

She desperately wanted to open the envelope but decided that she'd better consult her boss, Mr. Ian Avery, the fourth generation proprietor of the family that owned Avery & Lord. Somewhere along the line the Lord family disappeared from the firm, but the name hadn't.

Mr. Avery was not in the office that afternoon, so Liz carefully placed the envelope in the firm's safe for the night. The plan was for Ann to leave the envelope in the custody of Avery & Lord until Liz could discuss the matter with Mr. Avery in the morning.

The next morning Liz found Mr. Avery, gave him the background and showed him the envelope. Mr. Avery already had developed a level of confidence in Liz. He had received compliments from some of the senior people at the Rose School of Music, about her work ethic, her level of care and attention to detail and particularly her gift at research and sleuthing.

Mr. Avery said he'd contact Dr. Gingras at the St. Germain school to get instructions as to what the school would like the Avery & Lord firm to do with the envelope. Dr. Gingras, on behalf of the St. Germain school, entered into a tailored Engagement Letter with the firm which described the initial retainer fee and how ongoing fees were to be billed and paid. Mr. Avery and Dr. Gingras foresaw that this may be a long process so the Engagement Letter also addressed the manner in which future instructions were to be given. It stated that Dr. Gingras could provide written or verbal instructions and authorizations to the Avery & Lord firm, from time to time. His initial instructions were verbal, and he authorized Mr. Avery to do all that was necessary to determine what was in the letter.

Mr. Avery called Liz back into his office and relayed to her the instructions that he'd obtained from Dr. Gingras. He then asked Liz to start work on discovering what she could about the envelope after she finished up the assignment with the Rose School of Music. However, she was not to open the envelope...yet.

The following Monday, Liz was ready to start her research. She started with, what she thought would be the easiest lead, the name of Louis Chartier. The envelope had been found in the archives of the St. Germain school, so it was reasonable to assume that the envelope had some connection to the school.

Liz called Ann and asked her if she could provide any history on the St. Germain school and Louis Chartier. Not surprisingly, Ann's response was, "Well my friend, that will cost you another drink."

Liz agreed to meet her the following day thinking, 'Surely she won't have much new to tell me about this Jules fellow, so we should be able to get right to our business'. She was wrong. This time, though, Ann kept her gushing about Jules, down to about 10 minutes before addressing Liz's questions.

Ann already had a considerable amount of the information that Liz wanted from existing records. Louis Chartier had set up a French language tutoring business in London in 1805 after arriving from Paris, escaping the post-revolutionary troubles in France. Louis Chartier had a son, Charles, who had taken over the reins of the school in 1823, the very year of the post mark on the envelope.

That night in her flat, Liz mulled over the things Ann had told her. She conjectured that Gilbert Burns, the sender of the envelope, knew enough about Louis Chartier to know, or at least hope, that the envelope could reach John Murdoch by sending it to him c/o Louis Chartier.

Liz had learned from Ann that the address used by Gilbert Burns, **88 Porter Street, London, England,** was the address of the St. Germain school, from about 1820 to 1887. After that, the school had moved to its current location. She surmised that Gilbert Burns must have known enough to connect Louis Chartier with the St. Germain school. That might mean that the letter was more connected to the school than to Louis Chartier himself.

Liz then turned her attention to Gilbert Burns. His return address on the envelope was Bolton, East Lothian, Scotland. In Scotland, the Burns name was famous. It didn't take much sleuthing for Liz to postulate that this Gilbert Burns may have been the older brother of the famous poet, Robert Burns. The address matched where Gilbert lived for several years before he died in 1824. The post-mark on the letter was 1823. It seemed to fit.

Liz was now more than a little excited with her new project. Could this letter have something to do with the great Robert Burns?

So now Liz had figured out who Louis Chartier was and who Gilbert Burns might be, but who was John Murdoch? What could the connection be between the brother of the world-famous Scottish poet, Robert Burns, and John Murdoch?

She started researching Robert Burns rather than Gilbert Burns and quickly discovered that a John Murdoch had once been a teacher to both Burns brothers. Could this be the same John Murdoch to whom the letter was addressed?

Liz learned that an important source of information on all manner of things relating to Robert Burns and, to a lessor extent, John Murdoch, was the Burns Encyclopaedia. From that source, she discovered that a John Murdoch had been Gilbert and Robert Burns first teacher, hired by the boys' father William Burnes. Robert Burns would have been only six years old when Murdoch began teaching the boys. Apparently, John Murdoch had been Gilbert and Robert's teacher for at least two years. From what Liz learned from the Burns Encyclopaedia, various sites on the internet and other sources, Murdoch had introduced the Burns boys to their first non-religious literature, including, The Life of Hannibal, Titus Andronicus and the poetry of Alexander Pope. He had even taught them some French.

Liz was curious about this French connection and wondered if it might have something to do with the St. Germain school.

Liz also learned that John Murdoch had made quite an impression on the boys, particularly young Robert.

Liz thought she had learned about as much as she could from the information available to her without opening the envelope so she went back to Mr. Avery with her findings who, in turn, reported back to Dr. Gingras. Mr. Avery now advised Dr. Gingras that the next step would be to open the envelope and Dr. Gingras verbally agreed authorizing him to do so.

The next day, with Liz present, Mr. Avery donned a fresh pair of rubber gloves and carefully steamed open the flap of the 186-year-old envelope. Once opened, he looked inside. There were two items inside, one was a piece of paper folded in thirds, the other was another sealed envelope with the words '*TO JOHN MURDOCH, MY TEACHER, MY FRIEND*' written on it. These contents were not as brown and brittle as the main envelope, because they had been enclosed in their protective casing for all these years.

Chapter 23

Mr. Avery extracted the folded paper. It was a hand-written letter addressed to John Murdoch and signed by Gilbert Burns. It read:

November 19, 1823

Dear Mr. Murdoch,

I apologize for the extreme and unforgiveable lateness of my writing of this letter to you.

Enclosed is a poem written by my brother, Robert, in your honor. When he died, many of his belongings fell into the hands of his friends in Edinburgh. They somehow got misplaced and only recently have come to my attention and possession.

I have read my brother's poem and placed it in this sealed envelope for safer keeping during the mailing of it.

As you will see when you read his poem, Robert, like myself, was deeply affected by your teaching and friendship. You exposed our young minds to the beauty of literature and words themselves.

I also want you to know how grateful I am for the care and attention you gave in attending to the affairs of young William after his passing.

I have recently learned of your unfortunate financial circumstances and ill health. I am somewhat impoverished myself but would be happy to help you in some way if you require it.

I wish you all the best my/our dear teacher.

Gilbert Burns

The full impact of what they were reading was just dawning on Liz and Mr. Avery. Inside this next envelope was perhaps a Robert Burns poem that had never been seen or known about before.

They both sat in silence for a few minutes, lost in their own thoughts

Finally, Mr. Avery said, "We need professional advice on this, beyond what our firm can offer. I think we should advise the Centre for Robert Burns Studies at the University of Scotland in Glasgow of what we have in our hands. I don't think we should open this second envelope without a Burns expert being present."

Liz could only nod in agreement.

Mr. Avery again contacted Dr. Gingras to bring him up to date and bringing in Burns' experts. Dr. Gingras agreed and, again, verbally authorized the firm to proceed.

Liz was given the task of identifying the most senior person she could at the Burns Centre at the University of Scotland. Liz quickly realized Dr. Malcolm Crawford, the Chairman of the Burns Centre was that person. Mr. Avery reached Dr. Crawford that same day and related the whole story to him.

A somewhat incredulous Dr. Crawford fidgeted with some items on his desk and squirmed restlessly in his chair as he listened to Mr. Avery's story. A few, purportedly undiscovered, Robert Burns arrangements or reworkings of traditional songs and other writings had surfaced during Dr. Crawford's tenure, but none of them were as exciting as a new original Burns poem! Some of the 'discoveries' were fakes, but some were authentic. There was something credible and different about this story, he thought. And, in his line of work, this held the possibility of being something very thrilling.

Dr. Crawford knew that the second envelope needed to be opened in order to determine if there even was a Robert Burns poem inside. Assuming there was, it would need to be authenticated. If all of that happened, Dr. Crawford was well aware that such a find would become world-wide news and that the letter and the poem would have considerable value. Dr. Crawford secretly hoped that he might enjoy some of the fame that would be inevitably accompany such a find. It would most certainly enhance his career. He was already drafting the press release in his head.

Dr. Crawford agreed to meet with Mr. Avery and Liz Cullen. Before doing so, he said that the Centre would have to seek legal counsel on the matter of who might be the rightful owner of the Gilbert Burns letter and the Robert Burns poem if, in fact, there was such a thing in that second envelope.

Dr. Crawford suggested that Mr. Avery continue the safe keeping of the documents at his firm in London and that he would get back to him once he had obtained the solicitors' legal opinion.

It took one week for the Glasgow law firm of Fraser & Kennedy to get back to Dr. Crawford. The firm provided a 12-page opinion letter. The first portion set out the facts of the case. The second part discussed whether English or Scottish law applied. The firm concluded that English law applied based on the fact that the envelope was located in England when it was found. The bulk of the letter contained an extensive discussion as to who had the best legal claim to ownership. There were four candidates, the author of the letter, Gilbert Burns; the author of the poem, Robert Burns; the intended recipient, John Murdoch; and the possessor of the envelope, St. Germain School. The 11th page set forth the firm's conclusion. The firm opined that the best claim to ownership of the envelope and all of its contents, including the poem, was John Murdoch, subject to a long list of assumptions, qualifications and conditions set forth on the 12th page of their opinion.

After reading the qualifications and conditions, Dr. Crawford wasn't sure who the rightful owner really was. One of the firm's assumptions was that there was, in fact, a poem in the second envelope and that such a poem was written by Robert Burns and authenticated. One of the qualifications was that, since John Murdoch was now long deceased, the current lawful owner or owners would be his identifiable heirs, if there were any.

Dr. Crawford immediately called Mr. Avery to advise him of the solicitors' opinion and emailed a copy of the firm's opinion letter to him. Dr. Crawford also confirmed to Mr. Avery that the second envelope would need to be opened to determine what, in fact, was inside. He recommended that the opening of the envelope should take place at the Burns Centre at the University of Scotland where Thomas Campbell, an in-house Burn's historical specialist, should be present when the envelope was opened.

Mr. Avery told Dr. Crawford that he would require instructions from Dr. Gingras.

Mr. Avery called Dr. Gingras and, once more, brought him up to date. He emailed to him a copy of the Fraser & Kennedy law firm's opinion letter. On this occasion, Dr. Gingras did not immediately agree to anything, but advised Mr. Avery that he would need to consult his own legal counsel in London and that he would get back to him shortly. A few days later, he wrote an email back to Mr. Avery which said:

> Mr. Avery,
>
> *Further to our most recent telephone conversation, St. Germain École des Garçons hereby authorizes the firm of Avery & Lord to consult with the Burns Centre at the University of Scotland to further investigate the origin and authenticity of the contents of the envelope which is the subject matter of the Engagement Letter between our school and your firm.*
>
> *Thank you.*
>
> Dr. Pierre Gingras
>
> St. Germain École des Garçons

Mr. Avery wondered about the formality of the email, since all previous instructions had been given to him by Dr. Gingras verbally.

In any event, Mr. Avery called Dr. Crawford back and advised that they were ready to proceed as per his last recommendation. They set a meeting for 2 pm, Monday, August 9, 2010 in Dr. Crawford's office at the University of Scotland. Dr. Crawford, Mr. Avery, Liz Cullen and Tom Campbell would attend.

Liz and Mr. Avery flew to Glasgow on the weekend with their treasure in a secure valise that the firm had purchased just for this occasion.

When Liz and Mr. Avery arrived at Dr. Crawford's office, they introduced themselves and Dr. Crawford led them to a small conference room where Tom Campbell was already present.

Once the four of them were seated there was a nervous pause before Liz donned her rubber gloves and extracted the main envelope and its contents from the valise. She looked up as if to ask who she should give the envelope to. Dr. Crawford indicated that she should give it to Tom Campbell. He too had put on his rubber gloves and took the envelope. He paused, looked up and said, "Ok, is everyone ready?" They all nodded.

Tom Campbell looked briefly at the main envelope, then extracted the letter from it, examined it for a bit longer then laid it on the table. He pulled out the second smaller sealed envelope and studied it.

Tom turned on the small portable steamer he had brought for the occasion and aimed a small stream of steam toward the flap of the envelope for about 5 seconds and the flap loosened.

The air of anticipation in the room was palpable. Dr. Crawford, Mr. Avery and Liz all craned forward in their chairs to watch as Tom slowly and ever so carefully slide the contents of the second envelope out. Everyone was holding their breath.

It was a fragile looking piece of paper also folded in thirds. It looked more faded and delicate than Gilbert Burns' letter. That made sense to Liz as she watched. This piece of paper could have been several years older than the cover letter and may well have not been protected from the air during its lifetime.

Tom carefully unfolded the paper and laid it on the table. All four of them stood up to look at it.

It was a handwritten poem, showing the author to be Robert Burns.

Everyone was silent and just stood there staring at the paper. It was like they were looking at the Holy Grail.

Tom Campbell studied for it for several minutes without touching it further. He finally looked up at the others and said, "It looks legit but, of course, we'll have to submit it to a rigorous examination by experts to make a proper decision on its authenticity."

Everyone nodded in agreement and Tom continued, "It will likely take at least a couple of weeks to assemble the right team and for them to do the work required."

Everyone nodded again. Mr. Avery spoke, "Well, if we can all breath again, we'll need to decide next steps." After discussing matters for a few minutes, it was decided that the University of Scotland would take custody of the two envelopes, the letter and the poem to effect a full and complete process of authentication on each of them.

They agreed that Dr. Crawford and Mr. Avery would communicate with each other as soon as any significant developments occurred at either end.

Chapter 24

Dr. Crawford asked Tom Campbell to identify a team of top technicians and Burns experts as quickly as possible. Tom already knew exactly who should be on the team, besides himself. Two of them were in London and the other right there in Glasgow.

Dr. Noah Lucas was a scientist with the British Museum who had expertise in submitting historical documents to a range of scientific testing methods to determine authenticity.

Jack Oliver was a hand-writing expert with the London firm of Small & Pritchard.

Tom's friend, Leo Dwyer, was a professor of linguistics at the University of Scotland. He specialized in Celtic, particularly Scots Gaelic and early Scots dialect language forms.

Tom, himself, probably knew more Robert Burns history than anyone on the planet. He was the usual go-to person if the issue of provenance of a purported Burns work was in debate.

The four of them assembled at Tom's office at the University of Scotland and Tom showed the others the documents for the first time. They sensed that this was going be, at least, interesting if not exciting.

They each intuitively knew what the division of tasks would and should be, but they drew up a formal memorandum which described each of their duties, logistics and a timetable. Each of them would prepare a written report describing in detail, the work they had done, and their conclusions.

Noah would initially take the documents back to the labs at the British Museum in London where he would perform a detailed scientific analysis on the paper and the ink. Each document would be placed under the microscope. He would use infrared light and state-of-the-art chemical testing.

Then the documents would be transferred to Jack at Small & Pritchard for the handwriting analysis. Jack would check both Gilbert's and Robert's handwriting, comparing them to known authenticated historical writings by each of them. Jack would look at the slant and formation of each letter, their vertical positioning and spacing between the lines. He would look for evidence of tracing and smooth versus uneven flows of ink. The signatures would be compared to other known signatures looking for evidence that the signature fit the circumstances of the document and times. People had different forms of signatures in formal writings versus informal.

Next, the documents would be couriered back to Leo Dwyer at the University of Scotland. Leo's office was located in a building only a short distance from where Tom worked. Leo was the head of the Department of English and Linguistics. He would study the language form of both the letter and the poem. The poem was the real challenge. Whoever wrote this poem, had written it in an old Scots dialect and in the standard Habbie stanza form that Burns had used in much of his poetry. It was Leo's task to carefully study these things. He would assess whether the words in the poem were those that Burns might reasonably have used and whether the dialect and rhythm of the poem was consistent with Burn's known works.

Finally, the documents would be turned over to Tom for his analysis of provenance. Tom would check things like the type of paper used for the envelope, the letter and the poem. He would investigate the correctness of the stamp and post mark on the original envelope. He would check if everything agreed with the 1823-time frame. Tom would verify the circumstances surrounding the discovery of the envelope at the St. Germain École des Garçons. Tom would track the history of St. Germain and the Chartiers back to 1823. For that job, he recruited the help of Ann Benoit and Jules Marchand.

Once the work was completed, Tom organized a conference call which included the four experts and Dr. Crawford. The purpose of the conference call was to debrief each other.

Tom already knew the results from prior one on one conversations, but Dr. Crawford did not. Each of the experts verbally summarized their work and their conclusions.

Each expert advised that they had no reservation in opining that all of the documents were authentic and that a new Robert Burns poem had been discovered.

Dr. Crawford's heart began to race, and he began to perspire. He knew he'd have to change his shirt soon and maybe even his jacket before meeting anyone in person that day. Arrangements were made to have each of their written reports couriered to him.

Dr. Crawford called Mr. Avery that very afternoon and with no small amount of animation said, "I have some incredible news."

Mr. Avery interrupted him and said, "Please don't say anything further, I want to patch in Dr. Gingras and Liz Cullen. Once done, Dr. Crawford described the findings of the experts to the three of them. There were many congratulatory expressions made and then they paused.

Mr. Avery said, "Now we need to find the rightful and legal owner of this treasure. Does John Murdoch have any heirs? Dr. Gingras, do we have your authorization to continue and to conduct this ancestral research?"

"Yes, that would be fine," he answered.

It was then decided that the firm of Avery & Lord would conduct the necessary research to identify and locate heirs of John Murdoch, if any.

Based on her excellent track record, Liz Cullen was assigned the task. She was thrilled.

Chapter 25

Liz immediately started the task of finding the descendants of John Murdoch, if he had any at all.

Consulting the Burns Encyclopaedia and some other public sources, Liz had quickly learned that John Murdoch was born at Ayr, Scotland, had taught the Burns boys for more than two years in Alloway, Scotland and after a brief hiatus, again at Dalrymple School, presumably also in Ayr. The record then became sketchy. She did find occasional references to John Murdoch teaching at various Church of Scotland sponsored schools and secular adventure schools in different places in the country.

Liz learned that at some point, Murdoch went to London and started teaching French and for a time did well. However, with the influx of French refugees into England, escaping the troubles following the French Revolution, there were more native French speakers in London who were better qualified to teach French than John Murdoch. He began to fall onto hard times.

This is probably what Gilbert Burns was referring to in his letter when he said, "*I have recently learned of your unfortunate financial circumstances…*"

Now Liz began to wonder again what the connection was between John Murdoch and Louis Chartier and the St. Germain school in London. Had Murdoch been a teacher with or for Louis Chartier or his son, Charles? Had the Chartiers caused or contributed to Murdoch's financial hardship? Liz learned that there were no easy answers to those questions.

She also discovered that there were no easy answers to whether John Murdoch ever married or ever had any children.

Liz decided to call Ann again to see if she could help. It was now nearing the end of August and it had been several weeks since the girls has talked.

When they connected on the phone, Liz greeted, "Hi Ann, I'm wondering if you can help me with a few more bits of information?"

"Of course, I'll help in any way I can, but it might cost you another night out. What's up?" Ann said.

"Ok, well, I'm wondering if you have found anything further about John Murdoch and his connection to St. Germain and/or Louis Chartier?"

"Hey sister, you're in luck because just the other day, Jules, oh, I'll have to tell you more about Jules, when we get together," Ann said excitedly. Liz was happy that this was a phone conversation as she rolled her eyes.

Ann continued, "Well anyway, just the other day, Jules found a hand-written letter from Louis Chartier addressed to John Murdoch, dated, October 17, 1820 written in French advising him that they must part ways in the business of providing French language instruction."

Ann had always talked a lot and usually very rapidly and this time was no different. She rattled on, "I'll scan the letter and email it to you. Jules also found some employment records showing that a Robert Murdoch had been employed as a French teacher at the newly minted St. Germain École des Garçons starting in September 1823 but ending on November 1, 1823, only two months after the school year had started. We have not found any documentation explaining why his employment ceased so soon after starting."

Ann finally stopped to catch her breath and Liz was curious about all of this new and interesting information. Ann then suggested that they meet again for drinks later that evening, but this time, Liz declined. She was on a mission and was anxious to get back to work. She said, "Tell you what Ann, can we postpone for a bit? I'm really busy tonight and I need to pursue a few things right away."

"Ok, how about tomorrow night? Lord Byron's at 6?" Ann asked. It was clear that she had more to tell Liz about Jules.

"Sure, until tomorrow then", Liz said, and they hung up.

A few minutes later, Liz received the email from Ann, with a copy of the Louis Chartier's letter. It read:

> Le 17 octobre 1820
>
> M. John Murdoch,
>
> Je vous écris cette lettre pour vous aviser qu'il est nécessaire de mettre fin immédiatement à notre entente concernant l'enseignement de la langue française à notre école.
>
> Meilleures salutations.
>
> Louis Chartier

This information connected the Murdochs to the Chartiers, but now Liz had to figure out who Robert Murdoch was in relation to John Murdoch and what happened to Robert.

The girls met the next day at Lord Byron's again and Liz suffered through a two drink 85-minute detailed description of Ann's goings on with Jules. She felt that she had successfully faked interest in the whole affair with the occasional nod and the appropriate positive or negative response, as required. But Liz really just wanted to go home. Finally, she manufactured some excuse as to why she couldn't have a third drink and was able to extricate herself and go home. She was exhausted and went right to sleep.

Early the next morning, Liz was back to work.

Liz wondered if Robert was John's son. By 1823, John Murdoch would have been in his mid to late 70s and a son would likely have been in his 50s. Liz wondered if Robert might be a grandson to John, rather than a son. Liz wondered too, why Robert's employment at St. Germain was so short, only two months. Was there some bad blood between the Chartiers and the Murdochs?

Liz decided that she had to take the risk of committing to another drink date but needed to call Ann again. "Hi Ann, I really enjoyed our visit last night," Liz lied. "Listen, I need your help again. Was there any record of a middle name or initial for Robert Murdoch?" she asked.

"Hold on, I'll look again." A few minutes later she returned, "Yes, it is 'J'."

Liz held her breath, expecting another invitation. Thankfully, it didn't come. Instead, Ann said, "Oh, Liz, after you left the bar last night, Jules called me, and we hooked up and spent the night together. It was awesome but I'm only half here today, if you know what I mean."

Well, at least from Liz' perspective, there was one good result from that…she was not going to have to endure another two drink, lengthy recounting of the latest events, probably mushier than the night before, given what Ann had told her.

"Thanks again, Ann," Liz said with relief in her voice, that she hoped Ann wouldn't recognize.

Liz's avenues of investigation included general internet sites, ancestry sites (she had accounts with all the major sites of that nature). Over the course of 75 years, the Avery & Lord firm had at least some level of connection with most public institutions, particularly with the major churches, hospitals, police forces, etc., throughout the United Kingdom.

She knew that John Murdoch had been born in 1747 in Ayr, Scotland and that he had moved to London at some point. If he had children, it would be reasonable to put his child producing years in the range somewhere between 1767 and 1787. Liz wondered if John Murdoch would have even been in London yet during those years.

Liz started working the firm's Scottish connections first in the Glasgow area: churches, hospitals and other public records available. Nothing. Next, she worked the contacts in the Edinburgh area. Again, nothing. She was getting a bit discouraged. She started working connections the firm had in the north and had a hit.

It was a record from the archives of St Stephen's Church of Scotland in Inverness, Scotland of a birth to a John Murdoch (no middle name or initial) of a son, Alasdair John Murdoch in 1780. Luckily, the reference to John Murdoch had included the word, 'Teacher' following his name. There were hundreds of John Murdochs in the United Kingdom, but Liz thought that with the middle name 'John' given to the son and the reference to the father, John Murdoch, as a teacher, she might have the right man.

Liz had read that after leaving Ayr, John Murdoch had moved around Scotland in constant search for work. He could very well have gone to Inverness, which was a growing city after the troubles of the Jacobite Rising were over in 1746.

If Liz could now link Alasdair Murdoch to Robert J. Murdoch, then she would be sure that she had the right John Murdoch.

Continuing her focus on the Highlands of Scotland, it didn't take very long after, to discover another birth record, this time from the archival records of the Kirk of Keith, in Keith, Scotland another Church of Scotland church. This one showed the birth of another boy,

Robert John Murdoch on June 27, 1801 and recorded the father to be Alasdair John Murdoch. This birth record also indicated the father to be a teacher.

Bingo! Liz was now convinced she had the right John Murdoch and Robert Murdoch.

Now she conjectured that after Robert was born in 1801, his father, Alasdair, and his grandfather, John, had moved to London for work. She further postulated that John had started tutoring students in the French language in London and that his path had somehow crossed with Louis Chartier who had arrived in London in 1805.

Liz wondered how Robert Murdoch fit into this puzzle and what happened to him.

After a few more days of further research with no progress, Liz was beginning to get frustrated. She decided to change gears.

She had to call Ann again, "Ann, do you have full names for Louis and Charles Chartier?"

"Hold on." Again, only a few minutes later, "Here, let me see, ah, it was Louis Charles Chartier and Charles Wilfred Chartier."

"Thanks again, Ann," Liz said, again with relief. Then she added, "And, oh, Ann, if you run across any other info that might help me figure out what happened to Robert Murdoch, please let me know."

"Will do, friend," Ann said and surprisingly left it at that and hung up.

Liz wondered if something might have gone wrong in Ann and Jules's relationship for Ann not to offer to provide Liz with another long account of their sordid affair. She was not curious enough, however, to inquire.

Two days after that conversation, Liz found a reference from St. Bartholomew's Hospital in London of an admission of a Charles W. Chartier dated October 28, 1823. He was discharged on October 31. A follow up with the hospital's archive unit revealed no further information as to the nature of his illness or injury.

These were very interesting dates to Liz, because they immediately preceded the November 1, 1823 date of Robert Murdoch's cessation of employment at St. Germain.

Liz's working theory now looked like this: John Murdoch had been a French teacher in London for presumably several years; he had worked with or for Louis Chartier up until October 17, 1815 (the date of the 'we have to part ways' letter from Louis); Murdoch eventually had fallen onto hard times financially; Robert Murdoch had worked at the St. Germain school from September, 1823, ending abruptly on November 1, 1823; Charles Chartier spent three days in hospital from October 28, 1823 to October 31, 1823; the letter from Gilbert Burns to John Murdoch was dated November 19, 1823 and John Murdoch had died sometime in 1824, never having received the letter.

Liz' initial speculation that there may have been bad blood between Robert Murdoch and Charles Chartier was beginning to gel into a credible scenario. She wondered if Robert Murdoch harbored ill will against Louis Chartier and Charles Chartier for running his grandfather, John, into the poor house.

Then, according to Liz's theory: Robert Murdoch took employment at St. Germain either out of necessity or some idea of getting an opportunity for revenge; perhaps got into some kind of a confrontation with Charles; attacked and injured Charles; Charles has to go to hospital; Robert got fired; then Robert went on the lam to avoid the London authorities.

Liz's scenario continued: Gilbert Burns, not knowing anything of these events, wrote his letter on November 19, 1823 and sent it to John Murdoch c/o Louis Chartier, thinking that he was still working at the French school; when the letter arrived Charles refused to deliver it to John or to Robert, because of the ill will that existed between the families, so the letter remained unopened and placed in a file or box at St. Germain where it remained for almost 200 years until discovered by Ann and Jules.

Liz was satisfied that this scenario would explain why she was having so much difficulty finding anything about what happened to Robert Murdoch. He had disappeared. He was on the lam! Where had he gone?

Liz knew that if she didn't find out what happened to Robert Murdoch, the letter and poem might never get into the hands of the descendants of John Murdoch, if any the lawful owners.

One night, sitting in her flat, sipping on a French Pinot Noir, she decided to go to 30,000 feet and just review the main points of her theory: John Murdoch had left Ayr; moved around Scotland, at one-point landing in Inverness; had a son, Alasdair, in Inverness; Alasdair had a son, Robert, in Keith.

Even with a bit of a wine buzz, Liz suddenly realized that the answer was starring her right in the face and she hadn't seen it…Robert had escaped from the law in London after assaulting Charles Chartier and had gone back to Keith, Scotland, the city where he was born.

From that point, Liz renewed her focus on the firm's contacts in the north, particularly the Keith area. If Robert ran from London after the assault in 1823, he could well have arrived in Keith that same year or early 1824. Liz made the assumption that Robert escaped London childless and that if he did have any children, they would likely be born in Scotland. Liz then focused her research on the years between 1823 and 1840, his most likely years of Robert producing a child.

She knew that John Murdoch was a protestant and had taught in various Church of Scotland schools, so she searched for birth records in every Church of Scotland parish in the whole Highlands area. She found nothing that would fit that of a child of Robert.

Liz decided she needed to take another path. She started searching birth records in Catholic churches. She got another hit. She found a birth record in the St. Thomas Catholic Church in Keith. On April 14, 1831 a baby boy, named Colin John Murdoch was born to a Robert John Murdoch. Beside the father's name was the reference, 'Apprentice Stonemason, Strathisla Distillery'.

In all the records that she had culled through from the Shires around Keith: Moray, Banffshire and Aberdeen, the birth of Colin John Murdoch was the only one to a Robert John Murdoch between the years 1823 and 1840. She had found several references to a father, Robert Murdoch, but in every case the middle name or initial had been different from 'John' or 'J'.

There were two things though, that puzzled Liz about this information. First, why had the record been made in a Catholic Church. During John Murdoch's life, he had only ever been associated with the Church of Scotland. John Murdoch was definitely not Catholic, and Liz doubted very much if Robert was. The other thing that puzzled Liz was the reference to 'Apprentice Stonemason, Strathisla Distillery'. Robert was a teacher. He had been hired as a teacher at St. Germain, even if it only lasted for two weeks.

Based on this information, Liz had to create another scenario: Robert was on the lam, so he was motivated to change a few things, maybe, like changing his religious affiliation; Robert was either not able to find work as a teacher in Keith or he may not have wanted to and again, to hide his tracks, he looked for work in another field. One of Keith's largest employers was the Strathisla Distillery and it was reasonable to assume that Robert may have obtained work there as a stonemason.

The next day Liz contacted the Strathisla Distillery in Keith and inquired about employment records and construction projects at the site from back in the early to mid 1800s. She was told that most of the distillery's records were destroyed in a fire in 1879 but was directed to contact the London office of Chivas Brothers, the current owner of the distillery, to see what they might have. Fortunately, the Strathisla Distillery is the oldest continuously operating distillery in the Scottish Highlands, so there was hope that some records may still be in existence.

She was in luck. Chivas Brothers found a record of a Robert Murdoch's employment as an 'Entered Apprentice' from 1824 to 1832, a 'Fellowcraft' from 1832 to 1841 and then as a 'Master Mason' from 1841 to 1855.

Bingo, again! Liz level of excitement rose sharply. She could sense that an answer was within reach.

Now Liz just had to find out if Colin John Murdoch had any descendants. That turned out to be quite easy.

She stuck with the records of the St. Thomas Catholic Church in Keith and, sure enough, found another birth record that most certainly fit. On July 23, 1851, a baby boy named James Alexander Murdoch was born to a Colin John Murdoch. Beside the father's name was the reference, 'Stonemason, Strathisla Distillery'.

Bingo, yet again!

Unfortunately, the trail in that Catholic Church petered out and there were no subsequent birth records with James Alexander Murdoch as a father.

She expanded her search to the usual sources in the other Shires around Keith; Moray, Banffshire and Aberdeen. Nothing. She then went to the Glasgow and Edinburgh areas.

Liz' excitement began to fizzle, and frustration again set in. She felt that she needed to change gears, but to what now?

That night in her flat, she opened another bottle of Pinot Noir, poured a large glass and called Ann to bring her up to speed on her findings so far. Liz knew that this was likely to cost her, but she needed to bounce things off somebody, and Ann was her best shot at this moment.

It did, indeed, cost her, but not as much as she had feared. Ann did subject Liz, this time, to only a 40 minute, one-drink chronicle of her 'one of a kind romance' with Jules.

Liz knew that she had to take control of the situation and forced a change of subject. She summarized for Ann, her latest scenarios and that she was stumped at the point of James Murdoch.

It was Ann that broke the impasse. She said, "Liz, what if James emigrated out of the country…you know that millions of Scots were leaving the country back in those years. Have you checked Scottish emigration records?"

'Duh,' thought Liz, 'Why didn't I think of that?' Ann was ready to return to her favourite topic and gush on about Jules, but Liz wasn't even listening and wanted to get to work again. Liz stood up and announced, "Ann, you're a godsend and I'd love to hear more about you and Jules," she lied, "but I really need to get back to work now. I'll call you real soon and we'll gossip, ok?"

"Oh, ok then," Ann sighed.

When Liz returned home, she immediately got on the computer to start finding what she could in Scottish emigration records. She found herself quickly on the National Library of Scotland website and started her search. She started to zero in on the name James Alexander Murdoch and the dates after he would have turned 18, so after 1869.

After a few phone calls to the National Library the next day, she was told that her half hour of free staff service was more than used up and that she'd have to come up to Edinburgh to go through the archives herself.

It was time to report again to Mr. Avery, which she did. Mr. Avery, in turn reported to Dr. Gingras.

The flight from London's Heathrow to Edinburgh's EDI was only a little over an hour but the hackney trip at the London end was over an hour and in Edinburgh, just under an hour, so Liz spent basically all morning journeying. She had booked herself into the Fraser Suites and checked in. After freshening up a bit in her room, she went straight to the library.

She only had 3 hours left before the library closed so Liz really only got oriented on that first afternoon.

Liz spent the whole next day reviewing the emigration and passenger records to Australia. She found nothing. The following day, she did the same thing for Canada.

She found a record of a James A. Murdoch registering for passage to Halifax on June 23, 1873.

The Avery & Lord firm had developed working relationships with reputable archive firms in many other countries and after finding the reference to Canada, she called their firm's contact in that country. The firm was Bennett and Schwartz in Toronto. Liz was connected to one of the owners of the firm, Ms. Monica Schwartz. Liz summarized the relevant parts of the story to Ms. Schwartz and asked for help following up on the James A. Murdoch lead. Fees were discussed and agreed to.

Ms. Schwartz said she'd get back to her within 24 hours.

Liz flew back to London and spent another evening cozying up to a new bottle of Pinot Noir. After her second glass, Liz thought, 'Ann can have her Jules Marchand, I have my Pinot Noir.'

The next day, Ms. Schwartz called back and said that the only James Murdoch she could find in that time frame was a James Alexander Murdoch, born in 1851 and who been employed at a private school in Kingston, Ontario called Banffshire Academy for Boys.

Liz was certain that was the right person and asked if Ms. Schwartz could follow up on James Murdoch's descendants, if any. She again agreed and said she'd call her back within 24 hours.

Ms. Schwartz didn't get back to Liz the next day. Liz was getting both excited and anxious as to what Ms. Schwartz would come back with.

On the second day, Ms. Schwartz did get back to her and said, "I think you'll be pretty happy with what I've found, Ms. Cullen. I'll email you the full family tree but in a nutshell here's what there is: James Murdoch had a son, William, born in Kingston, Ontario in 1872, William had a son, Alexander, born in Kingston in 1894, Alexander had a son, John, born in Kingston in 1926. They were all employed at the Banffshire Academy for Boys, also in Kingston. There is no record of any child born to John Murdoch. If he's still alive, he would now be 83 years old."

"Oh, you don't know how happy I am to hear this and once this particular matter is settled and the file is closed, I'll tell you why. Thank you so much for your help."

Later that day, Liz received a series of emails from Bennett and Schwartz with attachments that contained all the particulars of the Murdoch family tree, names, births, deaths, marriages, etc., starting with James Murdoch and ending with John Murdoch. There were no records beyond James, but Liz already knew that history.

This part of Liz' job was now completed: John Murdoch of Kingston, Ontario, Canada, if he was still alive, would be the legal and rightful owner of the Gilbert Burns letter and the Robert Burns poem, according to the legal opinion of the Fraser & Kennedy firm in Glasgow.

Liz prepared a full report, backed up with all her references and sources. She brought her report to Mr. Avery the next morning and, together, they called Dr. Crawford to summarize Liz's findings and email to him a copy of her report. Dr. Crawford congratulated Mr. Avery and Liz on their firm's excellent work.

Following that conversation, Mr. Avery placed a call to Dr. Gingras. He was not in his office that day, so Mr. Avery sent him an email summarizing the findings and attaching a copy of Liz' report. He did not receive a response from Dr. Gingras.

The next decision was to make contact with 'Canada John Murdoch' as they decided to refer to him as, to distinguish him from the original John Murdoch, who they now referred to as 'Scotland John Murdoch'.

Again, Liz squirmed in her chair hoping to get that assignment.

She did.

That night, in her flat, she got on her computer. She wanted to find images of John Murdoch. She hoped that there would be photos of him on the Banffshire website. There was. Under the tab 'History' was a sub-tab 'Academic Staff'. There was his picture and a short bio. She was looking at the man who she hoped to see in person in a few days. In the photo, he looked to be in his mid to late 60s, so she assumed that it was taken of him at the end of his career.

It was a color photo and was a bust shot from mid chest and up. John Murdoch looked every part the professor. She could see that he was wearing a light brown herring bone sport coat. He had a collared shirt and a neck-tie with a logo on the tie. She recognized it as the Banffshire school logo because it matched the logo on the top right of each page of the school's website. He had the requisite professor's beard and bushy eyebrows. The centre portion of his head was bald and his remaining hair on the sides was longish and completely grey, as was his beard. He wore a pair of wire rimmed-glasses. Liz thought that he looked a bit like what she imagined John Lennon might look like if he had lived to this age. He even had John Lennon's long thin nose.

But what struck Liz the most was his eyes. They were light brown, inviting and warm.

The photo that Liz was looking at was likely taken more than 20 years ago. She wondered what he looked like now.

She would find out soon.

Chapter 26

Mr. Avery had asked Liz to determine if Canada John Murdoch was indeed still alive.

The first thing she did was to find a phone number and address. She got on her computer and went to the Canada 411 website and within minutes had a telephone number and an address for a John Murdoch in Kingston, Ontario. Fortunately, there was only one.

Next, she decided to call the property tax division of the City of Kingston to see if she could learn if this John Murdoch was a homeowner and was still paying property taxes. The young department clerk that Liz talked to had been taught to be discreet and to not disclose any personal information about the city's property owners, but she did happen to spill, "Oh, yes, Dr. Murdoch. Everyone in town knows him. He was just in here the other day, making an instalment payment on his taxes. Lovely old man."

"Thank you," was all Liz said, because she now had that last bit of information she needed. She had a phone number, an address and confirmation that he was still alive. She reported her findings immediately to Mr. Avery.

Mr. Avery decided that he would make the initial contact with Canada John Murdoch by telephone. It was 4 pm in London and 11 am in Kingston. The line was clear.

"Good afternoon…I'm sorry, Good morning. Is this John Murdoch?" Mr. Avery asked.

"Yes, it is. Who is calling?" John Murdoch answered.

"My name is Ian Avery. I'm calling you from London, England. I am the founder and President of the firm of Avery & Lord.," he said.

"Well, well! How can I help you?" John Murdoch asked.

"Are you the John Murdoch that was a teacher at Banffshire Academy for Boys?" Mr. Avery continued.

"Yes, I am," answered John Murdoch.

"Our firm assesses and manages archives for clients, among other things. In the course of our work, we often discover assets of historical significance and value. We have been engaged by a client here in London and we have, in fact, made such a discovery in the archive materials of that client," Mr. Avery said.

"Ok, that's interesting, and what does it have to do with me?" John Murdoch asked.

"Well, sir, we have discovered some documents that were delivered to a Scottish gentleman here in London by the name of John Murdoch. But he never received them," Mr. Avery continued.

John Murdoch chuckled at the mistake. "Oh, I've never been to London, I'm sorry to say. You must have the wrong chap," John Murdoch said.

"Yes, well, the documents date back to 1823 and we have conducted a considerable amount of historical research and have come to the conclusion that you, sir, are the only identifiable direct descendant of the original intended recipient. Let's call him Scotland John Murdoch, shall we?" Mr. Avery said.

"Oh, dear, that is a surprise! I had always planned to go to Scotland to look into my ancestry, but I never did and now, I have to say, I am too old to do so. I do hope that you can give me a copy of the research that you have done, I would very much appreciate seeing that," John Murdoch said.

"Of course, we can do that, but Mr. Murdoch, what will perhaps be more interesting to you than the record of your ancestry will be the documents themselves," Mr. Avery said.

"Now, I'm quite curious. What are they? Can you tell me?" John Murdoch said.

"I would rather that you see them in person," Mr. Avery responded.

"That would be fine. But, as I said, I'm too old to make that long of a journey. Can you mail or courier these documents to me?" John Murdoch asked.

"The documents are actually quite special, and we had hoped to personally deliver them to you in Kingston, Ontario. Would that be acceptable to you?" Mr. Avery said.

"My goodness, these must be important documents for you to do that. Why, yes, of course you can deliver them to me here, but I'm hoping that I don't have to pay any of your expenses for this trip," John Murdoch said.

"No sir, you won't have to pay anything to our firm or anyone else, for that matter," Mr. Avery said.

"Ok, then, when would you like to come?" John Murdoch asked.

"A young lady from our firm by the name of Liz Cullen will contact you tomorrow by telephone. You and Liz can set a time and place for her visit. She will come directly to your house with the documents if you wish," said Mr. Avery.

"That would be fine, I look forward to her call. Good-bye then and, thank you Mr. Avery," John Murdoch said and hung up the phone.

His old bald head was spinning, as he wondered, 'What in God's creation could these documents be that were so important that someone from London, England would personally deliver them to my house. And, documents from 1823!'

Before noon the next day, Liz had called John Murdoch. She was immediately impressed with the warmth of his voice. She thought to herself, 'His voice matches his eyes'.

"Hello, is this Dr. Murdoch?" she asked.

"Yes, it is. Are you Miss Liz Cullen?" he asked.

"Yes, I am, sir," she said, somewhat surprised.

"I was expecting your call. It's nice to hear from you," he said.

"It's nice to talk to you too, sir and I very much look forward to meeting you in person."

A meeting time was set for 2 pm on Thursday, September 30, 2010 at John Murdoch's home in Kingston, Ontario.

It didn't take Liz long to make the arrangements to fly from London to Kingston, with one stop in Toronto. She had never been to Canada before and she was very excited. The short layover at the busy and confusing airport in Toronto, however, so far hadn't given Liz any warm and fuzzy feelings about Canada. But she was patient and looked forward to reaching her final destination.

She carried the documents in the secure valise that the Avery & Lord firm had purchased for their safe keeping during that the first flight from London to Glasgow.

She arrived in Kingston in the early evening of September 29 and checked in at the Four Points Sheraton Hotel. It was too dark for her to see anything that night. She'd have to wait for the morning to get her first good look at Canada.

When she got to her hotel room, the first thing she did was place her valise in the safe in her room. The second thing she did was to order room service, a bottle of Niagara Pinot Noir. She was anxious about the meeting the next day and needed to cuddle up to her 'lover' to calm herself. She uncorked 'him' and drank with pleasure. It had been a long day and after a single, but large, glass of wine, she fell asleep.

The next morning, the sun was shining as she looked out her window. Her spirits rose, in anticipation of seeing a small bit of this new country and visiting John Murdoch.

Liz had several hours to do some sightseeing before the 2 o'clock meeting. She decided to explore the City of Kingston. She had the hotel concierge arrange a limousine to drive her to a few of the City's main sights. The driver drove her to the Royal Military College, Queen's University, some of the city's beautiful churches, City Hall and the Penitentiary Museum.

She still had two hours before the meeting with John Murdoch and asked the driver to take her to the Banffshire Academy for Boys. When they arrived, Liz got out of the car and continued on foot. She was impressed with the beauty of the grounds and the old limestone buildings. The campus was full of activity that afternoon. The boys in their white shirts, neck-ties, dark blue trousers and matching vests with brass buttons, were scurrying here and there, laughing and shouting. She recognized the school's logo on the ties of the boys. It was the same as she had seen on John Murdoch's tie from his photo on the school's website.

Liz began to imagine John Murdoch on this campus for 40 years, teaching English literature to boys like these. She had her own appreciation for English literature, having studied it in her university days. She felt a sort of admiration for this warm man and decided that she liked him before even meeting him.

Finally, it was 1:30 pm. Liz walked back to her limousine, instructed her driver to return to the hotel where she picked up the valise. Then they made their way to Canada John Murdoch's house.

A lump formed in her throat as she approached the door. She knocked three times.

Chapter 27

John Murdoch stayed seated after he hung up their old land-line telephone following his conversation with Mr. Avery. He didn't like to stand for very long.

He turned to his wife, who was standing beside him with an inquiring look on her face. He looked at her.

Sonya Gordon was still slim and her posture perfect. She looked stately for an 84-year-old woman. She still had her fair complexion but the skin on her face now sagged a bit and was sprinkled with a few age spots and skin tags of various sizes and types. She didn't wear make-up, she never had, her whole life. She had developed deep laugh lines around the outside of her eyes and grief lines on her forehead. Her once full lips were now thinned and her straight, slender nose had grown just a bit larger. She had let her hair grow long again and it was a beautiful steel grey color that matched her grey-blue eyes. They still glistened like pearls.

Sonya had overheard John's half of the conversation on the telephone and wondered what it was all about.

"Well, my dear, that was an interesting conversation. Come, sit down with me and I'll tell you about it," he said. Then he got up from his chair near the telephone, reached for her hand and they walked slowly together to the sofa in their living room.

He then related to her the conversation that he'd just had with Mr. Avery of the archive firm of Avery & Lord in London, England.

"And he didn't tell you what the documents were?" she queried.

"No, and they're sending a young lady, a Miss Liz Cullen, all the way over here to deliver them personally to me. Strange, isn't it?" he said.

"Hmm, yes, it is. I wonder what they are," Sonya said and squeezed his hand.

"Well, the young lady is going to call me tomorrow and we'll set a time for her to come and visit us. I'm sure it will be interesting," he said. He leaned toward her and placed his other hand over hers.

"John, did I tell you that Willie and Helen are planning to drop by this evening?" Sonya asked.

"No, you didn't. And now that they've retired from the farm and live so close to us here in Kingston, we get to see them more often," John said.

"Oh, and here's the best part! Little Sarah is with Willie and Helen this week. Maggie is involved in some big trial and Brad can't take the time off work, so we'll get to spend some time with her too," Sonya said, smiling.

"Why, that is wonderful! It will be nice to see the three of them again. It's hard to believe that Sarah will be five years old in January," John said.

When Willie, Helen and little Sarah arrived that evening, Willie gave his mom a big hug. Then he shook hands with John Murdoch. "You're looking good, Dr. Murdoch," Willie said.

"Thank you, Willie and, remember, you can just call me John. You're not in school anymore," John said with a laugh. Willie had called him 'Dr. Murdoch' since he was a student at Banffshire and couldn't get used to calling him 'John'.

Sarah jumped into her great grandfather's lap as he remained seated on the sofa. She gave him a huge hug and a wet kiss right on his hairy lips. She had only ever known him as 'Gramps'.

Sarah ran her little hands over John's bald head and through his white beard. He revelled in the child's touch and attention. It was an experience he had never had before. When Maggie was a child, she was not very affectionate, and she never seemed to want to be too close to him. Apparently, she was afraid of his beard and he had even thought of shaving it off at one point, but Sonya persuaded him not to. Sonya loved his beard. So, John treasured these few times that he had with Sarah, this beautiful child, so full of life.

When Sarah was finished exploring Gramps head and face, she climbed down and went to Grams. Sarah climbed into Sonya's lap and threw her arms around her neck and remained in that position for a full minute. Sonya didn't dare do anything to break that magical moment. When Sarah finally released her hug, Sonya put her out at arms' length and said, "Ok, my little princess, let me have a good look at you." Sonya then did have a good look at the little girl and remarked, "My, how you have grown. You're getting to be such a big girl now and soon you'll be five years old."

Sonya looked into Sarah's eyes. Of course, she had seen them before. They were the same as Robbie's eyes. They were dark blue and almost transparent. Tears began to well up in Sonya's eyes as she looked deeply into her great grand daughter's eyes.

Sarah saw Sonya's tears and was a bit puzzled. "What's wrong Grams? What are you starring at?" she asked.

Sonya let out a little laugh and said, "Well, sweetheart, I think I'm starring into one of the great mysteries of life."

Sarah's puzzled look deepened but then quickly changed to a look of hope as she jumped to a new topic and began to wiggle herself out of Sonya's lap. "Play for me, Grams. Play for me, please," she pleaded. It was a routine that Sarah demanded every time she visited Grams.

Sonya slowly rose up from her chair and went to the old piano, the very one Derek had bought for her many years before. She lifted the keyboard cover and sat down on the piano bench, which had been upholstered some years earlier. "Come and sit with me, sweetheart," she said, and beckoned for Sarah to join her. Sarah climbed up on the bench and snuggled up close to her. Sonya played Schumann's Traumerei with some assistance from Sarah's little fingers.

After the piano playing, Sarah had another important mission to attend to. She rushed into the kitchen to find some of Gram's home-made cookies. She knew where they were hidden.

They all spent a wonderful evening together, reminiscing and catching-up on and gossiping about the people they knew. Willie brought Sonya and John up to date on the happenings on the farm and that their son Tom and his wife Ella were managing it very well. They told how much they were enjoying their retirement in Kingston and being closer now to John and Sonya. They were planning a cruise to the Scandinavian countries next spring.

Sonya brought Willie up to date on her and John's life. Apart from the two mysterious calls of yesterday and earlier that afternoon, not much changed in their lives from day to day.

Sonya then asked Willie how Derek was. He reported that Derek had now been moved from the partial care facility in Maxville, to a hospice care facility in Perth, Ontario. Derek had been diagnosed about a year ago with cirrhosis of the liver and he was in the late stages of his life. It saddened Sonya, but she had come to her own terms with Derek's decisions that had led to this.

When their company left, John and Sonya carefully attended to their personal matters before going to bed, taking care not to slip and fall in the process. They climbed into bed, lying close to each other and nodded off. Sonya dreamt about Robbie and Sarah. She saw their dark blue eyes in her dream.

The next morning came quickly and Liz Cullen's phone call came in before noon.

"Hello, is this Dr. Murdoch?" she asked.

"Yes, it is. Are you Miss Liz Cullen?" he asked.

"Yes, I am, sir," she said, somewhat surprised.

"I was expecting your call. It's nice to hear from you," he said.

"It's nice to talk to you too, sir and I very much look forward to meeting you in person."

A meeting time was set for 2 pm on Thursday, September 30, 2010 at John Murdoch's home in Kingston, Ontario.

Finally, that date arrived. John and Sonya both woke with a sense of anticipation and nervousness. It was 6 am. What would that day bring?

They went through their morning routines, had tea and dry toast for breakfast, read the morning newspaper for an hour or so, then went for short walk around the block. What would take an able-bodied young person about 12 minutes, took John and Sonya about 35 minutes. They made the entire walk holding hands.

When they returned to the house, they had an early lunch of chicken noodle soup and then laid down for a short nap.

They woke up at about 1pm, returned to the living room and waited for Liz Cullen.

Finally, just before 2 pm, they heard three knocks on the door.

Chapter 28

John and Sonya both rose and went to the door.

John Murdoch greeted Liz with both hands outstretched to her. She took one look at him and reciprocated with both of her arms until their hands touched, the valise dangling precariously from her right elbow. She immediately thought to herself, 'Yes, he has the warm inviting look and aura that I expected'.

He introduced Liz to his wife, Sonya, and then escorted her into his living room.

Sonya offered her tea. Liz was grateful for the tea as she had gotten chilly in her walk around the Banffshire campus.

Sonya brought in the tea poured a cup for Liz, one for John and one for herself.

He invited Liz to sit in one of the chairs and he slowly made his way to the sofa and sat down beside Sonya. He fiddled for a bit with his hearing aid and then he reached for Sonya's hand.

There was very little small talk as they were all anxious to get to the reason for this visit.

Liz opened her valise and produced the original envelope, got up from her chair and handed it to him.

John Murdoch held the envelope in his hand for a moment and just looked at it. He could tell it was very old and the paper was brown and fragile with age.

He remained seated and carefully opened the envelope. He extracted the letter which was folded in thirds, unfolded it and read it slowly. He handed it to Sonya who also read it.

> *November 19, 1823*
>
> *Dear Mr. Murdoch,*
>
> *I apologize for the extreme and unforgiveable lateness of my writing of this letter to you.*
>
> *I am enclosing a poem written by my brother, Robert, in your honor. When he died, many of his belongings fell into the hands of his friends in Edinburgh and somehow got misplaced and only recently have come to my attention and possession.*
>
> *I have read my brother's poem and I have placed it in this sealed envelope for safer keeping during the mailing of it.*
>
> *As you will see when you read his poem. Robert, like I myself, was deeply affected by your teaching and friendship. You exposed our young minds to the beauty of literature and words themselves.*
>
> *I also want you to know how grateful I am for the care and attention you gave in attending to the affairs of young William after his passing.*

I have recently learned of your unfortunate financial circumstances and ill health. I am somewhat impoverished myself but would be happy to help you in some way if you require it.

I wish you all the best my/our dear teacher.

Gilbert Burns

When Sonya was finished reading the letter John Murdoch asked, "Who was this John Murdoch and this Gilbert Burns?" He started to reach into the envelope for the second envelope.

Liz stopped him. "Before you look at into the next envelope, I want to show you something and give you some background.

Liz then produced another single piece of paper from her valise that summarized the ancestral tree from Scotland John Murdoch to Canada John Murdoch. She handed that to him and said, "The John Murdoch that this letter was addressed to, was your grandfather, eight generations ago.

Name	Date of Birth	Place of Birth	Source of Records
John Murdoch	1747	Ayr, Scotland	Burns Encyclopaedia
Alasdair John Murdoch	May 22, 1780	Inverness, Scotland	St. Stephen's Church, Church of Scotland, Inverness, Scotland
Robert John Murdoch	December 11, 1801	Keith, Scotland	Kirk of Keith, Church of Scotland, Keith, Scotland
Colin John Murdoch	January 4, 1831	Keith, Scotland	St. Thomas Catholic Church, Keith, Scotland
James Alexander Murdoch	December 3, 1851	Keith, Scotland	St. Thomas Catholic Church, Keith, Scotland
William Alexander Murdoch	June 17, 1872	Kingston, Ontario	St. Mary's Cathedral, Kingston, Ontario
Alexander James Murdoch	February 14, 1894	Kingston, Ontario	St. Mary's Cathedral, Kingston, Ontario
John James Murdoch	January 31, 1926	Kingston, Ontario	St. Mary's Cathedral, Kingston, Ontario

John was impressed. He studied the ancestral tree for several minutes before continuing, "Well, isn't that something! I've always wanted to know more about my ancestry. I was going to get to it after my retirement, but this young lady," as he pointed to Sonya, "entered my life and I never did. At my ripe old age, I never thought I would know and here you've gone ahead and done all this work for me," he said with a chuckle and a look of satisfaction on his face.

Liz then gave them a summary of the entire story as it had unfolded. He and Sonya sat listening, with great interest, still not knowing what was in the second envelope.

When Liz was finished telling the story, she indicated to him that it was now appropriate to open the second envelope. He didn't say a word, then reached into the first envelope and pulled out the second envelope.

He opened the second envelope and slowly withdrew another fragile piece of paper also folded in thirds. He unfolded it. It was a hand-written poem. He held it out in front of himself and Sonya. They read it together:

TO JOHN MURDOCH, MY TEACHER, MY FRIEND

By Robert Burns

By John Murdoch I am bless'd.
By John Murdoch I was test'd.
He came whereo' I nest'd.
Lookin'. Wha' he found:
thrissles; my mind was mess'd.
He planted i' my ground.

In my ware he gently nurs'd it.
In simmer whipp'd and press'd it,
my mind he would no' rest it.
Wi' Dryden, Ramsay, Pope
he did his best to best it.
He never ga'e up hope.

By John Murdoch I am bless'd.
By John Murdoch I was test'd.
By hairst my mind conquest'd,
wi' his canie words
tha' he taught wi' pest an' zest.
I thank 'im wi' my words.

By John Murdoch I am bless'd.
By John Murdoch I was test'd.
Sae, my teacher lo'ed and trust'd,
I'll be indebt'd.
For wha' i' me he vest'd:
Curiosity whet'd.

At approximately 2:45 in the afternoon of September 30, 2010, the fragile piece of paper trembled in John Murdoch's hand. He became ashen faced, his body weakened, and he slumped in his chair. Sonya Gordon spilled her tea.

Chapter 29

Liz left the documents with John and Sonya and returned to London the next day.

Dr. Crawford issued a press release the following Monday following Liz Cullen's return to London.

> *October 4, 2010*
>
> ***New Robert Burns Poem!***
>
> *The Burns Centre - University of Scotland (BCUS) confirms that a previously unknown Robert Burns poem has been discovered. The poem, together with some other historically important documents, was found August, 2010 in the archives of St. Germain École des Garçons, London, England. The archive consulting firm of Avery & Lord, also of London, was engaged by St. Germain to assist in the investigation of the documents and BCUS was consulted to assemble a team of scientific and other experts to conduct extensive research on the documents to verify their authenticity and provenance.*
>
> *BCUS is pleased to announce that the documents, including the Robert Burns poem, have been authenticated. The poem is hand-written and has been verified to be in Robert Burns' own handwriting. The poem was written by Burns to his childhood teacher, John Murdoch. The poem is entitled "To John Murdoch, My Teacher, My Friend".*
>
> *BCUS has obtained a legal opinion to the effect that the rightful owner of the documents would be the descendants of John Murdoch. Ancestral research was conducted by the Avery & Lord firm who identified a descendant of John Murdoch to be a Canadian who resides in Kingston, Ontario, Canada. Coincidentally, the descendant's name is also John Murdoch, who is now in possession of the poem and related documents.*
>
> *This important new Robert Burns poem can be read on the BCUS website by clicking on the following link: www.us.ac.uk/bc/news/announcements*
>
> *BCUS wishes to congratulate the many parties who were involved in this exciting discovery, including the following:*
>
> > *St. Germain École des Garçons, London*
> > *Avery & Lord, London*
> > *Fraser & Kennedy, Glasgow*
> > *Small & Pritchard, London*
> > *British Museum, London*
> > *Bennett and Schwartz, Toronto*
> > *University of Scotland, Glasgow*
>
> *For further information, please contact*

Dr. Malcolm Crawford, Chairman of the Burns Centre, University of Scotland
Telephone +44 (0) 555 333 2200
Email: mcrawford@us.ac.uk

Within a week of the dissemination of the press release, 674 media sources around the globe, picked up the story of the new Robert Burns poem. Dr. Crawford's name was mentioned in all of them.

Over the following three months, John Murdoch received 23 offers to purchase the Robert Burns poem, the highest of which was USD $2 million from a private collector in the United States. He declined all the offers. In that same space of time, he received 34 requests for interviews from various media sources and he declined all of those as well.

PART III

Chapter 30

After Robbie Gordon's death, Derek's drinking spiked. Now, he drank every day and most days he drank heavily, starting in the early afternoon, not just in the evenings before bed time, as he had done in earlier days. He aged prematurely and his health deteriorated. His ability to maintain the farm was in direct inverse proportion to the amount of his drinking.

The stress level in their home was palpable, Derek was drinking, Sonya was grieving and neither of them was capable of helping the other.

The farm suffered. What had once been a successful business now became a neglected one. Financial issues began to crop up.

Sonya had returned to teaching Grade 2 at the Glengarry Public School, but her heart wasn't in it. Plus, Greta Schnurenberger was now the principal of the school and Sonya could hardly abide that. If there hadn't been a shortage of available teachers, Sonya was certain she would never even have gotten the job.

Willie finished his secondary schooling at Banffshire and was just starting the second year of a four-year degree program in agriculture at the University of Guelph. Willie had returned to the farm that first summer to help his father out, as he had done his whole life. But a large operation like the Gordon family farm required a full time, year-around, competent manager. Derek was not that person any longer and Willie's summer time help was not enough.

Sonya's relationship with Derek was deteriorating rapidly. She loved Derek but hated his drinking. She still had vivid memories of her childhood, her father's drinking and the hardships that he had inflicted on Lilian and her older brothers.

Like her father, Derek often became angry when he drank and had increasingly become violent with Sonya. He had struck her more than once in a drunken rage. Also, like her father, Derek was always repentant when he sobered up.

She had pleaded with him to join AA, but he would not. She pleaded with him to seek other types of help, but he flatly refused, somehow rationalizing that there really was no problem to deal with.

Sonya became increasingly detached from Derek, but what pained her more was that Willie was also withdrawing from his father. That father-son relationship had been one of the joys of both Derek and Willie's life. If that was lost, Sonya feared that Derek would come completely undone.

One summer night when Willie was home from university and Derek was at the bar, Sonya decided that she needed to have a heart to heart talk with Willie, a talk between two adults, not as a mother and son.

Sonya did most of the talking. Willie was mostly silent but knew what was coming and didn't argue with her. Sonya described Derek's increased drinking, his lack of attention to the management of the farm and the deteriorating financial position of the farm. She described a scenario where they would need to renegotiate the bank loans and lease out the farm, or lose it.

Finally, Sonya got to the most difficult part. She announced to Willie that she was planning to leave Derek and move to Kingston.

The remainder of that summer was very difficult for each of Derek, Sonya and Willie. They had a few three-way conversations and Derek was surprisingly compliant. He knew the grave he had dug for himself and his family and resigned himself to this fate. It was hard for Sonya to see him that way. It was clear that he was hurting but, unbelievably, he still refused to admit that there was a problem or to seek help.

An overall plan was hatched amongst the three of them and together they visited the banker and two potential lessees. Derek's pride was crushed, and he was mostly silent while Sonya and Willie did the negotiating. The pieces were all put into place, much the way Sonya and Willie had discussed them earlier in the summer. They signed a four-year lease with one of the neighbors, Jim Stewart.

By September, that painful summer was over. Willie returned to his studies at the University of Guelph.

The bright light in his life that year was that he met Helen Gerber, a lovely girl from Kitchener. She had just been accepted into the Doctor of Veterinary Medicine program.

Derek remained at the farm house and Sonya moved to Kingston.

Sonya rented a small house three blocks away from her new school and started teaching again.

It took Sonya three months of living in Kingston before she worked up the courage to call John Murdoch.

Chapter 31

Willie graduated with a Bachelor of Science in Agriculture from the University of Guelph. He returned to the family farm. For the remaining two years of the lease, Willie worked for Jim Stewart as a hired hand. Willie learned a lot from Jim.

Helen graduated with her Doctor of Veterinary Medicine degree and moved into the bunk house with Willie. The stars were now aligned. Willie had his Bachelor of Science degree in Agriculture and Helen was a veterinarian. The lease with Jim Stewart expired and Willie took over the farming operation. Two more qualified candidates couldn't be found to be in the agriculture business.

That summer was a busy time for Helen, because one month after she graduated, Willie and Helen got married.

They moved into the main farm house and Derek moved into the bunk-house. He was drunk most days. He arranged to have a liquor store in Maxville deliver booze to the bunk-house every week, sometimes twice a week.

Helen set up her veterinary practice right from the farm and Willie became the competent farmer that his father had once been.

Their first baby was a girl and they named her Margaret Lorraine Gordon. The name Margaret lasted for about a week and thereafter, and for the rest of her life, she was called Maggie.

Tom was born one year later.

Maggie was a strong healthy baby. The first time Sonya saw her new granddaughter, she remarked at how Maggie reminded her of the strong healthy baby that Willie had been when he was born.

As Maggie grew, Sonya, more than anyone else, could see the physical and personality resemblances to Maggie's father, Willie and her grandfather, Derek. Maggie was a tough, tom-boy type kid and very competitive.

When Maggie hit puberty, she was a big hit with the boys.

She was a natural blonde with a bronzy complexion. It looked like she was tanned but it was just her natural skin color. Her teeth looked whiter than they really were when she smiled because of the contrast to her dark skin. Her eyebrows and eyelashes were darker brown, not blonde, and she had dark brown eyes. She had the same strong nose and facial features of her father. She was muscular and curvy. By the time she was 18 years old, her percentage of body fat was at about 18%. She looked like a contestant in a fitness competition when she wore a bikini. And that's exactly what the boys, or anyone else for that matter, thought when they stared at her.

Maggie was used to competition. She was also used to winning. She had been an achiever since she was a little girl. She was always the top student in her class in grade school, the best in her gymnastics class, the top swimmer in her swim club and the Valedictorian of her high school graduating class.

She had graduated with honors in her B.A. degree in Political Science at McGill and had now been accepted into law school at the University of Toronto.

But swimming was what she really loved. Maggie learning how to swim was a precautionary measure, from Willie's point of view. From Maggie's, swimming was her passion. She not only learned to swim, she became an accomplished long-distance swimmer. She had swum the English Channel in the second summer of her undergrad and across Lake Ontario the following summer.

Maggie's Uncle Robbie had drowned in Lake Ontario when he was 13 years old, so her father was determined that she learn how to swim.

Maggie had heard many stories about Robbie Gordon when she was growing up. The description of Robbie and his behaviours varied depending on who told the stories. If her father, Willie, told a story about his brother, Maggie got a picture of Robbie as a vulnerable, strange but smart boy, who Willie had to protect from bullies, from time to time.

If Grandma Sonya told a story, Maggie formed an impression of Robbie as a mysterious, very special human being, bordering on genius. And Grandma never talked about Robbie without concluding with something like, 'Oh, how he could write poetry'!

But whoever recounted anything about Robbie, the ending was always the same. He drowned in Lake Ontario at 13 years old and the last poem he wrote was to Dr. John Murdoch, his beloved teacher at Banffshire Academy. Maggie had never seen the poem and, as far as she knew, no one else had either. For some reason, only her mom and Grandpa John had seen the last poem ever written by her uncle Robbie.

Chapter 32

Maggie met Brad Hall the second day of her first year in law school at the University of Toronto. The law school divided first year students up alphabetically into smaller groups for various administrative and study group purposes. Maggie was in the "F,G,H" group, which included Brad Hall.

When Maggie met Brad, they were in a study group with about 20 other students. He was the best-looking guy in the group and within seconds of her laying eyes on him, she had decided that he was her man. Two nights later they slept together.

Maggie and Brad made a good-looking couple. They almost looked like brother and sister. They had the same blonde hair, skin complexion, brown eyes and other facial features. The biggest difference was that he had a slim build, whereas Maggie was muscular and curvy.

The other main difference between them was their personalities. Brad was quiet and shy. He had a gentle, easy-going and kind nature. He loved animals and had a dog, Princess, back home in Windsor, who he missed very much. Maggie was bold, confident and competitive.

The started seeing each other on a regular basis. For Brad, Maggie was charming and so much fun. And the sex with this goddess was fantastic! For Maggie, Brad was sweet, kind and generous. The sex was ok, but she'd had a lot of experience in that department and Brad was not the best she'd had in bed.

Brad was in love. Maggie was not, at least not yet.

Maggie had joined the U of T swim team and was living in residence on campus to be near the pools. Brad had a modest one-bedroom apartment near the university. Maggie was spending increasingly more time at his apartment and he was urging her to move in with him. His motivation was love.

Maggie finally relented, gave her notice at the dorm and moved into Brad's small apartment after the Christmas break of their first year in law school. Her motivation was simply that she had never lived with anybody before and this would be kind of a novelty. Plus, Brad could cook, she couldn't.

Brad was a good student but was not in the same league as Maggie.

She breezed through the massive volume of the assigned readings. She easily comprehended the complexities of Contract Law. Maggie whizzed through Property Law, Criminal Law, Civil Procedure and the other first year courses.

Brad battled to keep up with the sheer volume of material, particularly the huge number of cases that he was expected to read for his Contracts course. That was the toughest course for Brad. He would ask Maggie to help him understand the cases. He was often bewildered as to how the majority and the minority decisions of the court could come to such opposite conclusions. He would often fail to see the rationale used by some judges when applying the doctrine of *stare decicis* from some earlier case. Sometimes, he thought, the judges just applied the judgment of an earlier case when it suited him or her, that there really was no logic. Maggie would try her best to find the rationale, if it existed, and explain it to Brad. But sometimes, she just had to concede that there really wasn't any. Not all cases made good law.

Some of the cases that were the most difficult for Brad to understand were those where the court applied some form of equitable remedy. He had trouble understanding when an equitable remedy was even appropriate.

Sometimes a judge would even venture into the territory of fairness. Fairness, it turns out, was 'as long as the judge's foot'. In those cases, *stare decicis* didn't seem to apply and no one could predict as to which side the scale of justice would tip.

Maggie, on the other hand, was always very interested in the cases involving equity and fairness. They fascinated her. To her, equity and fairness was the very essence and purpose of the law.

Amanda Fischer was in the same study group as Maggie and Brad. Maggie and Amanda had struck a friendship early on. The two girls decided to be partners and started entering several mooting competitions in first year. They had considerable success and enjoyed the top win rate and scores of all first-year mooters.

They finished their first year at law school. Maggie ranked 2nd and Brad 134th out of their class of 210. Amanda Fischer ranked 12th.

That September, Brad hoped that Maggie would stay in his apartment and that they would play house again for their second year in law school. She did, and he was happy. She was happy too. She had missed Brad over the summer.

They fell into the same routines as they had in their first year. Brad studied a lot. He needed to. Maggie didn't. Brad would stay home on weekends, and Maggie would swim, cycle and go out with her friends.

On a few weekends, she went back home to visit parents and her brother Tom on the farm in Maxville. Of course, she always liked to stop in Kingston to see her Grandma Sonya and Grandpa John. Many years before Maggie was born, her Grandma Sonya had divorced Maggie's Grandpa Derek and had remarried Grandpa John. Dr. John Murdoch had taught English at Banffshire where her father and Uncle Robbie had attended. She had grown to love Grandpa John, as she called him.

She rarely saw her Grandpa Derek. Willie had arranged for him to be moved into a partial care facility in Maxville in the hopes that the staff could somehow help him lessen his drinking. They couldn't and he didn't.

Maggie and Amanda continued to moot, and their collective debating and oral advocacy skills continued to develop.

Maggie had been on the pill but had become increasingly careless about taking them on a regular basis. Near the end of their second year in law school, Maggie announced to Brad that she was pregnant. Brad was ecstatic. Maggie was too but was also sick and threw up a lot in the month of April.

September of their final year in law school was a busy month. Brad and Maggie were busy with various things related to Maggie's pregnancy: doctors' appointments, ultrasounds, prenatal classes, Lamaze classes, etc. Added to those commitments, Brad and Maggie were planning to get married at Thanksgiving in October and Maggie and Amanda had won the right to compete in the Grand Moot competition in late September.

The Grand Moot was a big deal at the U of T Law School, and it was a huge honor for the girls to participate before a panel of three distinguished judges, one each from the Supreme Court of Canada, the Ontario Court of Appeal and the Ontario Superior Court of Justice. Both sides presented well researched and persuasive legal arguments. But in addition to their legal arguments, Maggie used the words of Lord Denning in the famous *High Trees* case and said '*the time has now come*' for fairness and for a new equitable remedy to be applied. She cited no precedents but made a passionate appeal to the court that the case cried out for fairness. All three Justices decided in favour of Amanda and Maggie. Madame Justice Ferraro spoke for the moot court panel and stated in her oral judgment that the Justices were persuaded by Maggie's eloquent argument that the case 'cried out for fairness' and applied the novel equitable remedy that Maggie had proposed.

After their win, Amanda and Maggie congratulated themselves and Amanda whispered in Maggie's ear, "*The time has now come*," and they both laughed.

Because Maggie was so busy with mooting, her pregnancy, and Brad studying so much, they planned a civil wedding with the bare minimum of to-do. They paid their $125 and arranged for a Justice of the Peace to perform the ceremony. Brad had asked one of his law school buddies and Maggie had asked Amanda, to act as witnesses. The five-some met in Brad and Maggie's apartment and they were married on the Saturday of Thanksgiving weekend in October. They didn't tell either of their parents.

Maggie's ultrasound in early November revealed that their baby was a girl.

It was only after that ultrasound that Maggie called her father and mother and told them that she had gotten married and was pregnant. Willie and Helen were each on a phone extension during the call and were shocked at this news. Neither of them knew how to respond. They hadn't even met this fellow, Brad Hall. In fact, they didn't even know that Maggie had been living with a guy. They had never visited Maggie in Toronto while she was in law school. Toronto was too big and busy for them to venture into. Maggie had always come out to Kingston to visit.

However, Maggie assured them that Brad was a wonderful, kind, loving man and that he'd make a great husband and father. For good measure Maggie added that Brad had a dog, named Princess, back in Windsor that he loved and missed very much. Maggie knew that her mom, being a veterinarian, would like to hear that. She did. Willie and Helen trusted Maggie enough to be satisfied that this Brad fellow was going to be just fine.

Maggie said, "Dad, would you please tell Grandpa John and Grandma Sonya. I'm just not up to talking to them right now".

"I'll do that dear", Willie said, "and I'll tell your brother, Tom."

"Sure, and Dad, can you tell Grandma that it's a little girl and I'm going to call her Sarah Sonya".

"Of course, I'll do that too. She will be pleased", he said.

After the shock wore off, Willie and Helen realized that they were looking forward to meeting their new son-in-law and they were especially looking forward to their first grandchild.

Later that day when Willie and Helen broke the news to John and Sonya, John said with a sigh, "Well, it's the times we live in," referring to the shotgun wedding.

Sonya had tears in her old eyes. She longed to see this new little bundle, her first great granddaughter, Sarah Sonya.

Sarah Sonya Gordon-Hall was born on January 4, 2006. She had the darkest blue eyes that Maggie had ever seen.

When Sarah was born, Maggie was in her last semester of law school. She had been so busy for much of the first semester and missed two weeks of the second with baby related matters. She finished 16th in her class and Brad finished 189th. Amanda Fischer ranked 3rd.

Within three weeks of Sarah's birth, Maggie's body pretty much looked like it did before she got pregnant. She was back to her pre-pregnancy muscular, curvy and sexy self.

Chapter 33

Maggie had wanted to be a litigator ever since she started law school. Now, with her and Amanda's win of the Grand Moot, she was pretty much committed to litigation as her career path.

Maggie had applied for an articling position at six different firms, all in Toronto. Three at large downtown full-service type firms and three at smaller boutique litigation firms.

She was offered a position by all six firms. She accepted the offer from the firm of Cohen, Widmore & Cohen. It was a 12-lawyer litigation firm. Their offices were not located in downtown Toronto but rather at the intersection of Yonge and Bloor.

Plus, the Cohen firm had a more tolerant policy for female lawyers with small children than the large downtown firms did. That suited Maggie just fine, now that Sarah was part of her life. The Cohen firm was also amenable to her deferring her articling start date until the end of January, the year after she graduated. That gave Maggie more time with her new baby.

Maggie learned that Mr. Lawrence Widmore, one of the senior named partners of the firm, would be her principal during her articling year.

Brad had applied for an articling position at twelve different law firms in the greater Toronto area. He received only one offer. It was with a four-lawyer real estate firm out in Markham. Of course, he accepted that offer. His office was some 25 minutes away from Sonya's, if you drove it in the middle of the night. At any time during a business day, it would be at least a 60-minute drive. Brad started his articles in May, right after graduating.

Brad and Maggie leased a small two-bedroom apartment in the southwest part of Scarborough. They needed a room for little Sarah. Their new apartment was approximately equi-distant to both of their offices.

They made arrangements for day-care for Sarah when Maggie started her articles in January. They took turns dropping off and picking up Sarah at the day-care.

Sarah celebrated her first birthday in the day-care. Brad and Maggie had planned a little birthday celebration with her that evening at home, but when Maggie picked her up, Sarah was in a foul mood and cried all the way home. She wasn't interested in the small birthday cake that Brad had brought home that evening and was asleep before they could even light the single candle and sing 'Happy Birthday' to her.

During her articling year, Maggie assisted several partners and senior associates in the firm on a number of complex litigation files. She was also given several minor cases to handle on her own. She quickly earned a reputation in the firm for being a competent litigator and particularly skilled in oral argument.

One of the files that she was handling on her own, was a particularly complex and difficult civil case. She expected to lose, but Maggie had spent several weeks in preparation. The trial was set for the last day that the court was sitting before the Christmas break. Her principal, Mr. Widmore attended the court room that day to observe her in a trial setting.

For her first big solo trial, Maggie wore a tailored light green business suit consisting of a small jacket, with a single button at her narrow waist, and a form-fitting skirt that came to the top of her knees. Under the jacket she wore a black sweater with a plunging V-neck made of fine-knit wool. For shoes, she wore black pumps with a two-inch stiletto heel. Her blonde hair co-ordinated perfectly with her green suit. She looked stunning.

Old Judge Walter Bedford paid close attention to Maggie during the three-hour trial and asked her many questions. On several occasions, he asked her to clarify information on a graph she had prepared and put up on a white board. This necessitated her walking back and forth from her counsel table to the white board.

She enjoyed a surprise victory. As soon as Judge Bedford rendered his verdict, Mr. Widmore rose from the gallery, went up to greet Maggie, shook her hand and congratulated her.

When they got back to the office, Mr. Widmore sent everyone an email describing Maggie's win. For the remainder of the afternoon, she received many congratulatory visits and emails. The office was closing for the day and for the Christmas break. Mr. Widmore came to Maggie's desk and invited her to join him, the other senior named partner, Mr. Samuel Cohen and the junior named partner, Josh Cohen for a drink to celebrate her victory. She hadn't had much in the way of socializing for some time now and gladly accepted. She called Brad to tell him about her good news and that the senior partners of the firm had invited her out for a little celebration. She asked him to pick Sarah up from the day-care.

Messrs. Cohen, Widmore and Cohen took Maggie to a posh lounge in Yorkville and toasted her success that day. Mr. Sam Cohen was getting on in years and was only able or willing to stay for one drink. Mr. Widmore said he had to leave as well. Family was arriving from Alberta for the Christmas holidays. The senior Mr. Cohen offered regrets at having to leave so soon but encouraged Josh and Maggie to stay for another drink, if they wished. Maggie was flushed with the excitement of the day and agreed to stay with Josh Cohen for one more drink.

They ordered second drinks and Josh downed his quickly. Maggie had barely taken two sips of hers and was just about to say something when Josh Cohen reached under the table and placed his hand on her thigh. She froze. There would have been a time when she wouldn't have minded that kind of advance from the right guy, but Josh Cohen was not that guy. Plus, he was married! She shuddered. She immediately took his hand and removed it. He carried on conversing with her as if nothing had happened. He ordered a third drink and Maggie decided to finish her second one more quickly than she normally would have. She wanted to leave as quickly as possible and hoped that his hand would not find its way to her thigh again. It did, this time higher than the first time and he gave it a firm squeeze. Maggie grabbed his hand, tore it from her thigh and slammed it down on the table. Without saying another word, she rose from her chair and stormed out of the lounge. She hailed a taxi and went home.

When she got home, Brad could immediately see that something was wrong. She was visibly flustered and upset. He asked her what was wrong, and she told him. He hugged her and said, "Bastard!"

Maggie was called to the bar at a ceremony at Roy Thomson Hall on a Friday morning, February 1, 2008. She was allotted five guest tickets. She had distributed them to Brad, her mom and dad and, of course, her Grandpa Murdoch and Grandma Sonya. Thankfully, Sarah didn't have to have a ticket, provided she didn't take up a seat. She sat on Brad's knee for the first while, then made her rounds to Grandpa Willie, Grandma Helen and Gramps John and Grams Sonya.

Maggie was able to purchase five more tickets because her bar call did not occur in September when the majority of students were called. She had given three of the tickets to lawyers at the Cohen firm who had helped her along in her career to that point, including Mr. Widmore. She gave the fourth ticket to her assistant, Kelly. She did not invite Josh Cohen.

Maggie gave the fifth and final ticket to her friend and moot partner, Amanda. Amanda had witnessed Maggie and Brad's wedding, and now Maggie wanted her to witness her bar call as well.

PART IV

Chapter 34

After being called to the bar, Maggie spent another 2 ½ years at the Cohen firm. From a professional development perspective, they were good years. She had gained considerable litigation experience, most of which was trial level civil litigation, as opposed to criminal. Maggie had also notched up a few appeal appearances as well, with about a 75% win-rate.

One of her appeals was a high-profile copyright expropriation case. Her client was a popular northern Ontario country singer-song writer, Mandy Cochrane, who had been sued by a large US music label who claimed that she had expropriated the melody of a song written some years earlier by one of the label's contracted-musicians. A law firm from Sudbury had acted for Mandy Cochrane. The US plaintiff had won at trial. Because the song had been a big hit on the Canadian charts for Mandy, she wanted to appeal her loss to the Ontario Court of Appeal. Maggie handled the appeal. The leading intellectual property law firm in Toronto, McKenzie Hoffman LLP, acted for the US respondents. The bad news was that Maggie lost. The good news was that Maggie learned a lot about copyright and property law. Plus, the press and the public were very sympathetic to Mandy Cochrane's position so Maggie got a considerable amount of positive publicity in the Toronto media.

But from another perspective, her time at the Cohen firm were difficult years. After the thigh grabbing incident during her articling year, Maggie tried as much as possible to stay clear of Josh Cohen. When they did have to interact, he was unfriendly and rude to her. This made her increasingly uncomfortable and her work environment unpleasant. Maggie knew he had a reputation for hitting on other female staff, making life uncomfortable for them as well.

After the high-profile appeal case, Maggie decided that it was time to leave the Cohen firm. She knew that she was competent and experienced enough to be marketable to any litigation firm in Toronto. So, Maggie announced to Messrs. Sam Cohen and Lawrence Widmore that she would be leaving the firm at the end of October 2010. They both expressed sadness at her decision.

Maggie had become very popular in the Cohen firm and both lawyers and staff were genuinely shocked and sorry to hear of her departure. The firm held a farewell party for her, and everyone bid her a tearful good-bye and wished her well in whatever she decided to do in the future. Josh Cohen didn't show up for the party and Maggie was relieved that he didn't.

Amanda Fischer started a solo litigation practice in 2007 after completing her articles. She located her new office in an 800 square foot sub-let space on the 4th floor of an office building downtown Toronto. In the last three years she had built up a very busy practice.

Maggie called Amanda the day after she had decided to leave the Cohen firm.

"Hey, Amanda, I don't think I've seen you since my bar call. I really appreciated you coming," Maggie said.

"Are you kidding? I wouldn't have missed it for anything! It was good to see you up there. You deserved that certificate! You were such a good student," Amanda said.

Maggie then proceeded to tell her that she was planning to leave the Cohen firm. She didn't explain the real reasons why. She just said that there had been some personality conflicts and that the office environment had become somewhat sour.

Maggie asked Amanda if she would have any interest in getting together to discuss partnering up.

Amanda knew Maggie's academic track record from law school and was intimately familiar with her advocacy skills from their moot court partnership, so, yes, she was very interested in pursuing the idea further and exclaimed, "Oh, man, let's get together and talk! You have no idea how good the timing is."

They made plans to meet at the Toad & Rooster, on Queen Street the following week, to discuss the matter further.

They greeted each other with a big hug, sat down and immediately ordered drinks, Amanda an Old Fashioned and Maggie a Whisky Sour.

"Wow, its nice to see you again, Maggie. I'm so glad you called," Amanda began after they had toasted. "How's Brad and that little girl of yours?"

"She's great! She'll be five in January," Maggie said, "I've got her in swimming lessons. She's already like a little fish! And, well, Brad is just a wonderful guy and great dad. He's doing well at a small firm out in Markham. Our only regret is that we're both so busy, we don't have enough time to spend with Sarah," Maggie continued.

"Oh, I'm so glad hear that you guys are doing well. You know, Sarah will be the beneficiary of a happy home even if you aren't able to spend the amount of time that you want with her," Amanda offered.

"Thanks," Maggie said. "Brad is actually thinking of leaving his firm too. He has one very loyal real estate developer client that he's already talked to who has promised to support him if he were to set up a sole practice from home. That way he could be a house dad and a lawyer all at the same time. Plus, he wants to get his dog, Princess, back from Windsor, to live with us!", she said and laughed.

"That would be great," Amanda said.

They gossiped about several of their classmates for the next half hour and then turned to the topic that brought them together.

Amanda started, "You know, Maggie, if you hadn't called me, I was just about to place an ad in the Law Society newsletter that I was looking for a partner or an associate. I'm very busy and have taken on more cases than I can handle. I'm mostly doing criminal and some small claims civil work. It's a paper war and I already have a staff of two paralegals and an assistant who doubles as my receptionist. I'm making a good living, but with a partner like you, if you were interested, I know that we could ratchet up the practice, especially on the civil litigation side, to a higher level of client. You were such a good student in law school, and we were so good together in the moot court competitions. And now you've had almost three years of litigation experience at the Cohen firm and some incredible publicity in the media. Hell, yeh, I'd be very interested in you joining me. My space is very small and all I could offer you is a small office that doesn't have much privacy. It does have a door," she said as she laughed, "and a glass wall so everyone can see in. It actually has a small exterior window too, and you'd have a wonderful view of the back side of the building across the alley," Amanda continued to laugh and paused to take a breath after her longish speech.

Maggie laughed along with her and felt very comfortable with Amanda. "Well, I don't really have any clients to bring to the practice but you're right, I do have a fair amount of litigation experience already, so, yes, I'm interested."

Then she paused before continuing, "Well, actually I do bring one matter with me. I don't know if it will go anywhere but it's a strange one. My grandfather, John Murdoch, has recently asked me to give him some advice on something."

"Oh, what is that?" Amanda asked.

"It's the craziest story you'll ever hear," Maggie said and then told Amanda the whole story of her gifted but strange uncle, Robbie Gordon, who had drowned in Lake Ontario at the age of 13. She retold Amanda the stories that she had heard growing up about her odd Uncle. She told Amanda about Robbie's strange dreams, his conversations with trees and creatures, his premonitions of things that had not yet happened and some of his other strange behaviours.

"Was he clairvoyant or something?" Amanda asked, with a frown and puzzled look on her face.

"I don't know what he was, but apparently, he had some kind of gift," Maggie said.

She told Amanda of his extraordinary ability to write beautiful poetry. Finally, Maggie told Amanda about the last poem that Robbie had written to his beloved teacher, her grandfather, John Murdoch.

"Ah, that's so sweet," Amanda said, "Robbie sounds like he was a very special boy."

"Well, yes, I guess you could say he was special, but I'm guessing he was also just a bit weird. But that's not the end of the story," Maggie said.

"Hey, wait a minute, before you go on. I'm confused about something. I thought you said that your Uncle Robbie's teacher's name was John Murdoch, but John Murdoch is also your grandfather's name. I don't get it. Are there two John Murdochs?" Amanda asked with a puzzled look on her face.

"Haha, no, it's the same guy. My Uncle Robbie's teacher and my grandfather are one and the same. After Uncle Robbie died, John Murdoch married my Grandma, Sonya Gordon. I've been calling him my grandfather my whole life, but my biological grandfather…ahh, never mind that for now, I'll explain that to you another time," Maggie said, and laughed again.

"Ok, then, carry on," Amanda said, urging her to continue.

"Well, some 46 years after my Uncle Robbie died, like only a month or so ago, a major discovery was made in London, England of a previously unknown poem written by the great

Robert Burns. The discovery was world-wide news because, of course, no one had ever seen or even heard about the existence of such a poem." Maggie said.

"Right, I remember hearing about this. So, then what happened?" Amanda asked, now leaning forward in her chair with intensified interest.

"Well, there was a whole big process of authenticating the poem and doing ancestral research to find the descendant of the person to whom the poem was originally written for," Maggie continued.

"Ok, and who was it originally written for?" Amanda asked.

"It was written for a John Murdoch. Remember, this poem was written some time during Robert Burns' lifetime in the 1700s," Maggie said.

"Ok, so who was that John Murdoch?" Amanda asked.

"Well, he was Robert Burns' childhood teacher," Maggie said.

"So, let me see if I've got this right", Amanda said, "Robert Burns' teacher's name was John Murdoch and he wrote a poem to him. Almost 200 years later, your uncle Robbie Gordon's teacher's name is also John Murdoch, who happens to be your grandfather, and your uncle wrote a poem to him."

"Yes, you've got it," Maggie confirmed.

"Ok, so what's the punch line in all of this?" Amanda asked.

"Well, here's where it gets interesting," Maggie said, "There's actually two punch lines to this story. The first is that it turns out that my grandfather, John Murdoch, is the only known direct descendant of the original John Murdoch, so my Grandpa is the legal owner of the Robert Burns poem. And, apparently, it's worth a fortune."

"Now I remember hearing about this too. John Murdoch lives right here in Ontario, in Kingston, as I recall, right? And, wow, he's your Grandpa! Was that the elderly gentleman at your bar call?" Amanda asked.

"Yes, Grandpa John and my Grandma Sonya were there," Maggie answered.

"Ok, what's the second punch line?" Amanda asked, now leaning even further forward in her chair.

"The second punch line is,…ok, this is very confidential. The poem that my Uncle Robbie wrote to his teacher, my grandfather, John Murdoch is apparently *exactly, word for word*, the same poem that Robert Burns wrote to his teacher, John Murdoch, almost 200 years earlier. No one has ever seen or known about my Uncle Robbie's poem other than my Grandpa John and Grandma Sonya. Last week he told me about it when he called. I've never even seen it yet myself," Maggie said.

"No way!", Amanda exclaimed.

"Way!" Maggie said.

"C'mon, how can that be?" Amanda exclaimed, "So you're telling me that now your grandfather has two identical poems, one written by your Uncle Robbie Gordon and the other written by Robert Burns, both to their teacher, John Murdoch? That's just hard to believe. It's a little spooky!"

"Yup," Maggie said.

"Is your grandfather, you know, ok mentally?" Amanda asked cautiously.

"Yes, I'm confident that he is. And so is my Grandma," Maggie said.

"So, either these two old people are colluding together to pull off one big hoax or it's true," Amanda said.

"I think it's true," Maggie said.

"And no one knows about your Uncle Robbie's identical poem," Amanda said.

"Nope," Maggie replied. "Grandpa and Grandma have kept it a secret. I'm not sure why. Maybe they thought that it would be too difficult for anyone to believe, so they just kept it to themselves. I know that Uncle Robbie's poem is very precious to both of them, and maybe for that reason too, they keep it as their own private treasure," Maggie said.

"So, what is your grandfather asking you for advice on?" Amanda asked.

"Well, some rich American from New York, by the name of Clarence Murdoch, has made several offers to my grandfather to purchase the Robert Burns poem from him. In fact, my Grandpa has received many offers from many different people, private collectors, museums and three universities in Scotland. My Grandpa declines every offer, but this Clarence Murdoch fellow keeps offering more and more money for the poem. If you can believe this, his last offer was for $2 million, US", Maggie exclaimed.

"Holy Cow! Who is this Clarence Murdoch?" Amanda asked.

"We have no clue," Maggie said, "Grandpa had never heard of him before."

"So, what does your grandfather need advice on, if he's just not willing to accept the offer?" Amanda persisted.

"Well, Clarence Murdoch is getting aggressive and the last time he spoke to my Grandpa, he threatened to consult a lawyer. That's when my Grandpa called me about a week ago and asked me what he should do. I told him to do nothing about Clarence Murdoch until he hears back from him or his lawyer. I told him that, if and when he does hear back from him, he should tell him that he has also retained legal counsel. And then I told Grandpa that if the Robert Burns poem is worth that much money, he should put it in a safe deposit box in a bank, or some place like that," Maggie said.

"I would say so," Amanda said, nodding her head, "but why would he threaten to consult a lawyer if all he's wanting to do is purchase the poem? If your Grandpa doesn't want to sell it, what good is a lawyer going to do? A lawyer can't force him to sell something that your Grandpa doesn't want to sell."

"You're right, and I don't know what he's up to," Maggie said.

"Well, whatever it is, it will be interesting to find out where this is going. I'd like to read this famous poem written by two different people almost 200 years apart," Amanda said.

"Well you can read the Burns poem on line and, well, I guess Uncle Robbie's poem is the same. Next time I talk to Grandpa, I'll ask him if he would be willing to send me a copy, copies, a copy, whatever!" Maggie said and laughed again.

Maggie and Amanda agreed to meet again the following week at Amanda's office and discuss joining forces in more detail.

Chapter 35

On December 1, 2010, the law firm of Fischer & Gordon LLP was formed. It was located in Amanda' 800 square foot sub-let office on the 4th floor of an old building in downtown Toronto. Maggie moved into her new office with the glass wall, that everyone could see into, and an exterior window with a wonderful view of the back side of the building across the alley.

One month after that, Brad gave his notice to leave his firm. Now Brad and Maggie wanted to let the Scarborough apartment go and move downtown, closer to Maggie's office. Brad didn't need to be in any particular location as he could do most everything, he had to do from a home office. Quality apartments in downtown Toronto didn't come cheap. Maggie and Brad had both just quite their jobs and were starting fresh and landlords don't like that. So Maggie humbled herself and asked her parents if they would help. Willie and Helen had grown to love and trust Brad, so they were happy to. Plus, they had the money!

Willie had made their farm, near Maxville a success and now they were retired. They had purchased a beautiful home in Kingston near Grandpa John and Grandma Sonya. Maggie's brother, Tom, had recently taken over management of the farm.

Willie agreed to co-sign for Maggie and Brad on the lease of a nice apartment on Wellington He also agreed to help them with the rent for a few months, until they got re-established in their new law practices.

Brad drove down to Windsor and collected his beloved dog, Princess, and the little family of four now occupied their new apartment on Wellington.

Amanda had given Maggie some of her civil cases and Maggie was grateful for the work. Within three weeks of Maggie's arrival, both lawyers were as busy as Amanda had been before Maggie arrived. Amanda focused mostly on criminal cases and Maggie on civil cases.

Maggie needed her own full-time assistant. She called Kelly, her former assistant at the Cohen firm, and asked if she'd be interested in leaving and coming to work for her at her new firm. Kelly didn't need to be asked twice. Two weeks later she started her first day at Fischer Gordon. Now there were six people crammed into the little Fischer Gordon law office.

It was late December 2010 when Maggie's Grandpa, John Murdoch, called her again. Actually, it was her Grandma, Sonya, who made the call.

"Hello, is this Maggie Gordon?" Sonya asked. This was the second time in her life that she had called a law office. The first was to engage a divorce lawyer some 40 years earlier.

Maggie immediately recognized Sonya's voice and could tell that she was nervous. "Yes, Grandma, this is Maggie. It's so nice to hear from you. How are you doing?" Maggie asked.

"Oh, hello Maggie. Well, I'm fine but your Grandpa is upset. He got another call from this man, Clarence Murdoch, and he's threatening to sue John and he doesn't know what to do," Sonya said.

"Ok, Grandma, can I talk to Grandpa," Maggie asked.

"Yes, he's right here," said Sonya, and then added, "How's my little Sarah?"

"Oh, she's doing fine. She'll be five next month, can you believe that?" Maggie answered.

"Give her a big hug from Grams," Sonya said and handed the telephone to John.

"This is John Murdoch here," he said.

"Yes, I know it's you Grandpa," Maggie said laughing, "How are you?"

"Oh, hello Maggie. I didn't know if it was you. I'm fine for an old man but I can't hear much anymore and I sure don't like this darn hearing aid. It's either too loud or not loud enough. Anyway, Maggie, I am troubled by the latest call from Mr. Clarence Murdoch." John said.

"What did he say this time, Grandpa?" Maggie asked.

"Well, he now claims to have evidence that he is the rightful owner of the Burns poem, not me. I don't know what to tell him, so I just told him that I would talk to my lawyer. That's you Maggie," he said, almost asking if that was in fact the case.

"Of course, I'm your lawyer, Grandpa," said smiling to herself, "Don't worry about a thing. I'll take care of everything for you. Did you give him my name and address?" Maggie said.

"Yes, I did dear, and we both want to thank you for helping out your old Grandpa and Grandma. You know, we're in this together," John said.

"I know you are Grandpa. I'll let you know if anything happens at my end and you keep me posted if anything happens at your end, ok?" Maggie said.

"Yes, I will, ok then good-bye Maggie and thank you again," John said then hung up the phone.

Chapter 36

It was about two weeks after that phone call that a letter arrived from the firm of Fleming Pankratz & Murrin LLP in New York.

Maggie Gordon finished reading the letter for the first time. "Damn!", she said louder than she had intended. Her door was open. She quickly looked up and through the glass wall of her office to see if anyone had heard her. She didn't think so and hoped not. Everyone seemed to be occupied with something or other.

She read the letter again.

Fleming Pankratz & Murrin LLP
Suite 6700, 88 Pine Street
New York, New York, 10005
Telephone: 212 555 1212
Facsimile: 212 555 1213
Email: info@fpmllp.com

Morris Pankratz
Direct Line: 212 555 1276
Email: mpankratz@fpmllp.com
Our File: 316672

January 7, 2011

PRIVILEGED AND CONFIDENTIAL   **Via Courier and Email**

Fischer & Gordon LLP
Barristers & Solicitors
421, 88 King Street West
Toronto, Ontario, Canada
M5H 1H1
Attention: Ms. Maggie Gordon

Dear Ms. Gordon

Re: Robert Burns Poem to John Murdoch

We confirm that our firm is United States legal counsel to Clarence Murdoch (hereinafter called "US Murdoch").

We understand that your firm represents Dr. John Murdoch, of Kingston, Ontario (hereinafter called "Canada Murdoch").

As you are aware, US Murdoch has made multiple attempts to negotiate the purchase from Canada Murdoch of the handwritten letter from Gilbert Burns to John Murdoch dated November 19, 1823, the handwritten poem by Robert Burns entitled '*To John Murdoch, My*

Teacher, My Friend' and the associated envelopes (together, hereinafter called the "Burns Documents"). The said John Murdoch was known to have resided from time to time in Scotland (hereinafter called "Scotland Murdoch").

Canada Murdoch has rejected all of US Murdoch's offers for the Burns Documents.

We hereby advise you that US Murdoch's last offer of USD $2 million for the Burns Documents is withdrawn, effective as of today's date.

We further advise you that US Murdoch has engaged an expert ancestral research team from The Church of Jesus Christ of Latter-Day Saints (hereinafter called the "LDS Team") to conduct extensive ancestral research on the descendants of Scotland Murdoch. The research by the LDS Team clearly confirms that US Murdoch, Clarence Murdoch, is, in fact the rightful heir to the Burns Documents, and that Canada Murdoch is not.

We enclose a copy of the ancestral research produced by the LDS Team.

Accordingly, we hereby make demand that your client forthwith deliver the Burns Documents to our offices using UPS' Critical Secure Service. We will cover all costs associated with the delivery. Please contact the writer immediately to make arrangements for this delivery.

If our office has not received the Burns Documents on or before, 5:00 EST, January 21, 2011, we have instructions to apply to the Superior Court of Justice of the Province of Ontario for an order compelling Canada Murdoch to give up possession of the Burns Documents and deliver them to US Murdoch.

Please govern yourselves accordingly.

Fleming Pankratz & Murrin LLP

Per: Morris Pankratz, Partner
MP/tg

"Damn!", Maggie scowled again. She leaned back in her chair as far as it would go, closed her eyes, took a deep breath and blew it out slowly.

This was not a good development and Maggie knew that this would be a terrible shock to Grandpa John and Grandma Sonya. Maggie took a few minutes to calm herself down before picking up the phone and dialing her Grandpa's number.

Sonya answered, "Hello."

"Hi, Grandma, this is Maggie. Grandma, can I talk to Grandpa?"

"He's taking a nap, but he should be getting up by now. Hold on, I'll get him."

The Mysterious Robbie Gordon

Maggie waited for a full three minutes before John Murdoch came to the phone. "Hello," he said very loudly into the telephone, "Hold on for a minute Maggie". Maggie could tell that he was fidgeting with his hearing aid. She waited for another few seconds then he came back on and said in a normal voice, "Sorry about that Maggie, I had to adjust this annoying hearing aid."

Maggie allowed herself a small smile before getting to the serious business at hand.

"Hi Grandpa, I received a letter today from Clarence Murdoch's lawyers. He's hired a big firm in New York City to represent him."

Maggie then proceeded to summarize the contents of the letter to him. John was silent for a long while. Finally, he said, "Oh dear. What should I do?"

"Well, for sure don't send anything to anyone," Maggie said.

"No, of course not," he replied.

"Grandpa, what I need now, is a copy of the ancestry report that the London firm gave you a few months ago showing you as the ultimate heir of the original John Murdoch. Do you still have that?" Maggie said.

"Yes, of course I do. It's with the poems. I did what you told me to do and I've put all of those things in my safe deposit box at the Bank of Montreal here in Kingston." He said.

"Good. Grandpa, can you go to the Bank and have them fax or email me a copy of that report? Oh, and Grandpa, while you're at it, can you also ask them to fax or email me copies of the two poems?"

"Yes, of course. I'll do that this very afternoon."

Before 3 pm that afternoon, Maggie received a long fax from the Bank of Montreal in Kingston. She instructed her assistant to open a new litigation file called 'Clarence Murdoch v. John Murdoch'.

She placed a copy of the letter from the New York law firm in the correspondence file and copies of the poems in the document folder of the file. She'd show the poems to Amanda later.

Maggie kept the two ancestry reports out and placed them side by side, on her desk. One was dated September 21, 2010 on letterhead of the firm of Avery & Lord, London England. The other was dated December 15, 2010 on letterhead of The Church of Jesus Christ of Latter-Day Saints, Salt Lake City, Utah.

She studied the summary page of the Avery & Lord report first:

Name	Date of Birth	Place of Birth	Source of Records
John Murdoch	1747	Ayr, Scotland	Burns Encyclopaedia
Alasdair John Murdoch	May 22, 1780	Inverness, Scotland	St. Stephen's Church, Church of Scotland, Inverness, Scotland

Robert John Murdoch	December 11, 1801	Keith, Scotland	Kirk of Keith, Church of Scotland, Keith, Scotland
Colin John Murdoch	January 4, 1831	Keith, Scotland	St. Thomas Catholic Church, Keith, Scotland
James Alexander Murdoch	December 3, 1851	Keith, Scotland	St. Thomas Catholic Church, Keith, Scotland
William Alexander Murdoch	June 17, 1872	Kingston, Ontario	St. Mary's Cathedral, Kingston, Ontario
Alexander James Murdoch	February 14, 1894	Kingston, Ontario	St. Mary's Cathedral, Kingston, Ontario
John James Murdoch	January 31, 1926	Kingston, Ontario	St. Mary's Cathedral, Kingston, Ontario

Then Maggie studied the summary page of the LDS report:

Name	Date of Birth	Place of Birth	Source of Records
John Murdoch	1747	Ayr, Scotland	Burns Encyclopaedia
Alasdair John Murdoch	May 22, 1780	Inverness, Scotland	St. Stephen's Church, Church of Scotland, Inverness, Scotland
Robert John Murdoch	December 11, 1801	Keith, Scotland	Kirk of Keith, Church of Scotland, Keith, Scotland
Joseph John Murdoch	May 17, 1822	Rochester, New York	Latter-day Saint Meetinghouse, Rochester, New York, now with Family History Library, Salt Lake City, Utah
John Cook Murdoch	December 29, 1842	Nauvoo, Illinois	Latter-day Saint Meetinghouse, Nauvoo, Illinois, now with Family History Library, Salt Lake City, Utah
Clarence Hyrum Murdoch	March 5, 1871	Salt Lake City, Utah	Family History Library, Salt Lake City, Utah
Joseph Clarence Murdoch	July 8, 1905	Salt Lake City, Utah	Family History Library, Salt Lake City, Utah
John Heber Murdoch	June 20, 1933	New York City, New York	Family History Library, Salt Lake City, Utah
Clarence Oman Murdoch	April 20, 1964	New York City, New York	Family History Library, Salt Lake City, Utah

Maggie's first observation was that the two ancestries agreed only for the first three Murdochs and then went in wildly different directions.

Her second observation was that Clarence Murdoch was likely a Mormon. In the LDS report, the birth places, source of records and names, after Robert Murdoch, almost tracked the history of the Mormon church in the United States.

'Oh, my god,' Maggie thought, 'I hope this doesn't turn into a battle against the Mormon Church.'

She got up from her chair, grabbed the letter and the two ancestry reports and went to find Amanda. She was just returning to the office from a court appearance she'd had that afternoon. Maggie followed her into her office, which was only slightly larger than Maggie's.

"Hey, Amanda, do you have a minute?" asked Maggie.

"Sure thing, what's up?"

"Well, I received this letter today," and Maggie handed her the letter from the Fleming firm in New York.

Amanda sat down and read it, then looked up and said, "Well, I guess it's game time now, huh?"

"Right, now have a look at this," Maggie said, and handed Amanda copies of the two ancestral reports.

Amanda studied the two reports for a few minutes, then started laughing. "You know that I'm Mormon, don't you?"

"No shit!", Maggie exclaimed, as she put her hand out to the wall for support to keep herself from falling down.

"Just kidding, but I had you going there for a minute, didn't I?" Amanda said, laughing, barely able to control herself.

"Why, I oughtta...," Maggie said as she raised her hand in a mock slap up-side Amanda's head.

"Who is this Clarence Murdoch anyway? Have you googled him?" Amanda asked, transitioning to a more serious mode.

"No, but I will now," Maggie answered, as she started to head back to her office.

"Hey Maggie," Amanda shouted after her, "Have you heard about this new musical called *The Book of Mormon*. It's opening soon in New York. It's supposed to be hilarious. You and I should fly out to the Big Apple for a weekend and have some fun, sort of like our first partners' retreat."

"Hmm, that does sound like fun. Let's do it," Maggie said.

"Great, I'll get one of the girls to look into tickets," Amanda said, "and, oh, Maggie, does your Grandpa have any money for legal fees?"

Maggie knew this was coming and cringed. "I don't really know what their financial situation is, but I know Grandpa John has a small pension from Banffshire and a modest home in Kingston and, of course, he is the proud owner of a Burns poem that's maybe worth millions!" she said, "But a lot of good that will do us."

"No worries," Amanda said, "I think we should do this pro bono. Depending on how this goes, we're going to get a lot of publicity, if nothing else."

"Right," was all Maggie could think of to say, as she returned to her office.

She got on the computer and typed in 'Clarence Murdoch, New York City'. She got six hits, but there was only one with the middle initial 'O'. She found a short bio on Clarence Oman Murdoch in Wikipedia and learned that he was a multi-millionaire who made his fortune as a fine art dealer and that he personally owned one of the world's largest private collections of first edition books by historically famous authors. He was also the President of the New York City Stake of The Church of Jesus Christ of Latter-Day Saints. He was married and lived with his wife on Park Avenue in Manhattan. He had five adult children.

'Hmm,' she thought, 'yes, it's game on, and I'm guessing that Mr. Clarence Murdoch is going to be a formidable adversary.'

Maggie looked at her watch. It was 5:30 pm, Toronto time on a Friday. It was too late to call London. She'd call Liz Cullen at the Avery & Lord firm early on Monday morning.

Chapter 37

"Hello, may I speak to Ms. Liz Cullen please?" Maggie requested when she'd made the connection early the following Monday morning.

"Yes, may I say who is calling?" the receptionist asked.

"My name is Maggie Gordon, please tell her that I am the solicitor for my grandfather, Dr. John Murdoch of Kingston, Ontario."

Liz immediately dropped what she was doing and picked up the phone when the receptionist told her who was on the line.

Maggie proceeded to describe her relationship to Dr. Murdoch and gave her a synopsis of the several offers he had received to purchase the Burns poem since Liz had visited him in September 2010. Then Maggie told her of the recent events as they related to Mr. Clarence Murdoch, the conflicting ancestral reports of the Avery firm and the LDS Church and his threat of a law suit.

"Oh, my," Liz said when Maggie was done. "How can I help?"

"Well, I'm not sure yet. I think we'll just have to wait and see if, in fact, we do get served formally with something from the Clarence Murdoch side. Then we can assess what our next steps will be. In the meantime, I just wanted to let you know what is happening and that you might be called upon at some point in the future to testify as to the merits and accuracy of your ancestral report. Of course, I'm hoping that you will be able to support your findings, if ever called upon to do so," Maggie said.

"Yes, of course, Ms. Gordon. I'll review the file, so that I'm prepared if and when you next get in touch with me," Liz said, "And, please greet Dr. Murdoch for me. I was very taken by his warm and gentle nature when we met last autumn."

"I'll do that and thank you Ms. Cullen. Good bye for now," Maggie said as she disconnected the call. She liked Liz Cullen.

The following Friday, Maggie received another letter on the Clarence Murdoch matter.

When she was finished reading the letter, this time she said, "God damn," again louder than she had intended. Her door was open, as it usually was. She quickly looked up and through the glass wall of her office to see if anyone had heard her. She didn't think so and again hoped not. Everyone seemed to be occupied with something or other. She thought to herself, 'I should really stop cursing so much.'

She read the letter again.

Cohen, Widmore & Cohen LLP
Suite 4000, 20 Bloor Street
Toronto, ON M4W 3G7
Telephone: 416 555 2121
Facsimile: 416 555 2131
Email: info@cwcllp.com

Josh Cohen
Direct Line: 416 555 6721
Email: josh.cohen@cwcllp.com
Our File: 14-3529

January 28, 2011

PRIVILEGED AND CONFIDENTIAL   **Via Courier and Email**

Fischer & Gordon LLP
Barristers & Solicitors
421, 88 King Street West
Toronto, ON M5H 1H1
Attention: Ms. Maggie Gordon

Dear Ms. Gordon

Re: Clarence Murdoch v. John Murdoch

We make reference to the letter dated January 7, 2011 from Fleming Pankratz & Murrin addressed to your firm. All words and terms defined in that letter, will have the same meaning herein.

We confirm that our firm is Canadian legal counsel to US Murdoch. Our firm will be acting as agents for US Murdoch's US legal counsel, namely, Fleming Pankratz & Murrin LLP.

We understand that your firm represents Canada Murdoch.

> **Your client has not complied with the demand, set forth in the said January 7, 2011 letter, to deliver, on or before, 5:00 EST, January 21, 2011, the Burns Documents to US Murdoch.**

Accordingly, on behalf of US Murdoch, you are hereby served with the attached Statement of Claim which we have filed in the Superior Court of Justice of the Province of Ontario. As you can see, we are seeking, among other remedies, an Order directing Canada Murdoch to deliver the Burns Documents to US Murdoch.

Please govern yourselves accordingly.

Cohen, Widmore & Cohen LLP

Per: Josh Cohen, Partner
JC/fl

Maggie didn't curse this time. She just leaned back in her chair as far as it would go, closed her eyes, took a deep breath and blew it out slowly.

There was a lot going on here and her mind was whizzing over the big picture items. She was more than a bit flustered and instead of just letting her mind whir about, she picked up her pen and started summarizing the main facts and issues on her note pad:

- *Dr. John Murdoch is my Grandpa. Do I/does our firm have a conflict?*
- *The Burns Centre at the University of Scotland has established the authenticity of the Burns documents.*
- *The London firm of Avery & Lord has conducted ancestral research that indicated that Dr. Murdoch was the rightful owner of the Burns documents.*
- *Several parties, including Clarence Murdoch, have made offers to Grandpa for the purchase of the Burns documents and he had consistently rejected all offers.*
- *Clarence Murdoch had been persistent in his offers and his last offer was for USD $2 million. Very high valuation? Do some research on this.*
- *Clarence Murdoch has engaged the LDS Church to conduct ancestral research that indicates that Clarence Murdoch is the rightful owner of the Burns documents, not Grandpa.*
- *Clarence Murdoch is wealthy and knowledgeable about historic documents.*
- *Clarence Murdoch is a high-ranking member of the LDS Church.*
- *Clarence Murdoch is now seeking a Court Order to force Grandpa to turn over the Burns documents to him.*
- *Clarence Murdoch is being represented by Josh Cohen. This is just great. I now have this creep opposite me in what could be the biggest law suit of my career so far!*
- *We're prepared to take this case on pro bono. It will involve a lot of time and may cut into fee paying files.*
- *Once the press gets wind of this case, there will be a lot of publicity for our new law firm. Could be good.*
- *Does the LDS church have anything more to do with this than just conducting the ancestral research?*
- *Is all of this connected, in some weird way, to the fact that my odd Uncle Robbie Gordon wrote the same poem as the Robert Burns poem???? Still weird!!!*

Maggie was just about to put her pen down when a sobering thought struck her, 'Grandpa Murdoch will be 85 years old soon and what if he dies? Who will her client be then? Who would be the legal owner of the Burns documents if he died? Grandpa Murdoch has no children, so who is his legal heir? I wonder if Grandpa has a will?'

Maggie had forgotten most of what she had learned in law school about estate law in the Province of Ontario, so she'd have to do a bit of research on that too, in the days to follow.

On Monday morning, Maggie dictated a letter in reply to Josh Cohen and gave the tape to her assistant. The letter simply acknowledged that she had received his letter and that she would be preparing a response within the next few days. She asked her assistant to have the letter ready for her to sign when she returned to the office that afternoon.

Over the next few days, Maggie began drafting a Statement of Defence to Josh Cohen's Statement of Claim. The substance of the defence was simple and straight forward. It denied that Clarence Murdoch had any right to the Burns documents and asserted that the rightful owner always was and remained, Dr. John Murdoch. The final paragraph asked the court to dismiss the claim, with costs.

Maggie instructed their paralegal to file the Statement of Defence at the courthouse. She then dictated a terse letter to Josh Cohen, enclosing a copy of the Statement of Defence. She chuckled to herself when she thought that maybe she should add a handwritten postscript at the bottom of the letter and ask him how his wife is doing. She didn't.

Just then, Amanda poked her head in Maggie's door. "Hey girl, guess what?" My assistant tells me that she can get two tickets for the Book of Mormon at the Eugene O'Neill Theatre in New York on Saturday, February 26th. Will that work for you?" she asked hopefully.

"Let me check my calendar," Maggie said. She went to check. "We're in luck! It doesn't look like Brad and I have anything special going on that weekend."

"Great, let's make it happen! We can fly out early on Friday and have two nights in the big city! I'll get my assistant to make all the arrangements. We're going to have a ball," Amanda gushed excitedly.

Three weeks later the girls were in New York.

"Oh my god, I've never laughed so hard in my life," exclaimed Amanda as they exited the Eugene O'Neill Theatre after watching The Book of Mormon.

"I loved it!" said Maggie and she started to hum the catchy tune to Hasa Diga Eebowai. "I can't remember the words, but then maybe that's for the good, because I'm trying to curse less," she laughed.

They laughed together and walked arm in arm down Broadway towards Times Square. They looked like two teenagers.

Chapter 38

Maggie told her assistant that she'd be at the Great Library at Osgood Hall for the morning. The library was at the corner of Queen and University, about a 10-minute walk from Maggie's office. She looked forward to the walk.

The small Fischer Gordon law firm did not have a library or any other legal resources, for that matter. They only had personal computers and the internet. So, for most legal research, they had to trek down to the Great Library at Osgood Hall.

At the library that morning, Maggie intended to research the laws of inheritance as they relate to a person who has no children and to a person who has no Will. In less than an hour, Maggie concluded that it really didn't matter whether her Grandpa had children or not, nor did it even matter if Grandpa and Grandma previously had a Will. Maggie would insist that they get a new or updated Will, and fast! That would eliminate all of the complexities and uncertainties.

She'd call Grandpa Murdoch when she returned to the office. She did and hoped that she'd catch him before his nap.

Her Grandma Sonya answered the phone. "Hi Grandma, it's Maggie. How are you?" Maggie greeted.

"Oh, hello dear," Sonya answered, "I'm fine, but Grandpa's not doing too well."

"I'm sorry to hear that. What's the problem?" Maggie asked.

"Well, he's come down with some kind of flu bug and you know, when somebody our age gets the flu its serious business," Sonya tried to make light of it, but it but she didn't sound very convincing.

"Can he come to the phone Grandma? I need to speak with him for a minute or two," Maggie said.

"He's in bed. I'll see if he can get up," Sonya said and left. Maggie could hear the receiver of the old wall mounted land line telephone swinging back and forth, hitting the cupboard and the wall as it did.

A minute or so later, Sonya returned and picked up the receiver, now hanging still, and said, "Maggie, I don't think he can talk now. He's just thrown up his soup."

"That's ok, Grandma. Let me ask you something. Do you and Grandpa have Wills?", Maggie asked.

"Yes, I'm sure we do," Sonya answered, "John had a solicitor here in Kingston do up Wills for both of us several years ago. I have no idea where they are, and I can't remember now what they say."

"Grandma, could you ask Grandpa about them when he's feeling better. It's important and now with this lawsuit, it's even more important to make sure that you both have them and that they're up to date," Maggie said.

"Oh, dear, yes, I will do that Maggie," Sonya said. "Maggie, how's my little Sarah? I hope to see here again soon. When will you be bringing her down to Willie and Helen's again?

"She's fine Grandma and I tell you what. You get back to me on this Will thing as soon as you can, and I'll plan to come down with Sarah and visit all of you soon, ok?" Maggie said.

"Ok, I will do that and please tell Sarah that I love her," said Sonya.

"I will Grandma and tell Grandpa that I hope he gets well real soon. Good-bye Grandma," Maggie said and disconnected the call.

Maggie had this uneasy feeling and it worried her. She hoped her Grandpa Murdoch would in fact get well real soon.

She finished her day by attending to the hundred other things that a lawyer has to attend to with a litigation practice, reading all the incoming correspondence, responding to it, meeting with clients, drafting this and that type of pleadings and settlement agreements, etc., etc., etc.

One week later, Sonya called Maggie back. "Is this Maggie Gordon?" She always asked that when they talked on the phone.

"Yes, Grandma, this is Maggie. How are you and how is Grandpa?"

"Oh, we're both fine. Did you know that John was sick last week, but he's feeling better now," Sonya said.

'Yikes,' thought Maggie. 'Does Grandma not remember that we talked about Grandpa's flu bug only a week ago?'

Before Maggie could respond, Sonya said, "Oh, silly me, of course you knew that he was sick. We talked about it when you called about our Wills, didn't we?"

"Yes, Grandma, we did talk about that. Were you able to talk about your Wills with Grandpa?" Maggie asked.

"Well, yes, that's why I'm calling. Here, I'll let you talk to John. He's right here," Sonya said and left the line. A minute followed with no one on the line. Maggie could hear her Grandpa mumbling in the background about 'this darn thing' and she knew he was fiddling with his hearing aid.

Finally, he had things adjusted to his liking and came on the phone shouting, "Hello Maggie."

Maggie smiled to herself and moved her phone away from her ear a bit while she turned down the volume. "Hi Grandpa. I hear you were under the weather for a bit last week."

"Oh, it was nothing. Sonya gets all worried at the smallest thing. I had an upset tummy one day and she thought I had the flu," John said and laughed.

"Grandpa, when I talked to Grandma last week, I had asked her about your Wills. Were you able to check that out?" Maggie asked.

"Yes, I did dear. I keep them in the safe deposit box at the Bank of Montreal, the same one that I keep the poems in. Your Grandma and I went down to the bank the other day to read them. We did them up 40 years ago, shortly after we got married. My Will leaves a small amount to Banffshire Academy and the rest to Sonya. Sonya's Will leaves a small amount to Banffshire and the rest to Willie. You and Tom weren't even born yet and, of course there were no grandchildren then either. Do you think we should update them?" he asked.

"Yes, I do Grandpa," Maggie answered, and before she could continue, John interrupted her.

"We thought so too. Sonya said that you and Sarah were planning to come and visit us soon, so you're a lawyer now and we thought you could do up new Wills for us when you come down," John said.

"Well, Grandpa, I don't do that kind of legal work and I don't think it would be appropriate for me to do up Wills for you and Grandma, even if I knew how to. I would recommend that you get new Wills done up by a solicitor right there in Kingston," Maggie said.

"Oh, that solicitor is long gone," John laughed. "He was old when we visited him 40 years ago."

Maggie smiled to herself again. "No, I didn't expect that you'd go back to that same solicitor. You'll need to find a new one. I can help you with that. I'll do some checking in our Ontario Law Directory and get a couple of names and telephone numbers for you. I'll call you back tomorrow. Is that ok, Grandpa?" Maggie said.

"Yes, that would be wonderful," John said and then said, "Oh, Maggie, please tell little Sarah that I love her and look forward to seeing her again soon."

"I will do that Grandpa. She loves seeing you and whenever she comes back from visiting you, she always tells me how much she loves rubbing your bald head and your beard," Maggie said.

She couldn't see the tears, but they welled up in John's eyes as they said their good-byes.

The next day Maggie called back and gave Grandma Sonya the names and telephone numbers of two solicitors in Kingston who, the Law Directory indicated, practiced in the areas of Wills & Estates. It took Sonya several minutes to write the information down. Maggie hoped that she'd written it down correctly and that she and Grandpa would, in fact, call one of them and attend to getting updated Wills drafted up. She also hoped that the lawyer would encourage them to do up Continuing Powers of Attorney for their financial affairs and personal care. She knew that this was pretty much standard practice now for lawyers practicing in those areas.

Two days later, the receptionist came to Maggie's office and announced that there was a Mr. MacDonald asking to speak with her about John Murdoch and Sonya Gordon.

Maggie immediately picked up the phone. "Hello, this is Maggie Gordon," she said.

"Good Day. My name is Rodney Howard MacDonald, 'upper case M, lower case a and c and upper-case D', he said, "You may call me Mr. MacDonald. I am a Barrister & Solicitor and member of the Law Society of Upper Canada. My practice is limited to areas of Wills & Estates. My office is in Kingston, Ontario." Maggie chuckled to herself at his formal manner.

He sounded quite senior. She speculated that he'd probably gone through that spelling clarification routine a thousand times in his life.

"Hello, Mr. MacDonald. How can I help you?" Maggie said, resisting the temptation to repeat the 'upper case M, lower case a and c and upper-case D' line.

"Yes, well, I understand that Mr. John Murdoch and Mrs. Sonya Gordon are your grandparents, is that correct?" he said.

"Yes, indeed they are," she said.

"I understand that you have referred them to me, and I want to thank you for that," he said.

Maggie didn't want to correct him, that she hadn't actually made a referral, but said, "Yes, I'm glad that they've come in to see you."

"Yes, well, you see, they have visited me and, if you don't mind, I would like to discuss a few things with you, if I could," he said.

"Surely," Maggie said. "What would you like to discuss?"

"Well, as you know, your Grandpa and Grandma are elderly and it is my practice to take certain precautions before having folks of that age sign a Will," he said.

"Oh, what kind of precautions?" Maggie asked.

"I like to get confirmation from a medical doctor that they are of sound mind. I like to discuss that issue with members of their family before I make that recommendation to the client. It is my experience that if I do so, there is less chance of people getting upset. So, when your Grandpa and Grandma visited me and told me that you referred them to me, I thought I had best talk to you about it. Another thing that I have learned in my long career ('Ah, there it was,' thought Maggie) is that if a member of the family advises the elderly client that this is something that I am going to recommend to them before I do, it softens the blow and then they are less likely to resist it, when I do make the recommendation. Does this make sense to you, Ms. Gordon?" he said.

"Yes, it does," Maggie said, "But, just so I'm clear, you have not made that recommendation to them yet and you're asking me to discuss it with them first."

"Precisely, yes," he said, "Do you mind, awfully?"

'Who talks like that?' Maggie thought, but found herself being entertained and enjoying his style of speaking.

"Not at all. I don't need to give you all the background but suffice it to say that it is very important that they have valid Wills, so I appreciate your precautionary approach to these matters. I'll discuss this with Grandpa and Grandma right away. Oh, and by the way, will you recommend that they also do up EPAs and PDs?" Maggie asked.

"Yes, of course, that is my practice," he said.

"That's great, and I'll confirm back with you after I've discussed the other matter with Grandma and Grandpa," Maggie said.

"Wonderful! Cheerio then, and I await your call back when the deed is done," he said, as he chuckled at his own joke. Maggie wondered if he'd done that a thousand times too.

Maggie called her grandparents later that same day and discussed the matter of seeing a doctor for the purposes described by Mr. Rodney Howard MacDonald. They were both completely amenable to the idea.

John said, "Well, I should probably do that anyway, just to make sure that I'm still the smart fellow that I think I am. I know Sonya is the same sweet intelligent woman that I met 40 some years ago! I'll make an appointment tomorrow with Dr. Robertson and, assuming we both pass the test, I'll have him send the certificates to Mr. MacDonald." Maggie smiled again to herself and hoped that she would have that same positive attitude and sense of humor when she was in her 80s!

"Thank you, Grandpa, good-bye for now," Maggie said.

One week later, the receptionist came to Maggie's office and announced that Mr. MacDonald was on the line again.

Maggie immediately picked up the phone. "Hello, Mr. MacDonald." This time she couldn't resist, "Is that with an 'upper case M, lower case a and c and upper-case D'?" she asked.

There was a long pause. "Well, yes it…, Why, that's very funny! Good for you!" he responded with a hearty laugh. She laughed along with him.

He then continued, "Listen, Ms. Gordon, I thought I would let you know that Dr. Andrew Robertson here in Kingston has just sent to me the results of the Mini-Mental State Exam that he has conducted on each of your Grandpa and Grandma. John Murdoch scored a perfect 30 out of 30 and Sonya Gordon scored a 27. Dr. Robertson has issued a certificate of good mental health for each of them and I have his documentation in my file. I will now be calling them to set up an appointment to discuss their instructions for the preparation of Wills, Enduring Powers of Attorney and Personal Directives."

"Thank you for the update, Mr. MacDonald. Please let me know if I can help with anything else," Maggie said.

"Yes. Cheerio then, Ms. Gordon," he said as he hung up the phone.

'Now there's a rare and, sadly, dying breed. Charming!' Maggie thought. She hoped someday to meet Mr. MacDonald, with an 'upper case M, lower case a and c and upper-case D'.

Chapter 39

When Maggie got to the office Friday morning, her assistant handed her an envelope which had just been couriered to the office.

She was finished reading the letter for the first time. Notwithstanding her commitment to curse less, she unconsciously let slip, "No fucking way!" again louder than she had intended. Her door was open, as it usually was. She quickly looked up and through the glass wall of her office to see if anyone had heard her. She didn't think so and again hoped not. Everyone seemed to be occupied with something or other. She reminded herself to stop cursing so much, but she just couldn't believe this letter.

Morton & Carry LLP
41 Baker Street, Marylebone
London W1U 7AM, UK
Telephone: +44 20 8956 3100
Facsimile: +44 20 8956 3299
Email: info@mcllp.com

George Pointer Morton
Direct Line: +44 20 8956 3105
Email: gpmorton@mcllp.com
Our File: 763079/gpm

March 3, 2011

PRIVILEGED AND CONFIDENTIAL   **Via Courier and Email**

Fischer & Gordon LLP
Barristers & Solicitors
421, 88 King Street West
Toronto, Ontario, Canada
M5H 1H1
Attention: Ms. Maggie Gordon

Dear Ms. Gordon

Re: St. Germain École des Garçons v. John Murdoch

Our firm is legal counsel in the United Kingdom to St. Germain École des Garçons.

We understand that your firm represents Dr. John Murdoch, of Kingston, Ontario.

You are, no doubt, aware of the handwritten letter from Gilbert Burns to John Murdoch dated November 19, 1823, the handwritten poem by Robert Burns entitled '*To John Murdoch, My Teacher, My Friend*' and the associated envelopes (the "Burns Papers").
As you may be aware, the Burns Papers' were discovered in the archives of our client, St.

> Germain École des Garçons. Our client has never relinquished ownership or legal possession of the Burns Papers.
>
> Our client's position is that the Burns Papers are wrongfully in the possession of your client and we have been instructed to recover them from your client.
>
> Accordingly, we hereby make demand that your client forthwith delivers the Burns Papers to our offices using our firm's account with Jet Worldwide. We will cover all costs associated with the delivery. Please contact Jet Worldwide to make arrangements for this delivery.
>
> If our office has not received the Burn's Papers on or before, 5:00 GMT, March 17, 2011, we have instructions to apply to the Superior Court of Justice of the Province of Ontario for an Order of Replevin compelling your client to give up possession of the Burns Documents and deliver them to US Murdoch.
>
> We would recommend that you proceed with care.
>
> **Morton & Carry LLP**
>
> George Pointer Morton, Esquire
> GPM/fr
>
> cc. McKenzie Hoffman LLP, Toronto, ON
> Attention: Mr. Charles C. Hoffman, QC

Maggie read the letter again. She had to literally bite her tongue to keep from cursing again.

She instructed her assistant to open a new litigation file called 'St. Germain École des Garçons v. John Murdoch'.

The letter was carbon copied to Mr. Charles Hoffman at the McKenzie Hoffman firm. Maggie was well familiar with that firm. It was the firm that she had lost her copyright appeal case to, when she had acted for the singer-songwriter, Mandy Cochrane.

'Poor Grandpa,' she thought. She'd have to break this news to him now and she really didn't want to do that. She was worried what the strain and stress would do to both Grandpa and Grandma. Maggie worked up the courage to call them later that day. She was right, the level of stress was weighing on them. Maggie's competitive, fighting spirit kicked in and she resolved to not let them down. She told them to not to worry and, certainly, to not send anything to this law firm. She again tried to comfort them and told them that she would handle everything.

Maggie's next step was to figure out what the hell replevin actually was. She needed to conduct some research on that. She walked again to The Great Library at Osgood Hall and enjoyed the 10 minutes trudge over the March snow, slowly melting into slush.

It took Maggie two hours of research just to learn what replevin was all about, another hour to figure out that there had actually been an Ontario Act called the Replevin Act, only to discover that it had been repealed and that now similar remedies were to be found in more modern legislation.

Section 2 of the old Replevin Act described replevin as

> Where goods, chattels, deeds, bonds, debentures, promissory notes, bills of exchange, books of account, papers, writings, valuable securities or other personal property or effects have been wrongfully distrained or have been otherwise wrongfully taken or detained, the owner or other person capable of maintaining an action for damages therefor may bring an action of replevin for the recovery thereof and of the damages sustained by reason of the distraint, taking or detention.

Maggie finally concluded that this replevin business was complex and that she was probably going to need help from an expert in the field, if the matter came to a trial. The more she researched, however, the more she began to wonder if replevin was even the correct legal remedy in a 2011 law suit. Replevin might be the proper remedy in England, but she wasn't sure that it was in Ontario. Wouldn't that be great if she could get this thing tossed out on a technicality! Well, she'd worry about that another day. They hadn't even been served with any formal court documents yet.

Two weeks later, the letter and court documents arrived from the MacKenzie Hoffman firm.

MacKenzie Hoffman LLP
Suite 5000, 180 Bay Street
Toronto, ON M5J 2J3
Telephone: 416 555 6100
Facsimile: 416 555 6211
Email: info@mackenziehoffman.com

Charles C. Hoffman, QC
Direct Line: 416 555 6111
Email: choffman@mackenziehoffan.com
Our File: CCH0311-52

March 18, 2011

PRIVILEGED AND CONFIDENTIAL   **Via Courier and Email**

Fischer & Gordon LLP
Barristers & Solicitors
421, 88 King Street West
Toronto, ON M5H 1H1
Attention: Ms. Maggie Gordon

Dear Ms. Gordon

> **Re: St. Germain École des Garçons v. John Murdoch**
>
> Our firm is acting as special Canadian legal counsel to St. Germain École des Garçons with respect to the above cited matter.
>
> We have been advised that your firm represents John Murdoch, resident of Kingston, Ontario.
>
> On behalf of our client, we have filed with the Superior Court of Justice of the Province of a Statement of Claim, a copy of which is enclosed for service upon your client. As you will see, we will be seeking, among other remedies, an Order of Replevin relating to the documents referred to therein.
>
> We await your response.
>
> **MacKenzie Hoffman LLP**
>
> **Charles C. Hoffman, QC**
> CCH/db

Maggie knew it would be coming so she didn't even curse this time. She was pleased with her self-restraint until her assistant came to her door and told her that another letter addressed to Maggie had just been couriered to the office.

Chapter 40

Maggie read the letter the first time and involuntarily exploded with, "For Christ's sake!" So much for her self-restraint. This time she didn't even care if anyone heard her. This was just too much.

She calmed down only about 30% and read the letter again.

Cowie LLP
11 Union St, Glasgow G1 3RC, UK
VP5V+G5 Glasgow, UK
Telephone: +44 333 555 7676
Facsimile: +44 333 555 8787
Email: info@cowiellp.com

Terrance B. Cowie
Direct Line: +44 333 555 7679
Email: tbc@cowiellp.com
Our File: TBC-1489

March 29, 2011

PRIVILEGED AND CONFIDENTIAL   **Via Courier and Email**

Fischer & Gordon LLP
Barristers & Solicitors
421, 88 King Street West
Toronto, Ontario, Canada
M5H 1H1
Attention: Ms. Maggie Gordon

Dear Ms. Gordon

Re: Freemason Lodge Stanecastle No. 1759 v. John Murdoch

Our firm acts for Freemason Lodge Stanecastle No. 1759.

We understand that your firm represents Dr. John Murdoch, of Kingston, Ontario.

For the last 216 years, our client has been in possession of a handwritten note by Robert Burns dated June 23, 1796 addressed to 'Barony Lodge Stanecastle, as it was then known. Our client, the Freemason Lodge Stanecastle No. 1759 is the successor to the original Barony Lodge Stanecastle. The Robert Burn's note states as follows:

"*My Dearest Brethren, I have enjoyed immensely my visit with you during my brief stay here in Irvine. I know that you are fully aware of my commitment to the noble causes of Freemasonry and to its teachings and convictions. My fellowship with you brethren has reinforced my faith in its ideals. For the great honor of bestowing upon me an Honorary Membership in Barony Lodge Stanecastle, I wish to give you a gift, as a token of my thanks. Some years ago, I had written a poem about my childhood teacher, John Murdoch, who I very much respected. The poem is entitled 'To John Murdoch, My Teacher, My Friend' and is currently in the possession of certain of my friends in Edinburgh. I had originally intended to give the poem to my teacher, but I have lost track of his whereabouts. As soon as I return to good health, I will instruct my friends to send it to you. Your Brother, Robert Burns"*

As you may know, Robert Burns died on July 21, 1796, a few weeks after writing this note. Our client never received the gift of the poem, as promised by Robert Burns. Our client is of the view that due to Robert Burns serious ill health following the writing of this note, he was never able to speak to his friends in Edinburgh about the gift. Our client is further of the view that some years later, when Gilbert Burns finally received the poem from Robert Burns' friends in Edinburgh, he sent it to John Murdoch in London, thinking that it belonged to him, not knowing about the gift of it to our client.

Our client's legal position is that Lodge Stanecastle No. 1759 is the rightful and legal owner of the Robert Burns poem entitled '*To John Murdoch, My Teacher, My Friend*'.

We understand that the said poem is currently in the possession of your client, John Murdoch.

Accordingly, on behalf of our client, we hereby demand that you advise your client to forthwith deliver the said poem to our offices not later than 4:00 pm GMT, April 12, 2011.

If the said poem is not delivered to our offices as aforesaid, we have instructions to seek one or more legal remedies from the Courts in the Province of Ontario to compel John Murdoch to deliver up possession to our client.

We look forward to your early positive response.

Cowie LLP

Terrance B. Cowie
TBC/mg

cc. Gastelum & James LLP, Toronto, ON
Attention: George H. Gastelum, QC

"Well, I wonder how many effing days after April 12 before I get a letter from Mr. Gastelum!" she said under her breath. 'At least saying 'effing' wasn't swearing,' she thought to herself and then laughed out loud.

She instructed her assistant to open a new litigation file called 'Freemason Lodge Stanecastle No. 1759 v. John Murdoch'

She had to unload on somebody, and Amanda needed to be informed anyway, so she turned off her computer, took her briefcase and coat and strode over to Amanda's office. She planted herself in the doorway and looked in. Amanda looked up and thought to herself, 'Oh, oh, something's up.' "Hi," she said, "What's up?"

"Hey Amanda, it's just about 5 o'clock and I desperately need a drink. Care to ditch early and join me?" Maggie asked.

"You've read my mind. Let's get out of here," Amanda said, got up, grabbed her coat and followed Maggie out the door.

The girls went to their favourite pub, the Toad and Rooster on Queen Street, got a table and ordered. Amanda ordered an Old Fashioned and Maggie a Whisky Sour.

When the drinks arrived, Amanda said, "I can't quite tell if you're just flustered about something or mad as hell. What's going on?"

"Ha, I'm both," Maggie said, then held up her left arm with her hand open, and said, "Wait." With her right hand she grabbed her Whisky Sour took a not-lady-like gulp, took a deep breath then continued, "Ok, now I can talk," and they both laughed.

Maggie proceeded to recount the crazy situation that had developed on her Grandpa Murdoch's case. She ended with "God Amanda, now we're fighting a wealthy US art collector, maybe the Mormon church, a prominent French school in London and the Freemasons in Scotland!"

By the time Maggie finished her longish account, the girls were already working on their second drinks.

Amanda said, "Hold on! Let me see if I've got this. So, everyone is claiming that they own the Robert Burns poem. Clarence Murdoch from New York says he owns it because, according to an LDS ancestry report that he commissioned, he is the heir to the Burns poem, not your Grandpa, right?"

"Right."

"And the St. Germain school in London is claiming that they own it because the poem was found at their school, and they've never relinquished their rights to ownership and possession, right?"

"Right, again."

"Ok, now this Freemason Lodge in Scotland is claiming that they own it because Robert Burns gave it to them as a gift, but they just never received it."

"Right, once more."

"And, of course, your Grandpa thinks he's the owner because of the ancestry findings of the Avery & Lord firm in London."

"Right, right, right and right!" Maggie exclaimed.

"Well, I'm surprised you haven't heard from some descendants of Robert Burns or Gilbert Burns yet, claiming that they own it," Amanda said laughing.

"Don't laugh, they could be coming," Maggie said laughing with her, but then wondering about that.

"And, all of these claimants have lawyered up. Both sides of the Atlantic," Amanda said shaking her head.

"Yup."

"Well this is not just game on. This is looking like the War of the Roses!", Amanda said laughing again, "Or is it more like the family feud of the Hatfields and McCoys? I don't know my history well enough, but I do know that this could be one complicated, long, drawn out affair."

This time Maggie didn't laugh and sat silent for a few minutes. She did, however, order a third drink for Amanda and herself.

Finally, she said, "I'll tell you one thing Amanda, the lawyer in me sees this as a very complex legal case. If this ever goes to trial, it'll be one for the books, one they'll study in every English common-law law school in the world. There's choice of law issues, property law issues, copyright issues, inheritance issues, contract/gift issues and, hell, there might even be some criminal law in there somewhere!" Then she paused for a moment, seemingly deep in thought.

Then she continued, "But, you know Amanda, ever since our law school days, I've always been interested in the concepts of equity and fairness. Even without doing a speck of research, this looks to me like a case where there are just too many conflicting claims in law. Law, Shmaw. I'm wondering if this might be a case for an equitable solution. Don't know, just wondering."

"Hmm, yes, I wonder too," Amanda said, "Remember, it was your equity argument that won the Grand Moot for us back in law school!"

"Haha, yes, it was. I almost forgot that," Maggie said, laughing again.

It suddenly occurred to Maggie that when she and Amanda were together, they laughed a lot. They were not just partners in the practice of law, they were best friends.

Maggie came out of her reverie and said, "But the granddaughter side of me, just wants this to go away and for Grandpa and Grandma to enjoy their remaining years."

"I know what you mean, Maggie. I'll be there to support you all the way, you know that. You're the best lawyer your Grandpa and Grandma could ever wish for. And if nobody tells them that, I will!" Amanda said.

"Thanks Amanda," Maggie said, relaxing a bit, "Here's mud in your eye!" as she raised her glass to Amanda to toast their friendship. Their glasses met, clinked and they downed their third cocktail.

They had both risen from their chairs and were just ready to leave the bar when Amanda stopped, tugged at Maggie's sleeve and said, "Maggie, can we sit down again, just for a minute? I have a question."

"Ok, what is it?" Maggie asked.

"This is going to sound a bit strange, but there's another thing that I keep wondering about," Amanda said and then she paused before continuing. "What, if anything, does this have to do with the poem that your uncle, Robbie Gordon wrote. It's just such a curious thing that all this high-level litigation is setting to launch over a Robert Burns poem, when the very same poem was written almost 200 years later by a kid who knew nothing about the Robert Burns poem. It's absolutely weird!" Amanda exclaimed. "Can you see any connection between the two poems?"

"Honestly, I've been thinking a lot about that myself and it's a total mystery to me. Maybe it's just one of those things that there's no answer to," Maggie said, "No one even knows about Uncle Robbie's poem, so I can't see how there can be any connection."

Chapter 41

Maggie was right, the next 'effing' letter came right on time from the Canadian law firm engaged to act for Freemason Lodge Stanecastle No. 1759. She didn't even curse this time.

Gastelum & James LLP
Suite 250, 495 Jarvis St
Toronto, ON M4Y 2G8
Telephone: 416 555 7580
Facsimile: 416 555 7590
Email: info@gastelum.com

George Homer Gastelum, QC
Direct Line: 416 555 7588
Email: ghgastelum@gastelum.com
Our File: 14894-GHG

April 13, 2011

PRIVILEGED AND CONFIDENTIAL   **Via Courier and Email**

Fischer & Gordon LLP
Barristers & Solicitors
421, 88 King Street West
Toronto, ON M5H 1H1
Attention: Ms. Maggie Gordon

Dear Ms. Gordon

Re: Freemason Lodge Stanecastle No. 1759 v. John Murdoch

Our firm acts as Canadian legal counsel for Freemason Lodge Stanecastle No. 1759.

We understand that your firm represents Dr. John Murdoch, of Kingston, Ontario.

We refer to the letter of Cowie LLP, Glasgow, UK to your firm dated March 29, 2011.

We have been advised by Cowie LLP that, as of today's date, they are not in receipt of the Burns Poem as demanded in the said March 29, 2011 letter.

As a consequence, we have received instructions to file with the Superior Court of Justice of the Province of Ontario an Application for a Mandatory Order compelling Dr. John Murdoch to release possession of the Burns Poem to our client. A copy of the Application is enclosed for service upon your client.

We await your response.

Gastelum & James LLP
George Homer Gastelum, QC GHG/ef

Maggie called her Grandpa that very afternoon and gave him the latest. Then she said, "Grandpa, would it be ok if I came out this weekend to visit you in person to discuss this face to face?"

"Of course, that would be wonderful! Can you bring Sarah?" he answered.

Maggie called her Mom and Dad and they made arrangements to all get together for a big Gordon family dinner at Willie and Helen's on Friday night. There would be ten of them for dinner, Grandpa John, Grandma Sonya, Willie, Helen, Tom and his new girlfriend, Monique, Brad, Maggie and Sarah.

Then Maggie had another idea.

She went down to Amanda's office and said, "Hey, have you ever been to Kingston?"

Early Friday afternoon, Brad, Sarah, Amanda, Maggie and Princess piled into Brad's Toyota Prius and headed out to the 401 towards Kingston for the weekend.

When they arrived three hours later, without a doubt, the biggest and most excited greeting was between Sarah and her Gramps and Grams. She ran to Gramps first, jumped on to his lap, as he remained seated on the sofa. As always, she gave him a huge hug and a kiss right on his hairy lips. Then she ran her little hands over John's bald head and through his white beard. And, as always, he revelled in the child's touch and attention.

When Sarah was finished exploring Gramps head and face, she climbed down and went to Grams. Sarah climbed into Sonya's lap and threw her arms around her neck and remained in that position for a long while.

When the hug was finally over, Sonya looked into Sarah's dark blue eyes, as she always did. For just a brief moment her memory clouded, and she thought she was looking into Robbie's eyes. Her tears came.

Sarah saw Sonya's tears and asked, "Why do you always cry when you look at me Grams?"

Sonya let out a little laugh and said, "Well, sweetheart, it's the same answer that I always give you. I think I'm looking into one of the great mysteries of life."

The evening was a wonderful time for the Gordon family. Amanda fit right in as if she had been a member of the family for years. They caught up with the events in each other's lives, gossiped about people that they all knew and reminisced about shared times and experiences in the past. There was so much talking going on that to an outsider, the scene appeared chaotic.

At the end of that evening, Maggie made plans for her and Amanda to visit Grandpa John and Grandma Sonya in their home, the next morning. They said their good-byes and Brad drove Grandpa and Grandma back to their house, a few blocks away.

Chapter 42

Maggie and Amanda arrived at John and Sonya's house at 10 am, as planned.

John and Sonya sat close together on the same sofa that they had sat on when Liz Cullen had visited them only a few months ago. John adjusted his hearing aid, then reached for Sonya's hand as he often did.

Maggie did most of the talking and gave as much background to the three lawsuits as she thought was necessary to help her Grandpa and Grandma understand the entire situation. She tried to explain the merits and weaknesses, as she saw them, of the legal case of each of Clarence Murdoch, St. Germain school and the Freemason Lodge. Amanda contributed comments from time to time.

For the most part, John and Sonya sat and listened quietly, occasionally nodding as if they understood.

When Maggie didn't seem to have anything more to say, there was a long pause. Maggie and Amanda looked at John, waiting for his response.

Finally, John leaned forward, placed both his hands on his knees and slowly started to speak, "Well, your Grandma and I have been giving this a lot of thought lately. On the one hand, we don't look forward to a long court case." He paused again before proceeding, "But, on the other hand, we believe that Robbie's poem and the Robert Burns poem belong together. It's a very strange thing that the two poems are identical, and we've been pondering that mystery for the last several months. We can't explain it, but it is what it is. We feel that to honor Robbie, the poems simply must be kept together."

He paused again before continuing, "We also treasure the Burns poem because it was written for my great, great, …how many is it, Maggie? And if it now belongs to me, then we want to keep it for that reason, as well. So, as much as we would like to avoid a long court case, we are prepared to fight, aren't we dear?" He then turned his head to look at Sonya, leaned back on the sofa and took her hand again. Sonya nodded and squeezed his hand as she had done a thousand times before.

Everyone remained silent for another minute and John continued yet again, "There is one thing that does bother us though. Your Grandma and I don't have much money to pay you young ladies the legal fees that you would normally charge for a complex file like this. You need to make a living."

Amanda spoke, "Dr. Murdoch, Maggie and I are not expecting you to pay us any legal fees. We'd like to do this, for you, because you're family." She hadn't realized, until the words were already out of her mouth, that she had inadvertently included herself as part of the Gordon family. She laughed, self-consciously and looked around to see everyone's reaction.

Maggie finally spoke, "I understand and agree with everything you've said Grandpa and, as Amanda has said, we are happy to fight this battle for you and Grandma. You told me one time, Grandpa, that you and Grandma were in this together and now Amanda and I want to support you both in this battle."

"Thank you dear. That means so much to John and me," Sonya said.

"Grandpa, can I ask you a question?" Maggie asked.

"Of course dear."

"Grandpa, did you and Grandma get new Wills done up with Mr. MacDonald?"

"Yes, we did and we both gave most of our…."

Maggie interrupted him, "Grandpa, I don't want you to tell me what you've done in your Wills, I just want to remind you that whoever you've designated as the beneficiaries in your Wills are people you care about, right?"

"Why, yes, of course, we love them very much," and again he turned and looked at Sonya who nodded in agreement.

"And you also understand that when you pass away, whatever you own in your estate will go to those loved ones, right?"

"Yes, we understand that, but we don't have much."

"Well, the Burns poem may be worth a considerable amount of money, so when you pass on, it will become part of your estate. So, in addition to the good reasons you've already talked about, this is a battle worth fighting for the benefit of your loved ones."

"We hadn't thought of it that way, did we dear?"

Sonya shook her head and said with a smile on her face, "Well then for all these reasons, let's go to battle!"

"That's great! Yes, let's fight this! Maggie and I will take care of everything and we'll report to you when there's something to report and we'll get your instructions when we need them. We don't want you to worry about anything," Amanda said.

Maggie got up to leave but Amanda tugged at her sleeve and said, "Could we stay a bit longer?" she asked and turned to John and Sonya. "Dr. Murdoch and Mrs. Gordon, would you mind telling me about Robbie. Maggie has told me some stories, but, if you don't mind, I'd really like to hear from you. You knew him the best."

Maggie sat back down and now it was her turn to nod in agreement.

Sonya and John spent the next hour relating their respective stories and anecdotes about Robbie Gordon. These were interesting to both Amanda and Maggie, but it was their emotional memories of the intimate times with Robbie that touched them the most. There were a few times during the hour where all four of them were tearing up.

Maggie got up to leave a second time but Amanda tugged at her sleeve again and said, "I have one more request. I have never seen the poem that Robbie Gordon wrote to you, Dr. Murdoch. Maggie has a copy at the office and has promised to show it to me one day, but she hasn't done that yet," and she wagged her finger scoldingly at Maggie.

John said, "Yes, of course. The original is in my safe deposit box at the Bank, as per Maggie's instructions, but let me get something for you. Just a minute." He rose up from the sofa and slowly made his way to their bedroom. He came back a few minutes later with an old scrapbook in his hand. The front cover of the scrapbook had the words '*Poems by Robbie Gordon*' in bold letters.

He handed it to Amanda, then said, "Sonya and I put this scrapbook together many years ago. It contains all of the poems that Robbie wrote, at least all of the poems that we know of. There are some 25 of his poems in this scrapbook. Most of them were written by Robbie in my English classes at Banffshire, but some were written elsewhere. Sonya found some in his bedroom at the house on the farm and some were found in his dormitory room at Banffshire. The last two pages of the scrapbook contain Robbie's last poem '*To John Murdoch, My Teacher, My Friend*' and Robert Burns poem of the same name."

Amanda opened the scrapbook to the last two pages. Robbie Gordon's poem was on the left side and on the opposite page was the poem by Robert Burns. The handwriting was different, but the poems were exactly, word for word, the same. Even the punctuation was identical in each poem.

She shook her head slowly. "That is just incredible!" she said very quietly. "I don't know some of the words, but what I do understand is beautiful! By the way, what does 'canie' mean?" They all laughed.

"Have you ever considered publishing a book of Robbie's poetry?" Amanda asked.

No one answered. John and Sonya just looked at each other and Amanda decided to not press it any further.

For the third time, Maggie got up to leave and this time was successful. They said their good-byes and left.

It was time for John and Sonya's nap anyway.

For the balance of the afternoon Maggie and Amanda decided to visit Banffshire Academy. Maggie had seen the campus a few times during her childhood. Her father had taken her there on occasion when there was an alumni dinner or a fund-raising function. Amanda was impressed with the beauty of the grounds and the old limestone buildings. The campus was full of activity that afternoon. The boys in their white shirts, neck-ties, dark blue trousers and matching vests with brass buttons, were scurrying here and there, laughing and shouting.

They toured the beautiful Inverness Library and the Great Assembly Hall. They walked around the campus and then Amanda said, "Maggie, can you show me where your Uncle Robbie drowned?"

Maggie said, "I'm not sure exactly where they found him, but I know that it was near the senior boys' dormitory." They walked in that direction and approached the shore of Lake Ontario. "I think it was somewhere near here." They stood looking out over the water and a strange feeling came over them. It was as if they both felt a presence. They looked at each other and both laughed nervously. Maggie said, "I think he's still here!"

Chapter 43

The next few weeks were a flurry of activity at the Fischer Gordon law firm. In addition to the dozens of other cases that Amanda and Maggie had on the go, they both busied themselves with researching statutory and case law pertinent to the three lawsuits against John Murdoch. They were both getting confused with the complexity of the issues.

It was Maggie who first suggested that they should make a motion to consolidate all three lawsuits into one. Since all three cases were commenced in the Superior Court of Justice and all three dealt with the same property, it made sense to her that they should be combined and heard together.

After several weeks of Maggie wrangling with the Canadian counsel for the three plaintiffs, and two court hearings, Justice Ogorek of the Superior Court of Justice, made an order for the substantive consolidation of the three actions. In the process, Justice Ogorek required all three plaintiffs to recast and refile their pleadings, partly to accommodate the consolidation and partly to comply with his decision that some of the original pleadings did not properly comply with Ontario's Rules of Civil Procedure. Maggie was particularly pleased that Justice Ogorek made a specific reference to the erroneous pleadings filed by Josh Cohen. 'Fool!' she thought to herself.

Shortly after the motion to consolidate was ordered by the court, the Toronto Globe and Mail picked up the story and ran an article about the three lawsuits over the ownership of the Robert Burns poem. Maggie, the law firm of Fischer Gordon and Dr. John Murdoch's name were all named in the piece.

Amanda saw the article first and rushed into Maggie's office, threw the paper down on her desk and exclaimed, "Here we go, we're already starting to get some publicity out of this case, just as we thought!"

Maggie read the article and said, "Yup, here we go!"

The day after the Globe story was published, 67 more media sources in Canada, the US and the UK ran similar stories.

Two days after the Globe story was published, a journalist for the Kingston Whig-Standard called John Murdoch. Sonya answered the phone.

"Hello, may I speak with Dr. John Murdoch? My name is Keith Davidson and I'm a journalist with the Kingston Whig-Standard."

"Yes, I'll get him," Sonya said.

A few minutes later John came to the phone and shouted, "Hello, this is John Murdoch. Hold on a minute." He then proceeded to adjust his hearing aid.

That done, he returned to the phone in normal speaking voice, "Sorry about that. Hello Mr. Davidson?"

"Yes. Dr. Murdoch, you may not remember me, but I'm Keith Davidson. I was one of your students many years ago."

"Oh, how nice! But I'm very sorry Keith, I don't remember all of you young people."

"Well, sir, I'm not so young anymore, I've just turned 61. I was in the same class as Robbie Gordon and I'm sure you remember him."

"Why, yes of course I remember him. How can I help you?"

"Sir, as you know, your name had been in the media several times over the last few months. Last October there were several articles relating to your inheritance of the Robert Burns poem and now the article in the Globe yesterday about various lawsuits against you over the poem. You may not recall this either, but in October, I had called you and asked if you would give me an interview and you declined. I know you were inundated with requests then, but, sir, I was hoping that you might reconsider and allow me to come over and visit you to talk a bit about these lawsuits and the Burns poem."

"Haha, yes, Keith, I had dozens of requests for interviews. I'm an old man and I don't have an appetite for that, but now that you've told me that you were one of my students, I'd be happy to see you again and have a visit."

Arrangements were made to meet the following morning.

Sonya had already left for Willie and Helen's house when Keith Davidson arrived. She planned to spend the day with them.

After arriving, John invited Keith to sit down on a chair in the living room. John said that he had already made some tea and asked Keith if he would like a cup. Keith said that he would so John went into the kitchen to fetch the tea tray. While he was in the kitchen, Keith spotted a scrapbook on the coffee table in front of his chair, with bold lettering on the cover, '*Poems by Robbie Gordon*'. It had been laying there since the day John had brought it out of their bedroom to show Amanda and Maggie.

Keith picked it up and started to flip through the pages of the scrapbook. He wasn't reading the poems, just flipping through the pages. When he got to the last two pages and saw the two identical poems, one by Robbie Gordon and the other by Robert Burns. He stared at the one then the other. He had seen a copy of the handwritten poem by Robert Burns online, but he wasn't sure what he was looking at when he saw the Robbie Gordon poem. It was entitled, '*To John Murdoch, My Teacher, My Friend*', the same as the Robert Burns poem.

When John returned with the tea, Keith quickly put the scrapbook back down on the coffee table, but John had already seen that he had been looking at it. He served the tea and both men were silent while he did so. He then walked to the sofa and sat down.

John Murdoch realized that his long held, almost sacred, secret was out. He sat silent for several minutes thinking about what had just happened, then said, "Well, I see that you've been looking at my scrapbook. I'm sorry, I hadn't intended for it to be laying about when you got here but I forgot to put it away."

For the moment, Keith decided to change the topic and said, "Dr. Murdoch, after speaking with you yesterday, I ran a quick historical search at our newspaper for articles with your name in them. Of course, I found the three or four articles that we had printed about the Robert Burns poem last fall, but then I found a short article from 1964 about Robbie

Gordon's drowning and you giving the eulogy at his funeral. I remember that you had a special relationship with Robbie, but I didn't know that you had given his eulogy."

"Well, it was a small funeral and yes, Robbie was very special to me. It turns out that I was very special to him too."

"Oh, how is that sir?"

"Well, the poem, you know."

"No, sir, I don't know. What poem?"

"The poem he wrote to me just before he died."

"I'm sorry, I don't know anything about a poem that he wrote *to* you."

"Well, I think that you may have just been looking at it in my scrapbook there," and John pointed to the scrapbook on the coffee table. He continued, "Robbie wrote that beautiful poem to me. It was called '*To John Murdoch, My Teacher, My Friend*'. Go ahead, please pick it up again and have a closer look."

Keith picked up the scrapbook again, turned to the last two pages and looked again at the two identical poems, then he said, "Sir, there seems to be some mistake. This poem," and he pointed to the left side of the page, "says its written by Robbie Gordon."

Part of John Murdoch wanted to pretend to agree with him that, yes, there was some mistake, but it was not in his character to deceive or tell a lie. "No, there is no mistake, that poem was written by Robbie.

Keith continued, "Sir, am I to understand that Robbie Gordon wrote this poem to you in 1964?"

John Murdoch slowly nodded his head.

"And this is Robbie Gordon's handwriting?"

"Yes."

"Are you then saying that this poem, written by Robbie Gordon in 1964 is the same poem that Robert Burns wrote in the 1700s?"

John Murdoch slowly nodded his head again.

"But sir, how can that be?"

"I can't explain it Keith," he said.

Keith looked at the two poems, one on each side of the open scrapbook, and thought to himself, 'Even if I were to write a story on this, it would not be believable,' But he asked anyway, "Sir, could I take a copy of each of these poems and write an article in our newspaper about them?"

John Murdoch thought about that for a minute or so and then said, "I think that I would like to talk to my granddaughter about this. She's my lawyer too, you know."

"Yes, I know, I saw her name in the Globe article yesterday," Keith said.

"I'll try to get back to you tomorrow," John Murdoch said.

That's the way they left it that day and as Keith Davidson was returning to his office he thought, 'I'm going to have to talk to my editor about this.'

Chapter 44

Within minutes of Keith Davidson leaving John Murdoch's house, he called his editor and John called Maggie.

"Nicole, this is Keith," Keith Davidson said to his 31-year-old boss, Nicole Stark, at the Kingston Whig-Standard. He then proceeded to tell her the story of Robbie Gordon and his poem to John Murdoch. He concluded by asking her advice on whether she thought he should write a story about it.

"An identical poem written by a 13-year-old kid in 1964, eh? Well, that is a challenge!" she said, and he could hear her exhale a sort of breathy whistle, like she was thinking, 'What do I do with this?'. She continued, "As you well know, Keith, the Kingston Whig-Standard is a conservative, respectable newspaper and we don't run tabloid type articles. On the other hand, pretty much everyone in this town knows who Dr. John Murdoch is and, as far as I know, he's well regarded and credible. Would you agree with that?" she said.

"Yes, I would," Keith responded.

Nicole continued, "I guess there are three possibilities: one, Dr. Murdoch is lying, and that doesn't seem likely; two, he's senile or delusional or something; or three, it's true. Does he seem of sound mind to you, Keith?"

"Yes, he seems very lucid to me," Keith answered.

"With this whole Robert Burns thing going on, I'd love to break this story, but I'm not prepared to do it unless we can somehow get some additional comfort that Murdoch isn't lying and some third-party evidence that he's ok in the head," she said.

Keith responded, "Well, even if we got that kind of evidence, we still need Dr. Murdoch's permission to run the story and he said that he wanted to talk to his granddaughter, Maggie Gordon, who is also his lawyer."

"Maggie Gordon! I know her from McGill. She's a lawyer now? And she's Dr. Murdoch's granddaughter? Huh, small world, eh?" said exclaimed. "Ok, so let's wait and see if we get Dr. Murdoch's permission to even run with the story and if we do, then maybe you can talk to Maggie and see if you can get more background on him and this Robbie Gordon. In the meantime, is there any way you can think of to get evidence on Murdoch's mental state?"

"Well, I happen to know Dr. Murdoch's medical doctor. Dr. Andrew Robertson was a classmate of mine and, co-incidently, also of Robbie Gordon, at Banffshire. Of course, Dr. Robertson won't disclose any confidential information, but I can just raise the subject and see where it goes," he said.

"That's great Keith! Keep me posted, eh?" Nicole said and disconnected the call.

While the conversation between Keith and Nicole was going on, John was on the phone to Maggie.

He recounted the events of his meeting with Keith and concluded by asking her advice on whether he should give him permission to write a story about the Robbie Gordon poem.

Maggie thought about it for a moment and a light seemed to turn on in her head. She wondered if revealing the Robbie Gordon poem to the world at this point might in some way help their legal case. She wasn't sure how, she just had the thought that it might.

Then she said, "Grandpa, from a personal point of view, I think that this is entirely your decision. I know that you've kept Uncle Robbie's poem a secret all these years and that you regard it as your and Grandma's private treasure. But now that it's slipped out, maybe it's time to share your treasure with the world," Maggie said.

"Ok, thank you dear. I'm going to talk it over with Sonya when she gets home. She's at your father's today. I'll let you know what we decide. Good-bye for now Maggie," John said.

The next day John called Maggie back. "Maggie, your Grandma and I have discussed this matter and, together, we've decided that we are prepared to share our treasure with the world. With all the publicity surrounding the lawsuits, we thought that Robbie's great talents should share in some of the limelight," he said.

"Ok, Grandpa, if that's your decision, you should call Mr. Davidson and tell him that he can go ahead and write his story," Maggie said. "I look forward to reading it!"

During that conversation, Keith Davidson was on the phone to his old classmate Andrew Robertson. "Hello Andy, Keith Davidson here. It's been a while."

"Yes, indeed, good to hear from you, Keith!" Andrew said.

"Listen, we should get together and get caught up. Would you be able to join me for a drink at the Boar's Crown later this afternoon?" Keith asked.

"That would be great, it just so happens that my clinic closes early today, so I could meet you there at 4ish. Would that work for you?" Andrew asked.

They met at the Boar's Crown pub and after a half hour of catching up on the news of their lives, and those of their and families and friends, Keith purposefully steered the conversation to Banffshire Academy. They reminisced about some of their classmates and then Keith said, "I saw Dr. Murdoch the other day. Do you remember him? I wonder how he's doing these days. He must be in his mid-80s by now."

"Oh, yes, of course I remember Dr. Murdoch. I didn't do so well in his English classes, but he was a wonderful man. And I happen to know that he is, in fact, doing quite well. He has stayed in touch with me over the years," Andrew said.

"Really? He's not stayed in touch with me over the years. My feelings are a bit hurt. He must have liked you more than he did me, and I did quite well in his classes. In fact, he's a big reason that I went into journalism," Keith said and laughed.

"No, I'm sure he doesn't like me any more than he does you. Dr. Murdoch has stayed in touch with me because I'm his doctor," Andrew said.

"Ok, then, that makes me feel better. When I saw him recently, he looked and sounded great. So many people his age now are suffering from some sort of dementia or Alzheimer's, but he sounded quite with it," Keith fished, hoping Andrew would offer some more information."

"Yes, I can tell you that he is doing well both physically and mentally. I just saw him recently and his hearing is failing, but other than that, he's as healthy as a horse," Andrew said.

That was all Keith needed to hear. They stayed for a second drink, but Keith's mind was wandering for the remainder of their time together. He was already writing the story in his head. Now he just needed Dr. Murdoch's blessing to print it.

No sooner had Keith and Andrew parted company and Keith received a call from John Murdoch.

"Hello, is this Keith?" John shouted.

Keith recognized the loud voice and knew what the reason was for it but didn't care. He anxiously answered, "Yes, it is Dr. Murdoch. How are you today?"

"Listen, Keith, would you mind dropping by the house again and I'll tell you what we've decided about Robbie's poem," John said.

"Yes, sir, of course I can do that," Keith said, his excitement mounting. He assumed that 'we've decided' meant what Dr. Murdoch and his lawyer and granddaughter, Maggie Gordon had decided.

They made arrangements to meet the next day.

Keith arrived at John's house the following day and was greeted by both Dr. Murdoch and his wife, Sonya Gordon. Keith had never met Sonya and after introductions were made, he said, "It's very nice to meet you Mrs. Gordon. Are you related to Robbie Gordon or Maggie Gordon?"

"Yes, I'm Robbie's mother and Maggie's grandmother," she said calmly.

Keith thought, 'Ok, this is getting weirder', but didn't say anything to that effect.

The three of them sat in the living room, John and Sonya close together on the sofa and Keith across from them with his notepad and tape recorder. The scrapbook, '*Poems by Robbie Gordon*' lay on the coffee table between them.

For the next two hours, Keith interviewed the couple about Robbie Gordon. He learned about Robbie's mysterious behaviour as a child, his ability to write beautiful poetry, his poem entitled '*To John Murdoch, My Teacher, My Friend*', his premature death and Dr. Murdoch's inheritance of the Robert Burns poem. As they talked, Keith became very aware of how important the Robbie Gordon poem was to them both. The elephant in the room, of course, was that neither Dr. Murdoch or Sonya Gordon talked about the fact that the two poems were identical.

Keith knew he had to tread carefully with his next question, "Dr. Murdoch and Mrs. Gordon, how do you explain that Robbie's poem was the same as the great Robert Burns poem?" It was Sonya who answered. She looked towards John, reached for his hand and turned back to Keith Davidson.

Then she calmly started to speak, "Mr. Davidson, I think at some point in our lives we all have to admit that there are things that cannot be explained. You could say that Robbie was clairvoyant, or that he was psychic or had some kind of extrasensory perception. But I choose to believe that there are just some things that cannot be explained, and I no longer try to. As a young mother, I puzzled over and worried about Robbie's behaviour during his short life. But for the last 40 years, I've just come to accept it for what it was, and I have peace about that. I can't explain it, but it happened. And there you have it. So, go ahead and write your article. You can say whatever you want to say, but just know that my son was a very talented and special human being. John and I loved him very much. His poem '*To John Murdoch, My Teacher, My Friend*' is as valuable to us as the Robert Burns poem is. We cannot explain why Robbie's poem is identical to Robert Burns poem. It is a mystery. All we know is that together, they have great sentimental value to us, and we wish for them to be kept together."

A lump developed in Keith's throat and he decided that there wasn't much to say after Sonya's speech so all he did then was turn to Dr. Murdoch and say, "Dr. Murdoch, do I have your blessing to write the article?"

"What she said," he said and laughed at his own clever response. They all laughed, and Keith was grateful for the relief.

Keith asked if he could take the scrapbook with him and make a copy. He promised to return it within the hour. John and Sonya agreed to that as well.

Chapter 45

Keith worked on the story for the next two days and showed the draft to Nicole Stark for her approval. She made that breathy whistling sound again and said, "I hope I don't regret this, but let's go with it!"

On May 12, 2011 the Kingston Whig-Standard published Keith's article on the third page.

John Murdoch Reveals Poems After 47 Years

In October 2010, Dr. John Murdoch of Kingston became famous as the inheritor of the Robert Burns poem entitled '*To John Murdoch, My Teacher, My Friend*', recently discovered in London. Robert Burns (1759 -1796) wrote the poem in honor of his boyhood teacher in Scotland, also named John Murdoch. The Burns poem can be found, with a photo of the original, on this newspaper's website: www.kingstonpost.com/category/news/burns

The elderly Dr. Murdoch is now being sued by three different parties, each claiming ownership of the Burns poem. Dr. Murdoch's granddaughter, Maggie Gordon, is a Toronto lawyer, at Fischer Gordon, and is acting as defence counsel in the court proceedings.

Dr. Murdoch was an English teacher at Banffshire Academy for Boys, in Kingston, from 1951 to 1991. One of his students was a local boy named Robbie Gordon who drowned in Lake Ontario in 1964 at the age of 13.

Young Robbie Gordon was also a poet. His poems have been in the possession of Dr. Murdoch and his wife, Sonya Gordon, who also happens to be Robbie Gordon's mother, since Robbie Gordon's death in 1964. For the first time in 47 years, Dr. Murdoch and Mrs. Gordon have revealed, exclusively to the Kingston Whig-Standard, some 25 of Robbie Gordon's poems. The scanned poems can be found on this newspaper's website: www.kingstonpost.com/category/news/murdoch

One of Robbie Gordon's poems is entitled '*To John Murdoch, My Teacher, My Friend*' written in honor of his teacher, John Murdoch. What is shocking about this poem is that it is identical to the Burns poem of the same name, written almost 200 years earlier. Every word, and even the punctuation, is exactly the same as the Burns poem. Only the handwriting is different.

When questioned about the two identical poems, Robbie Gordon's mother, Sonya Gordon said, "...*I think at some point in our lives we all have to admit that there are things that cannot be explained. You could say that Robbie was clairvoyant, or that he was psychic or had some kind of extrasensory perception. But I choose to believe that there are just some things that cannot be explained, and I no longer try to. ...Robbie Gordon was a very talented and special human being and John and I loved him very much. His poem 'To John Murdoch, My Teacher, My Friend' is as valuable to us as the Robert Burns poem is. We cannot explain why Robbie's poem is identical to Robert Burns poem. It is a mystery. All we know is that together, they have great sentimental value to us, and we wish for them to be kept together.*"

Within three days of the Kingston Whig-Standard article, 182 media sources around the world ran some variation of the story of the two identical poems. Many of the pieces expressed some level of skepticism. Some were out and out mocking but a few credible sources treated it as a serious story worthy of more investigation.

In addition to the 182 news stories, there were several editorials, a few of which commented on Sonya Gordon's comments about Robbie possibly being "...*clairvoyant, or that he was psychic or had some kind of extrasensory perception.*" The most prominent editorial was in the New York Times, which entitled their article, "*The Mysterious Robbie Gordon*".

The Canadian Broadcasting Corporation called Maggie Gordon and asked if they could do a story on the Robbie Gordon poem complete with an in-depth interview with Dr. Murdoch and Sonya Gordon. They proposed shooting the interview at Banffshire Academy with shots of Lake Ontario where his body was found. Maggie declined the invitation on behalf of her Grandpa and Grandma, but CBC went ahead and did a 12-minute segment on the story anyway and aired it on their popular Sunday night show, *The Passionate Eye*.

Chapter 46

For the next several months, the litigants filed motions for this and that, went through the torturous discovery process and even explored, then abandoned, notions of mediation and pre-trial conferencing.

During the discovery process, Maggie had introduced the Kingston Whig-Standard article on the Robbie Gordon poem. She anticipated that it would be challenged as irrelevant to the case by opposing counsel, but no one did. Besides a few snide remarks from Josh Cohen about the apparent strangeness of Robbie Gordon, the article didn't garner much attention or discussion.

Clarence Murdoch's counsel, on three different occasions, tried to settle the whole affair by offering each of the litigants substantial amounts of money in return for them relinquishing their claim to ownership of the Burns poem. No one was in the mood to settle, so finally a trial date was set for January 2012, with Superior Court of Justice, Chief Justice Kuebler presiding.

The trial was scheduled for three days. It lasted for seven.

For witnesses, Clarence Murdoch's counsel called three experts from the LDS ancestry research team. Counsel for St. Germain École des Garçons called Ann Benoit, Jules Marchand, Dr. Pierre Gingras and Ian Avery. Counsel for Freemason Lodge Stanecastle No. 1759 called their Grand Master. Maggie called Liz Cullen and Dr. John Murdoch.

As soon as Maggie met Liz Cullen, she knew that they would also become friends. Liz provided very professional and credible testimony, both under examination and cross-examination. On the other hand, under Maggie's skillful cross examination, the LDS experts fumbled on the accuracy and veracity of some of their ancestral findings.

During her Grandpa John's testimony, Maggie prompted him to talk mostly about Robbie Gordon and his ability to write beautiful poetry and his great interest in reading and reciting the poems of Robert Burns. His testimony was interrupted on several occasions by counsel for the plaintiffs objecting on the grounds that Dr. Murdoch's testimony about Robbie Gordon was irrelevant to the case. But Justice Kuebler was fascinated by Dr. Murdoch's accounts and overruled each objection.

By the end of March, Justice Kuebler rendered a 12-page decision.

The first part of the decision was an explanation that Dr. Murdoch's and Clarence Murdoch's claim to ownership of the Burns poem could only be as good as the claim of the original John Murdoch. So, if the claim of the original John Murdoch was flawed, then both Dr. Murdoch's and Clarence Murdoch's claim were consequentially flawed.

With respect to the conflicting ancestral reports of the Avery & Lord firm and the LDS team, Justice Kuebler noted that the Avery & Lord report had supporting documentation for each and every one of their findings. The judge pointed out that at the point of departure in the two competing reports, the LDS research lacked a crucial piece of evidence. While the LDS report showed the father of Joseph John Murdoch to be a man by the name of Robert John

Murdoch, their research had provided no supporting documentation that that Robert John Murdoch had ever emigrated from Scotland to the United States, where Joseph John Murdoch was born. Justice Kuebler went on to state that with that vacuum in the LDS report, he had to conclude that their Robert John Murdoch was a different Robert John Murdoch. Avery & Lord's documentation supported Robert John Murdoch being the father of Colin John Murdoch, the ancestor to Dr. John Murdoch. As a result, Justice Kuebler dismissed Clarence Murdoch's claim on the grounds that the ancestral research of Liz Cullen of the Avery & Lord firm was more complete and accurate than that of the LDS research, so therefore, more credible.

The judge ruled against St. Germain École des Garçons on the grounds that the school was only a custodian of the Burns' poem, it never had a valid claim to ownership.

Finally, as between Dr. Murdoch and Freemason Lodge Stanecastle No. 1759, Justice Kuebler ruled in favour of the Lodge on the grounds that whatever intention Robert Burns may originally have had to give the poem to his teacher, John Murdoch, was changed by Burns' own words in his June 23, 1796 note to the Lodge where he said, *"I had originally intended to give the poem to my teacher, but I have lost track of his whereabouts. As soon as I return to good health, I will instruct my friends to send it to you."*

Chapter 47

Both Maggie and Amanda wanted to appeal. They were of the view that Justice Kuebler had erred in law on the grounds that the gift to the Lodge was never consummated.

While it wasn't a formal protocol, the practice in Ontario was that the law firm who handled the trial did not also handle an appeal of the same case. But Amanda and Maggie were not prepared to yield this file to anyone else, so they were willing to continue with the appeal.

Maggie and Amanda made another trip to Kingston to explain Justice Kuebler's decision to John and Sonya and to discuss the question of appealing the decision.

After Maggie and Amanda had finished speaking, John turned to Sonya, and she simply nodded her head. Then John said, "Ladies, we've come this far and if you think we should go all the way, then it's fine with Sonya and me, isn't it dear?" Sonya again nodded.

Maggie and Amanda knew that this appeal would likely be the final verdict on the matter, so what they did in preparation for it was of great importance.

Maggie filed a Notice of Motion for Leave to Appeal with the Court of Appeal for Ontario, and it was granted. Maggie, Amanda, Kelly and, in fact, everyone in the Fischer Gordon law firm pitched in to prepare and bind all of the documents required to effect an appeal under Ontario's *Rules of Civil Procedure*. But Maggie did all the work on the factum, the document that set out the facts, issues and arguments of their case.

Appended to her factum, Maggie included, among other documents, several decisions of the Supreme Court of Canada and the House of Lords on the law relating to gifts, the note by Robert Burns to the Freemason Lodge Stanecastle No. 1759, copies of the Gilbert Burns letter, the Robert Burns poem, the Robbie Gordon poem, a copy of the Kingston Whig-Standard article, the scrapbook entitled '*Poems by Robbie Gordon*', several quotes from Jeffrey Berryman's *Law of Equitable Remedies* and selected quotes from The Laboratories for Fundamental Research in Palo Alto, California on precognition. Maggie's *pièce de résistance* though was the decision of, and extensive quotes from, Judge Berry in a 1927 New Jersey case called *Burr v. Bloomsburg*. Maggie based much of her equitable argument on that case.

In the factum, Maggie had drafted a sentence where she snuck in the words of Lord Denning from the famous *High Trees* case, the same words she had used years earlier in the Grand Moot competition, '*the time has now come.*' She then proceeded to wax eloquent that this Murdoch case cried out for fairness emphasizing several of the key passages from the *Burr v. Bloomsburg* case.

In her oral presentation to the Court, Maggie again used Lord Denning's words, '*the time has now come*' and quoted several of Judge Berry's passages. Amanda watched in ah as Maggie spoke. Her oral advocacy skills were that of a veteran lawyer with many years' more experience than Maggie had.

17 months later, on September 10, 2013, Court of Appeal for Ontario Chief Justice Esther Longhi, Justice Peter MacMillan and Justice Michael Kaplan rendered a split decision.

Justice Kaplan wrote a short dissenting decision stating the he agreed with all of the considerations and conclusions by Justice Kuebler at trial and that he would dismiss the appeal.

Madame Justice Longhi wrote the majority decision on behalf of Justice MacMillan and herself.

> "…*There are three elements required to perfect a gift. First, the donor must intend to make a gift; second, the gift must be delivered by the donor to the donee; and third, the gift must be accepted by the donee.*
>
> *Clearly Robert Burns intended to make a gift. However, we agree with the arguments made by counsel for the Appellants that the gift to Freemason Lodge Stanecastle No. 1759 was never consummated on the grounds that the poem was simply never delivered and therefor the gift to the Lodge fails.*
>
> *The giving of instructions by Burns to his friends in Edinburgh, to send the poem to the Lodge, was a prerequisite to the delivery of the gift. The instructions were never given, the gift was never delivered and therefore, the gift fails.*
>
> *On the other hand, we find that the gift to the Appellant, Dr John Murdoch succeeds.*
>
> *Robert Burns wrote the poem to his teacher John Murdoch and his original intention was to give the poem to John Murdoch. He not only said so in his note to the Lodge, but he entitled the poem, 'To John Murdoch, My Teacher, My Friend.' Robert Burns' original intention remained intact, that is, it was never interrupted by the giving of instructions to his friends in Edinburgh to deliver it to anyone else.*
>
> *When the poem came to Gilbert Burns' attention and possession, he would have logically assumed that his brother's intention in writing a poem entitled, 'To John Murdoch, My Teacher, My Friend', was that it be given **to** John Murdoch. Gilbert Murdoch did just that and thus effected the delivery of the poem.*
>
> *The Respondent argues that the fact John Murdoch was not alive at the time of the delivery negates the delivery. We are satisfied that the acceptance of the Robert Burns poem by the Appellant, Dr. John Murdoch, the legal heir of the original John Murdoch, constitutes acceptance. Furthermore, the common law has historically deemed that a gift is accepted, unless there is evidence to the contrary. We find no such evidence.*
>
> *We wish to offer the following comments by way of obiter dictum.*
>
> *Appellant's counsel has reminded this court of the famous words of Lord Denning in the 1946 High Trees case, '…the time has now come…'. In that case Lord Denning was referring to the fact that the time had come to introduce a new equitable remedy, because the circumstances in that case required fairness.*
>
> *We agree with Appellant's counsel that this case also requires a measure of fairness. The law does not always provide that.*

Accordingly, even if we are wrong on our decision, as set forth above, we believe that fairness would direct us to decide in favour of the Appellant.

We are compelled by the statement of Mrs. Sonya Gordon when she said, "...I think at some point in our lives we all have to admit that there are things that cannot be explained. You could say that Robbie (Gordon) was clairvoyant, or that he was psychic or had some kind of extrasensory perception. But I choose to believe that there are just some things that cannot be explained, and I no longer try to. ...Robbie Gordon was a very talented and special human being and John and I loved him very much. His poem 'To John Murdoch, My Teacher, My Friend' is as valuable to us as the Robert Burns poem is. We cannot explain why Robbie's poem is identical to Robert Burns poem. It is a mystery. All we know is that together, they have great sentimental value to us, and we wish for them to be kept together."

Conventional science may not recognize the existence of 'precognition', the subjective experience of acquiring information from a past or future space-time point, because it cannot be scientifically proven. Mrs. Gordon used the words, 'clairvoyant', 'psychic' and 'extra-sensory-perception'.

We are not prepared to recognize the existence of precognition, but nor are we prepared to dismiss the concept. We agree with Mrs. Gordon when she says, "...there are just some things that cannot be explained..."

In any event, a court of equity, which this is, is not in the business of science, it is in the business of fairness.

Counsel for the Appellant provided a very interesting case for our consideration, the 1927 case from the Court of Chancery of New Jersey called Burr v. Bloomsburg. It was a case involving a family dispute over the ownership of a ring. The ring in that case is comparable, in our view, to the Burns poem in the case at hand. I'd like to quote a few passages from the Burr case. Berry, V.C. said:

'...It is also insisted that mere sentiment or personal desire for a particular object affords no basis for an equitable action such as this. That may be true as an abstract proposition; but when that sentiment or desire is based upon or born of facts and circumstances which endow the chattel with a special, aside from intrinsic, value, to the extent of *pretium affectionis*, it is not true.... how can the sentiment, the imaginary value put upon it by the complainant's fancy, because of her affection for the one from whom she obtained it, be valued in terms of money any more than could a value be placed upon the "touch of a vanished hand" or "the sound of a voice that is still?" The real question here is whether or not this ring has a *"pretium affectionis."* If it has, whether because of sentiment, desire, or what not, provided it be real, "not...founded in weakness and folly", and not assumed for the occasion, then this court has jurisdiction, and relief should not be denied.

"Pretium affectionis" is defined in Wharton's Law Dictionary as:

"The imaginary value put upon a thing by the fancy of the owner in his affection for it."

In Bouvier's Law Dictionary, it is defined as:

"An imaginary value put upon a thing by the fancy of the owner in his affection for it, or for the person from whom he obtained it." (Emphasis mine.)

...There is here an abundance of proof to establish a *"pretium affectionis"* in this ring...That it does have a real and not a pretended sentimental value is evidenced by the fact that the complainant cherished it from then until now; that she refused to sell it even to her own brother...These facts show conclusively to my mind that the ring has had the *pretium affectionis* impressed upon it. To the defendant, it is merely a piece of jewelry, necessary to the gratification of envy or avarice, but to the complainant it recalls the daydreams of youth and the childhood memories of maturer years...."

We see many similarities between the Burr case and the case at hand.

We believe that there is an abundance of proof to establish a 'pretium affectionis' in the Robert Burns poem. Dr. John Murdoch and his wife, Mrs. Sonya Gordon, have cherished the Robbie Gordon poem for over 47 years and when they received the Robert Burns poem, they treasured them together more than if they were to be separated. Even if the poems were not identical, we can understand that Dr. Murdoch would attach a sentimental significance to it because his student Robbie Gordon, loved and emulated the poetry of Robert Burns. But the fact that the two poems are identical gives the Burns poem special meaning to Dr. Murdoch.

Further proof of a 'pretium affectionis' for the Burns poem is the fact that Dr. Murdoch declined all of many offers to purchase the poem, including the offer from Mr. Clarence Murdoch of USD $2,000,000. That he declined an offer of that much money, to us, is ample evidence that Dr. Murdoch placed a higher sentimental value on the poem than monetary value.

We agree with counsel for the Appellant that 'the time has now come' to provide an equitable remedy for Dr. Murdoch, based on the principal of 'pretium affectionis', and that it is fair and equitable that he be entitled to retain ownership and possession of the Burns poem.

Judgment in favour of the Appellant."

The next morning the Globe and Mail captioned their front-page article, '*Murdoch Wins the Burns Poem Case*' in size 18 font.

Maggie and Amanda read the full decision together in Maggie's small office. When they had both finished, they looked at each other, stood, hugged each other and for the second time during their career and friendship, Amanda whispered in Maggie's ear, "*The time has now come!*" Then they laughed and cried together.

EPILOGUE

Shortly after the decision of the Ontario Court of Appeal, John Murdoch and Sonya Gordon donated the Robbie Gordon and the Robert Burns poems to Banffshire Academy. They had each bequeathed the two poems to the school in their Wills, but they decided not to wait.

The school had commissioned the construction of a specially designed, high security, protective glass cabinet to display the poems. The display case was installed in the Inverness Library. One of the old globes was removed and replaced with the new cabinet. It was situated at the end of the table where Robbie used to sit, directly under the stained-glass window of Robert Burns.

In the largest and most elaborate public ceremony Banffshire had ever had, the poems were unveiled, and the name of the Inverness Library was changed to the Robert Allan Gordon Memorial Library.

Later that same year, the name of the Avery & Lord firm was changed to Avery & Cullen. Liz planned a return trip to Canada to spend some time with Dr. Murdoch, Sonya Gordon and her new friend, Maggie.

Ann Benoit and Jules Marchand had married the spring following the revelation of the Robert Burns poem and early that summer they had their first baby.

The size and importance of the cases that the Fischer Gordon firm were engaged to act on, ratcheted significantly upwards following the publicity of the Murdoch case. Amanda and Maggie signed a head lease for 4,000 square feet of posh new office space on the 53rd floor of one of Toronto's premier office towers on the corner of King and Bay. They both had corner offices with magnificent views of Lake Ontario. Maggie Gordon was awarded the 'Queen's Counsel' designation, the youngest lawyer in the history of the Law Society of Upper Canada to receive it.

John and Sonya spent one more winter in their house and decided to sell it the following spring. They moved into the Kilmory Seniors Lodge in Kingston. Every day, they could be seen walking slowly up and down the halls, hand in hand.

Robbie Gordon and Robert Burns became friends and continued writing poetry.

Manufactured by Amazon.ca
Acheson, AB

14917006R00101